Henry's Stories: Volume 2

Henry's Stories: Volume 2

Henry Melton

Short fiction collected from the pages of the ***Henry's Stories*** online magazine

Wire Rim Books
Hutto, Texas

Printing History First Edition: March 2013
ISBN 978-1-935236-45-0
ePub ISBN 978-1-935236-46-7
Kindle ISBN 978-1-935236-47-4

Printed in the United States of America

Wire Rim Books
www.wirerimbooks.com

Contents

Introduction

Scott A. Cupp

In my house, there are many, many books. Of these, a large number are signed. Thinking about this volume, I was reminded of collection of Keith Roberts short stories entitled Kaeti and Company which was published by Kerosina Press in 1986. The signed limited edition featured the title character speaking to the reader. She says "Cor! Ain't you the lucky one?" and then the limitation numbers were shown.

She might be talking to you today. In your hands, you have the new collection of stories by my friend Henry Melton. I have known Henry since August 1970 when we were introduced by Sue Vannoy, a mutual friend who thought we had similar tastes. Sue was an amazingly perceptive person. I was 18 and away from home and small classes for the first time. I had been a military brat which meant making and breaking friendships with some ease. The breaking was the easier of the two. Your family packed up and you moved many miles away, rarely if ever to return. And, since most of my friends were from military families, they wouldn't be there if you went back anyway.

Henry and I spent a great deal of time together, listening to music. He introduced me to Dave Brubeck and "Take Five" and One Stormy Night by the Mystic Moods Orchestra, both a far cry from the psychedelic rock I loved then and now. I expanded his rock and roll knowledge.

After that first year, he got married to the wonderful Mary Ann. Together they tried to make sure that I survived my college years. I rarely had much money and was in a variety of awful jobs, but they represented a sort of calm in the storm. I was in their wedding and they stopped into San Antonio to visit while on their honeymoon.

We attended our first science fiction conventions together and, in 1976 the three of us, along with our friend Clay Phennicie, went to our first World Science Fiction Convention. It was in Kansas City and it was magical.

We both wanted to be writers and we worked at it a great deal that first year. We wrote some truly awful things that might have been stories and were both glad to leave much of it behind. When Henry finally began to sell stories to Analog and other markets, I was pleased for him. Jealous but pleased. His first sale preceded mine by at least 15 years. So, in Kansas City, he was a published, if unknown, writer.

Over the years we went our separate ways. He and Mary Ann had a couple of kids and stayed in the Austin area. I moved around the state. I got married and, coincidentally, on our honeymoon, Sandi and I stopped in to see Henry and Mary Ann

I liked his short stories quite a bit. They were infrequent, but always thoughtful. When his novels began coming out, I thought I would see how he had progressed. I remembered some of our awful attempts from 35 or so years earlier and there was a faint hint of dread.

I should never have doubted it. Emperor Dad, his first novel, was a compelling read. I loved it from the start and read obsessively until I was done. It was a YA novel in the vein of the old Winston juvenile series or the YA works of Heinlein. Subsequent novels have been just as good.

But here we want to talk about short fiction. Henry is a fan of the short story. I know we discussed and read hundreds during those college days. He has written quite a few.

So, like Kaeti in that collection I mentioned earlier, I know that you are the lucky ones. Enjoy these pieces and then pick up one of his novels. I like them all, but I can tell you that I have a fond spot for Emperor Dad and Follow That Mouse. Check them out.

One of my regular writing gigs is for MissionsUnknown.com where I review Forgotten Books and Films. I have reviewed three or four novels from Henry over the years and wished I could do more. Actually, I wished that I would never have to consider his work "forgotten" or "unknown". Perhaps these stories will help that task along.

"Cor! Ain't you the lucky one?" indeed.

Scott A. Cupp

The Attorney for Passenger Pigeons

This is a simple "What if...?" story. What if our legal system decided to treat animals not as property, or even as people, but as equivalents, and what kind of event would be necessary to trigger it?

"What's this?" asked Blake Springdale, as his secretary handed him the thin package of legal-sized sheets.

Shirley shrugged. "I thought it was a *pro bono* case at first, but it isn't like anything I have seen before."

He scanned the front sheet, and then dropped it like it was dipped in poison.

It was a legal summons. Boiled down, he was to appear before the UN Intra-Species Arbitration Board (ISAB). The matter at hand was:

Homo sapiens (common name Humanity)

vs.

Ectopistes migratorius (common name Passenger Pigeon)

Represented by Blake Springdale, member United States Association of Environmental Law

Oh no! I've got an ISAB assignment.

Then he saw the date.

"This can't be right. That's only a couple of weeks away. I can't be ready by then. USAEL said that everyone would probably get one of these, but they said we'd have 90 days to prepare!"

"There was a cancellation."

The case had been assigned to a firm in Boston. They held it two months and then cancelled. The ISAB then sent it to the next person on the list, him. He scowled as he read the final sentence.

"It is the policy of this board that due to the depth of the case load, no extensions to these proceedings will be granted."

They weren't going to give him any time. His only choice was to hit the ground running. Or cancel.

I can't cancel. The USAEL had been very clear on the issue. Members in good standing had to serve their turn at the ISAB, or lose their certification. Maybe that Boston firm had other cases to deal with, but he was new in the Environmental Law specialization. He needed the certification to survive.

He picked up the phone.

"Hello, Stan? I wondered, have you ever had an ISAB case? Do you know anyone who has? I'll buy lunch for a little guidance."

After that call, he tapped the phone with his fingers for a minute, and then called his wife.

"Barbara, I've got an urgent case that will put me in New York on the 19th."

"That's Aunt Margaret's birthday!"

"I know, that's why I called you as soon as I found out about it."

"You promised. We're her only family, and we do so little as it is."

Blake tried to pacify her, but she wasn't listening very well.

Not that it really makes any difference. His wife's great aunt was in her late nineties, and since her stroke two years earlier, she was unresponsive. This birthday party was just something to make his wife feel better. If Aunt Margaret had any awareness of her surroundings, she gave no sign.

. . .

Steaks put the trio of lawyers in a good mood.

"ISAB cases can be fun," said Gordon Potter. "The UN pays for your stay. It was their Declaration of Species Equivalence that started the whole ISAB process in the first place. And, if you can win a big judgment for your clients, your cut can be a nice piece of change indeed."

"No doubt about that," agreed Dan Fieldstone. "Just look at the ISAB surcharge on these steaks. Just a few cents, but for every steak dinner, and every dairy delivery, and every leather shoe, it adds up. And their negotiator gets a cut."

Blake asked, "And the cows get to admire their bank accounts before going to the slaughterhouse? Or do they get custom decorations on their cow-bells?"

Dan shook his head. "No. That's the thing. The rules are that you negotiate for the benefit of the species, not for any individuals of that species.

"In fact, domesticated animals don't generally do very well in the mediations. *Homo sapiens* negotiators are good. The UN pays top dollar to defend the rights of humanity, and unless an animal species has its own advocacy group, their lawyers are draftees, like you and me. The chance for a big settlement is really the only thing that keeps the process honest.

"Repeatedly, the case has been made that domesticated animals have already gained a significant benefit from their historic association with humans. There are more cattle now than there would have been if the species had been ignored by humans. We provide them food, water, protection from predators, medical care.

"It's the wild species that go extinct, not some rancher's livestock."

"Then why the ISAB steak tax?"

Dan smiled. "The cows lucked out. Their negotiator made the case that long-term domestication had harmed their ability to survive in the wild. By breeding repeatedly for placid beasts that could be easily handled, we've reduced their chances of surviving without us.

"That's why there are now preserves on each continent where cattle are being bred back to wild variants that can hold their own.

"Personally, I think the judgment was excessive, but the tax is minor, and few other species can use it as legal precedent. From what I have heard, a New York firm has appealed the sheep award, citing the cow case. But it'll likely be twenty years or so before they can get on the docket."

"No sooner?"

Gordon shook his head. "No. There's an automatic review—but only as a check for incompetent representation. One of the first cases was handled by an old geezer who thought the whole thing was silly and bungled the case for some frog. The case was resubmitted, the frogs won a part ownership of some marshland in Texas, and the original negotiator was censured by his state licensing board."

Blake shook his head. "I can't say I don't have qualms myself. Taking fairness to the snails and oak trees is a little outlandish."

Dan looked down at his plate, and stirred the butter in his potato. "Oh, law isn't about fairness anyway. It's about self-protection. Without laws, it's 'might makes right'. We protect the weak because tomorrow, we might be the weak, and we want all the right safeguards in place before we need it."

Blake nodded. It was the Magellanic War. Proof that aliens existed had changed so many things. Everyone knew that those lights the astronomers saw a zillion light-years away could only be some vast battle in space. But if there were space aliens with powerful weapons in the Magellanic cloud, then there could easily be others, closer to home.

With humanity's technological upper hand, any kindness to animals had been purely voluntary. But if humans weren't the most powerful beings around, the idea of intra-species conflict being settled by strength of arms didn't sound so good any more.

Dan smiled at Blake's frown. "A few popular animals have their own advocates, but for the rest, we lawyers have to handle them *pro-bono*, just like we do for the incompetents of our own species.

"It may not make any difference if we bump up against aliens, but if we can talk, then we at least avoid having our own behavior used against us."

Blake nodded. "I think I understand the basics. But I need nuts and bolts advice."

"Do your research. Humanity lawyers have a big staff, and you can be sure they know more about your client than you do. You said yours is some kind of bird? Then check for habitat reduction, or hunting. That's the big thing."

Gordon added, "And be prepared for any case where your animal harms humanity. In the smallpox case, it was ruled that its near extinction was appropriate self-defense by humanity."

"But it didn't hurt the rattlesnakes," said Dan. "In their case, the ruling was that any harm to humanity was incidental to human encroachment."

Gordon asked, "What was your species again?"

Blake looked at his notepad. "*Ectopistes migratorius*, the passenger pigeon."

Gordon looked at Dan. Dan tightened his lips.

"What is it?" Blake asked.

"Passenger pigeons are extinct," Dan said.

"What? How can that be?"

Gordon nodded, "It's true. They died out a hundred years or so ago."

Blake sat back in his chair, his mind in a whirl.

"How can I possibly represent a dead species? It this a mistake?"

Dan shook his head. "No. I knew this was coming. I just didn't know they'd drop it on you.

"The UN noticed several species being deliberately hunted to extinction once the ISAB was set up, so they ruled that extinction, per se, was no bar to ISAB judgment. No fair winning the case by killing the plaintiffs.

"But the side effect is that extinct species have to go through the same ISAB process."

"But how does this work? How can I argue for a judgment to benefit my client, when it doesn't even exist?"

Dan shook his head. "I don't know. Your case is the first one of this class. Yours will set the rules. But you know," he frowned, "you have to win this. Yours is the precedent for all the other extinctions. No award and people will know that it's okay to push the marginal species over the edge. You can't let that happen."

...

Blake dove into the Internet.

Everyone knew that passenger pigeons were extinct, except him. There were even pictures of the stuffed birds, mostly in private collections.

Many articles sang the same song. Evil greedy humans had hunted the bird to extinction and we should all be ashamed.

Other sites were different. The bird had apparently been beautiful, and impressive in its numbers, and its extinction had moved many people to poetry.

Finally, he located a site with a large unorganized collection of facts. He studiously went from page to page, reading and copying everything.

The prize, to his mind, was John J. Audubon's writings. A patron saint of the environmental movement, Audubon's descriptions reeled and soared through Blake's mind's eye, letting him glimpse just a bit of what it must have been like to see thousands of flocks fly overhead, for hours on end. One image, that of a flock wheeling in unison, one moment showing the azure of their combined breasts, and then turning as one, to show the purple of their backs, stuck with him. It must indeed have been a beautiful sight, uncountable flocks overhead changing colors like jewels.

But Audubon's narrative was also dangerous. The scientist could not imagine their extinction, but like the careful observer he was, he considered the effects of the massive hunting, and observed the grand flock recovering easily from a harvest. And it had been a massive hunt—a million killed. Blake couldn't quite get his mind around that.

He glanced at the clock. His wife should still be up. He picked up the phone.

"Barbara. I'll be late getting home. I'll probably be late working on this case every night right up to the last minute. But, I was wondering if it would be okay to have Aunt Margaret's birthday party this week. I would like to see her."

"You do?" She was rightly suspicious. Aunt Margaret had been her favored friend when she was a child, but by the time she'd married, her great aunt had gone downhill. Blake had no pleasant memories of the lady.

"Yes. I don't know why, but I'd like to see her, and I really hate it that this case has made me go back on my promise."

"Okay, if you really mean it."

"Yes, I do."

...

Aunt Margaret's room was spare. Paintings hung on the walls and flowers sat on the little desk next to the bed—his wife's contributions.

She looked smaller every time he came, and the pillow below her head looked huge. She appeared comfortable, and the bed was cranked up to a sitting position, but he suspected the nurse who had arranged her hair had also arranged her thin frame on the bed with all the care of someone creating a flower arrangement.

Barbara gushed over her 97th birthday, carefully omitting that it was actually several days early. She talked about little Judy, and told her about how she was learning to walk, and getting into all sorts of trouble. The old lady breathed, but showed no other signs of life.

"Blake is here with me." She waved him closer.

"Hello, Aunt Margaret. Happy Birthday." He tried to make it real, although she'd never quite remembered who he was even before the last stroke.

"I was thinking of you the other day. You have seen a lot of history.

"The world must have been quite a different place when you were young. The machines have changed, and the people have changed. There are different ideas now, so different from when you grew up."

Barbara watched him, listening.

Blake looked at the old wrinkled face, not that there was response to his words. But she was alive, and who knows, maybe she could still hear what was going on around her.

"I have a case, a legal case, about passenger pigeons. Do you know about passenger pigeons? They were almost totally gone by the time you were a little girl, so I suspect you haven't seen them any more than I have. But your parents did. You lived in Kentucky, Barbara told me. They must've presented a spectacular sight when they came through. Did your father tell you about them? How they came in flocks that blocked out the sun?

"I wish I could see them. They're long gone, but you can be sure I'll tell my daughter about them, when she gets older and can understand. If your father told you about them, then you are really blessed to get descriptions by someone who was there, who saw them in person."

It was just his imagination, he was sure, but it seemed like there was a glisten around the edge of her old eyes.

Barbara smiled and squeezed his hand.

...

He'd invited his wife to come to New York with him, maybe take in a show after his job was done?

"No, I still think I should be there for her birthday."

It was just as well. He was up all night working and reworking his presentation. His brief was turned in by the deadline, and he'd managed to be suitably offended at the memo from the humanity lawyers complaining about their deadlines. It was all gamesmanship. Their memo and his written response were spare ammunition to be used if necessary to argue their good-faith efforts.

The ISAB proceedings were held in a new building near the UN. There were five separate courts, each running their own agendas. His assigned assistant, Joe Neeley a young man barely out of high school, looking prim in his blazer, showed him his temporary office and filled him in on the workings of the court. The *Homo sapiens* negotiators had an entire floor in the same building, with easy access to an extensive law and science library. He was given access as well, but there was no time to use it.

He entered the courtroom, and his eye caught the wooden calendar on the wall, with May 19 in black incised letters—Aunt Margaret's birthday.

Three arbitration judges arrived shortly before 11AM, strangely attired in colored robes more reminiscent of his professors' gowns at graduation than the black of US judges. It was a reminder that he was arguing before an international tribunal, and he shouldn't expect US custom to prevail.

He felt alone on his side of the aisle, while a team of four sat confidently on the other side.

Who are the people in the gallery? I wonder if there are any Passenger pigeon fans out there? I could use the support.

He was up first, presenting his opening argument. He argued that *Ectopistes migratorius*, as an equivalent species to *Homo sapiens*, had been unfairly reduced in numbers and driven to extinction by the actions of 19th century American commercial hunting and land development, and that the governments of the United States and Canada should pay 100 million dollars into a fund to be used to reconstruct the genetic sequence of passenger pigeons from the taxidermically preserved remaining members of the species.

"And when technology and research reach appropriate levels, the species should be recreated and reintroduced into the wild." He felt odd, pushing such an agenda, but regeneration was really the only course open. How else to benefit his client?

Judge Engelmann, on the left, barely looked his way, taking notes all the while. Judge Mbeya, in striking dark orange robes, stared at him with hardly a blink. And on the right, Judge Park rested her chin on her fist, as if her forearm were propping her head up. Surely, she wasn't asleep, but she moved so little it was a disturbing thought.

The lead negotiator for *Homo sapiens* then presented, and it was a point-by-point knockdown of everything he had said.

"*Ectopistes migratorius* no longer exists," the gray-haired lead-council began, "and there can be no question of an award by this board, since there is no species to receive its benefit."

Reconstruction was a myth, he argued, since earlier attempts had used DNA with helper sequences from host animals and the result was not equivalent to the original species. It would just be a chimera, an entirely different species, and one which would be entirely dependent on *Homo sapiens* for its existence and care.

He went on to undermine humanity's guilt in the extinction. Yes, there was large scale hunting, but from all historical records, the species abruptly declined in numbers, well in excess of any expectations. An avian disease could well have caused the species extinction, or some parasite totally unrelated to the hunting losses.

Audubon was trotted out with due reverence and his passage explaining that the passenger pigeon could survive the hunting was recited. Records from state legislatures from the mid 1800's were entered into the record, showing that protection for the species was considered, investigated, and determined to be unnecessary.

"Humanity had been careful. Humanity had been prudent. By every science of the day, the birds were studied and found healthy, but still they died. We didn't do it. Some defect of *Ectopistes* itself was likely to blame for their extinction.

"Extinction happens to all species. It is not humanity's role to play God and reverse that."

As he summed up, Joe Neeley edged up to Blake's table and handed him a small notepad.

"Phone call from Barbara Springdale:

"Aunt Margaret died this morning. Made it to her birthday on her own. Everything under control here. Come home soon, but do a good job for the pigeons. Love, Barbara."

He slipped the note under the other papers, trying to shake off the feeling of failure. *No. It's not over yet.*

...

Judge Engelmann called him to answer questions.

"Mr. Springdale, I'm interested in the statement in your brief that an award to a trust organization for the passenger pigeon would be the same thing as an award to the species. In other cases, a trust organization is the appropriate administrator of an award, since the individuals of that species are incompetent. However, I fail to see how a trust for a class of incompetent individuals is the same as a trust for a class of nonexistent individuals. How do you resolve this difference?"

Blake felt his mind race. He'd thought long and hard about this one.

"Your Honor, what, exactly, is a species? It is a mistake to think of a species as a set of individuals. If so, the species is different from one moment to the next as individuals die, and are born, or hatched." The judge cracked a slight smile. "Under that definition, the species of March fruit flies is a different thing than the species of May fruit flies, since no individual lives longer than a few days.

"Nor should I think a copy of the genetic code to be enough to be considered a species, otherwise the Human Genome database would have to be considered a part of humanity, and the existence of Martha, the stuffed bird in the Smithsonian could be considered evidence that the Passenger pigeon is not extinct.

"No, the idea that a species can be 'extinct' gives us the clue that 'species' is a process that can be extinguished. Put simply, a species is the process that preserves the existence of a genetic code.

"And by that definition, the *Ectopistes migratorius* has never quite gone out of existence.

"When their population crashed, people were concerned. Efforts were made to collect the birds and breed them in captivity. When these last individuals died, they were preserved for study. And when the last one died, people cared. In the historical exhibits, are the poems and the passionate writings by people expressing their loss.

"I submit that as hopeless and ineffectual as it seemed, those early efforts were part of the process that now has a real hope of preserving the genetic code of *Ectopistes migratorius*. For a brief time the spirit of the passenger pigeon has left the flesh of its native host, but it has the chance to return!

"The details of my proposal explain the rest. A trust entity would, upon the grant of the award, become *Ectopistes migratorius* for legal purposes, providing the process that would eventually preserve this genetic expression."

The judge asked for more details about the trust, forcing him to think fast. There were indeed pitfalls. Fund administrators could hold the species hostage and preserve the trust even when the technology was ready to restore the birds.

But, he was able to describe remedies. At least in his own mind, he sounded like he'd been working on the idea for years. Who knew what the judges thought?

There were many more questions:

"What is your reasoning for placing the levy on the jurisdictions indicated?"

"How did you choose the 100 million dollars? That's a nice round number. Did you pull it out of a hat?"

"What makes you think the species can be reintroduced into the wild, given the changes to the land in the last 150 years?"

"Council for Humanity has described the effects of the large flocks as horrific—flocks scavenging food so completely that nothing is left for other animals, nesting so heavily that all the trees are broken down, droppings collecting several inches deep. Why should humans pay to re-introduce such a plague on themselves?"

Blake tap-danced as hard as he could to answer their questions, and smiled when he stumbled. They knew he was a last minute substitution, or at least they should. He could only do his best.

Then, it was Humanity's turn to be grilled. Blake took careful notes. He had only one chance left, in his summation. He had to hit every weak point that the judges had left un-demolished.

There was a pause in the proceedings, as he collected his notes. His mind was overflowing with data, important points to make, and a dozen different strategies. There wasn't time to do it all.

"Mr. Springdale? Your summation."

He nodded, as his mind suddenly went blank. Still he rose from his desk and stepped to the center.

The only thing he could think about was Aunt Margaret's tear, when he had talked about the passenger pigeons. Did her death today, on her birthday, mean that she'd been aware of what he said? What had she been thinking? What memories had he stirred?

He faced the judges.

"I am here today to speak for the passenger pigeon, and to speak against humanity.

"But more importantly I am here to speak for justice. We have created Declaration of Species Equivalence, and to that I must speak.

"No one denies that the 18th and 19th century Americans killed *Ectopistes migratorius* in large numbers. No one denies that the prime habitat for these birds, the large beech forests, were largely cut down to make farmland. No one denies that in 1914, Martha, the last known passenger pigeon, died.

"What is debated is the cause of this extinction, and humanity's culpability in it.

"One part was the harvesting of so many birds. I say 'harvesting' because hunting was hardly involved. Millions of birds at a time were shipped to the cities of the East Coast. But this couldn't have been the sole cause. Killing a million out of a population of three billions is still only one out of 3000. No, this can only be part.

"The loss of the beech forests is likely a much greater cause of the population crash, but still—not all the beeches are gone.

"No, there is something more.

"Council for Humanity has alluded to some defect in the species. The passenger pigeon just wasn't good enough to survive this misfortune."

He looked from judge to judge to judge.

"But species equivalence is more than just the name of a law. It is the underlying principle of this proceeding. We cannot say, 'This species is defective, because it didn't tolerate human instituted changes.'

"The passenger pigeon may have needs that were beyond the ken of 19th century science. They were a grand social animal. Their flocks flew as one being. They ate together, they few together, they nested for the night together. They were a species of flocks, more than individuals.

"Just because we humans can breed and thrive in small numbers if we have to, does not mean that another way is defective.

"Audubon noticed that in the great American flocks the birds always produced two eggs, but puzzlingly, among the birds sent to England, they never produced more than one egg. Yes, there are mysteries here, but just because they don't act human, doesn't mean they are any less deserving of legal protection than any other species."

He looked at his empty hands. "There is one other, very compelling point.

"We all know that we are guilty.

"I did not know about passenger pigeons until I was assigned this case, but I felt no shock that a species whose numbers were in the billions just 150 years ago, are now entirely gone. Of course we did it! You know, and I know, that species are killed off every day, and that humans are the cause.

"We didn't mean to do it. It was out of ignorance. It happened long before any of us were born—but we know we are guilty.

"I submit that in Audubon's day, this dark side of humanity was not a part of the world's consciousness as it is today. No one back then thought the birds were in any more need of protection than ants.

"In the Garden of Eden, man was made caretaker of over all the animals, but it is only in the last hundred years that that duty has become clear to us.

"The extinction of the Passenger pigeon changed us! I submit it is the root of the environmental movement. It is the root of the very declaration on which this court exists. It is the root of a change of mind, one that may well be our species salvation in the future."

He hit his fist into his open palm.

"Humanity owes *Ectopistes migratorius* something. More than just punishment for our own wrongdoing, we owe them something good for the change that has happened to us. Great good has come from their death, but even greater good can come from their redemption.

"I have a daughter, only a year old. When she is older, I will tell her about this bird, who flashed like jewels in the sky, and blacked out the sky by their numbers, and whose wings caused the air to hum for hundreds of miles.

"I will also tell her how we were careless, and caused them to die.

"It would be a great thing if I could also tell her about the rebirth of this bird, and it would be even greater if she could see this marvel in her own lifetime, so that when she is old, the thought of the passenger pigeon would bring a smile of joy and pride to her face, and not a tear of regret."

...

Blake retired to his seat and suffered through the opposition's closing remarks. He was done. Anything he had left unsaid would remain unsaid. He tried to ignore the points that were being made, but no doubt about it; humanity's negotiators were good. Point by point, he could feel his own statements being undermined, and doubts being seeded.

Finally, the argument phase was done. The judges retired, and with a nod to the other team, he went back to his temporary office. He put his head down on the desk and dozed.

...

Two hours later, he was called back in.

The mediators entered and the court was called to order.

Judge Park, who had not participated in the question and answer session, called him and the other lead negotiator to the center. Her clearly enunciated English had a distinctive Korean accent.

"In the matter of *Homo sapiens* vs. *Ectopistes migratorius*, this mediation board finds for the plaintiff as follows:

"(1) *Ectopistes migratorius*, commonly known as the passenger pigeon was driven to extinction by various environmental stresses, and that *Homo sapiens* bears the primary blame for this.

"(2) *Ectopistes* is acknowledged to be a species under the terms of the UN Declarations of Species Equivalents using the definition of species as an ongoing process to preserve a genetic code, and thus, (3) is entitled to redress by what measures this board recommends."

She looked up from her paper and nodded to him. He was still absorbing the idea that he had won.

"Mr. Blake. The board found that your remedy was sound in principle, but that the proposed amount of the award was far in excess of the need, due to the lack of urgency of the remedy. The goal of restoring the species will not be measurably compromised if it is done twenty years or a hundred years from now. If individuals of the species were still alive, and on their last legs, then urgent action, requiring a larger outlay would be more appropriate."

He could feel his heart start to sink. Did that mean he won, but it was just an empty victory, with no teeth?

But she continued, "Accordingly, this board recommends a substantive award of ten million dollars, which should fund the research and genetic material collection phases."

Then her voice notched slightly louder, angrier.

"However, this board finds that extinction of another species for economic gain is unacceptable, and that in spite of the unintentional nature of this extinction, punitive damages shall be added to the award, trebling it to thirty million dollars.

"The board acknowledges that no current individual is to blame for this extinction, and that it was done through ignorance, for if it had been otherwise, the punitive damages would have been much greater."

And as quickly as that, the court was adjourned.

There was a splattering of applause, he turned to see who it was, and didn't recognize anyone. However, one of the humanity team gave him a surreptitious thumbs-up.

A court official spoke with him for a minute to clarify the details of the award. He nodded, and accepted the papers.

...

It took him another hour to leave the building. Several of the spectators had been reporters, and they all wanted a few words with him. He made it to the hotel, finally, and was able to call his wife.

She was dealing with the funeral arrangements, and was suffering from the mix of relief and grief that comes when an elderly invalid dies. She was happy to talk about his trip.

"So, you won, but not everything?"

"Yes. It counts as a win, and it looks like I have a new client, for I'll have to be a part of this new species trust. Money-wise, it's wonderful. I just have a feeling that I didn't do enough. The passenger pigeon is still dead."

"I know." Barbara's voice caught. "Aunt Margaret was special, and I know I'll never be able to tell people what a beautiful person she was."

...

As he checked out of the hotel next morning, he couldn't take his eyes off the USA Today newspaper he had found in front of his door.

There was his picture, and next to it was a photo of Martha, the Smithsonian's stuffed passenger pigeon.

"$30 Million ISAB Award for Extinct Bird."

He read the article, and it was like an old friend. Audubon's poetic descriptions tickled his imagination all over again.

There was another paper in the stand, the New York Times. It showed another of the famous stuffed birds, George. Its story was about the impact the ruling would have on currently threatened species. Judge Parks words, on reflection, added up to a formidable threat if any species was deliberately bulldozed out of the way.

The hotel clerk handed him his final tally, and added. "By the way, congratulations Mr. Springdale. You did a good job for the birds. I'm going to tell my kids about it when I get home."

"Thank you."

He went out to meet his taxi, and as he stepped outside, there was a flutter of wings. He caught sight of a pair of common rock pigeons taking wing.

But he blinked his eyes, and felt spirits in azure and purple, swooping overhead in ancient and grand array.

Duck and Cover

Some stories are exercises. I had heard one too many jokes about 1950's Civil Defense exercises, you know the one where school children were taught to hide under their desks to avoid blast effects. That was back when people thought *about how to survive rather than wave their hands and scream in panic that we're all going to die. So I thought, how would I survive? The house in this story is my house, and the resources available to Clark and Ginger are my resources.*

They were half-way to Lake Granger when the sky lit up.

"What is that?" Ginger screamed.

Clark didn't reply. He immediately swerved off the highway and drove the Jeep across the ditch and through a wooden fence. As soon as he had a hand free, he shoved her down. "Stay low! Don't look at it!"

Ahead was a deserted farmhouse. He ignored the wood-frame building and pulled the Jeep up next to the brick and concrete shed next to it. Only when he stopped and saw the shadows moving on the ground did he realize there was another one.

Ginger's eyes were wide with panic.

"Come on." He held out his hand and pulled her out.

"Clark, what's going on?"

He made her huddle down with him next to the concrete. "Nukes. One in Austin, the other north. Maybe Fort Hood."

"Oh, God! We're going to die!"

He held her close, trying to put his own thoughts together. The two of them, dressed for boating and picnicking on the lake, were caught in an open Jeep with no shelter in sight.

"We'll make it. But first we've got to wait for the shock waves."

"What do we do?"

"It'll all be..."

Before he could complete the sentence, a tornado force wind blasted through the area from the south. They huddled tighter into the shelter of the wall. He kept his arms around her.

"Duck and cover," he laughed. The air was like opening an oven. But although it was still filled with dust and debris, it passed.

"What?"

"I'm wishing for a school desk, like in those old Civil Defense films where school kids ducked under their desks." It had appeared funny then, but it wasn't now.

"That was the Austin blast. The other shouldn't be too long."

"But what about the fallout? Won't it kill us anyway?" she was shivering.

He patted her shoulder. "Two more minutes. Then we'll head for shelter."

The shock wave from the north was severe, but less so than the Austin one.

"Come on. It's time to move."

He checked the Jeep. It had rocked, but the wall had kept it from flipping. The engine was still running. He hadn't thought to turn it off.

"Check the radio. See if you can find anything." He glanced at their picnic supplies in the back seat, but the ice chest and the basket were still intact. He wrapped the towels around the basket.

He'd probably thrown the wheel alignment off when he'd jumped the ditch, but it got back up to highway speed with no more than a slight wobble. There were cars off the road, some overturned, some burning, but there was other traffic, going in all directions. Ginger pulled out her cell phone, but there was no signal. He suspected the system was down.

There wasn't a good choice on which way to flee. He'd seen two blasts, one upwind and one downwind, but the weather could change at any time. If there'd been just one blast, he'd head cross wind as far and as fast as he could manage, but there were two. Two meant that this was a widespread and co-ordinated attack. San Antonio, Houston, Dallas, and any number of other cities were likely showing their own mushroom clouds. Fallout would be widespread. He couldn't outrun it.

"Where are we going?" Ginger was staring at the car radio. It was scanning, and scanning, and scanning. All the stations were off the air.

"My Uncle Fred's house."

She nodded, and switched from the FM to the AM band. Shortly, she found a broadcast—an announcer saying what they already knew. Many cities had been hit, all at once. There'd been no missiles, no warning. No one knew who did it.

The back-country roads were filled with hazards, and other cars racing, like him, at dangerously high speeds. There was smoke everywhere, as either accidents, or blast effects had triggered so many fires that there was no one to put them out. Dangerous gray clouds were high in the sky, and although they weren't glowing any more, Clark knew they were deadly.

"Ginger!" he yelled over the road noise.

"What?"

"Make a breathing mask. Make one for me too. Fallout will be coming in minutes. We don't want to breathe in that stuff."

She nodded, looking relieved to be able to do something. She dug into her bag and ripped the sleeves off of a blouse. She wrapped one around her face, and then carefully, she did the same for him as he drove.

The house he remembered was not too far. He crossed the creek and found the cross-road.

Soon he was bouncing down the long gravel driveway into the five acre property. There was no car in the driveway. He hadn't expected one.

"Ginger, we're probably already dusted with some of the fallout." He led her to the back porch. He pointed to the swimming pool, still as blue and inviting as he'd remembered before. The property was down in a little valley and much of the force of the blast waves must have passed by overhead. "Our clothes are contaminated as well as our skin and hair." He pulled off his shoes and then his shirt. "Strip down and wash in the pool." He didn't look her way as he stripped to the buff and jumped in. Her splash came a few seconds later.

He scrubbed hard at his hair, and then pulled himself out. She was doing what he'd asked, even if there was a suspicious look on her face. "Leave your clothes on the porch, and come inside."

He dashed through to the den. His uncle had never locked his doors, and this time was no different. Padding with wet footsteps, he went straight to his uncle's office and rummaged until his found what he'd remembered from a visit three years before—a little Geiger counter. The battery was dead, but there were replacements. He had it clicking after a minute.

Ginger was waiting, her arms bundled across her chest. He came up and ran the little device over her. "You've still got some in your hair."

"Back to the pool."

"No. There's still probably some water pressure in the lines. Go use the shower and shampoo. I've got to get the food out of the car."

It was uncomfortable to dash out into the sunlight naked, but there was no time for anything else. He moved the ice chest and basket to the back porch. With a garden hose, he rinsed them off and checked them with the counter. The basket was still hot. He unpacked the wrapped sandwiches and tubs of food and rinsed them separately. After another dunk in the pool, he moved everything he could indoors.

All the windows had been closed, and for that he was grateful. The fallout hadn't gotten inside.

But that didn't mean the clicks on the counter weren't climbing dangerously high.

He found Ginger and confirmed that her hair was clean. "Good. I'd hate to have to cut it off."

He pointed to the closets. "Find clothes for you and me. We'll be stuck in tight quarters for several days. I've got to find the most secure place in the house."

This was Central Texas, so there was no basement in the house, and it was much too late to dig a fallout shelter. He surveyed the house. Centrally located, with no exterior walls, was a second bathroom. With the electricity out, it was dark inside, but he stoppered the drains and started filling the tub and sink. They would need all the water they could hoard.

He looked at the central air conditioning cabinet. There was a cozy, if dusty, space under the actual air conditioner equipment. It might be good enough.

Ginger arrived with a bundle of clothes. She'd already dressed in an over-sized shirt. "There weren't any women's clothes."

"Sorry." He stuck the Geiger counter inside the air conditioner vent and the clatter of clicks dimmed a bit.

"Do we get in there?" She didn't sound happy.

"We need to find the place that has the most mass between us and the outside. There's no fallout inside, but it's already getting deadly hot outside, and those clicks are blasting right through the walls. Every wall, or box or brick we can put between us and the dust will make us live longer. This hallway is not good enough, not for the next few days. The bathroom is better, and so is this air conditioner cavity."

"Is there any place else?"

He considered. On the other side of the wall common to the bathroom and the hallway was the garage. But he'd better check.

"Stay here in the bathroom and turn off the faucets when the sink and tub gets full. We're collecting water."

"Put this on." She handed him one of his uncle's khaki shorts.

"Sorry." He slipped them on. They were a little loose, but they'd work.

He kept the counter on, wincing at the clicks when he went through the laundry room to get to the garage. But the garage was interesting, a warehouse so full of boxes that no car, nor likely a motorcycle, would be able to get in. And there was a stairway up to the attic.

Don't go there. He wanted to go down, not up. He wanted mass over his head. But climbing over some boxes, he found the corner near to where Ginger was waiting on the other side of the wall. There, under the staircase, was an untidy little room that contained the hot water heater. It might be tight quarters, but not as bad as the space under the air conditioner.

He checked with the counter. *Good. This is it.*

He pushed aside some boxes to make it easier to get in and then dashed back to get her.

She'd found a flashlight.

"Good. We'll need that. I found a better place." He led her to their shelter.

"How long are we going to be here?"

"Get inside and we'll talk." She went in and they crouched in the dark. He checked the clicks and showed her the scale.

"I really wish I knew all the answers, but I never thought I'd actually have to deal with it. I remember just a few things. One is that the exposure adds up. See, inside here, we're in the blue range. So it'd take us...two weeks or so to accumulate a fatal exposure."

"So we're still not safe?"

He took her hand. "The thing is, the fallout peaks. It burns itself out. In a hundred hours, it'll only be one percent as hot. Something like that. I don't remember exactly. But in just a couple of days it won't be deadly. We'll probably only have to hide in here for three or four days to be safe. And by that time, the fire department and the government people with all the fancy protective gear will be out in force, and we'll probably get better instructions on the radio.

"All we have to do is stay safe for just a few days."

He was telling her the most optimistic version, but they needed to keep hope alive.

Ginger nodded. "Okay, but it's nasty in here. There's mice droppings and stuff."

"We'll clean it up. I'll have to make runs through the house to get food, and mattresses, and stuff like that. I'll bring a broom first thing. But you have to say put. Understand?"

She looked at him with a funny expression. "Why you? We can both get that stuff."

"I'm not going to risk it."

"Why not?"

He sighed. "Ginger. I hate to be the one to break the news, but you're a girl."

She took in a breath, ready to do battle.

He put his fingers on her lips. "And because you're a girl, you've got all the egg cells you're ever going to have already. And I don't want them damaged by radiation. I make new sperm cells all the time. It's less of a risk for me. Understand?"

She didn't like it. But she nodded. "Okay, but you be careful."

"Oh, I will be! I hate going through the laundry room. With it's window to the outside, it's already unhealthy in there. I want to zip through there in a flash."

She leaned close, and they kissed. With his heart beating fast from all the activity, it notched up still higher. He'd had hopes for some making out time on the picnic, and her bikini had been all that he could have wished for. But everything had changed. How they'd feel about each other after this ordeal wasn't something he'd want to put money on.

He gave her a squeeze. "Okay. Broom. Then bedding to make this concrete floor less deadly on my knees, then what?"

She smiled. "Another flashlight? Food, I didn't get lunch. Something to drink."

He nodded and headed out.

He wasn't kidding about the laundry room. The house was limestone brick, so windows were the most dangerous places. He was sure it had been a good idea to have a nice window, so the room was well lit while working, but for the next few days, he'd not be doing anything there.

...

With a broom, sandwiches and cokes, they took a lunch break. Clark checked the radiation with the door open and closed and there was little difference when they were both sitting. The warehouse boxes filling the garage probably made a nice radiation shield from that direction. While they ate, with the door open for lighting, he tried to visualize the house. For one thing it kept him from dwelling on just how tasty Ginger was, dressed in nothing more than a man's shirt.

Nothing was coming through the ground, obviously. To the south, the clutter in the garage was good protection. In the opposite direction, there were four interior walls and the exterior limestone, plus whatever furniture was in the way. The west had two interior walls, limestone, and a very cluttered closet protecting in that direction. The east was a problem, as was the attic. He knew there were storage boxes up there, but he didn't know if it was enough. There was a metal roof, but it probably wasn't as good a shield as the limestone walls.

So east and up are the major risks. He looked up. That was the stairway.

He finished up his sandwich.

"Are you done sweeping?"

"Not quite."

"Well, in a few minutes, I'll be bringing in a mattress and we'll be putting it right here, under the stairs."

"Why there? There's more headroom here where we're sitting."

"Because before I'm done. That's going to be the safest spot, and that's where I want to be spending most of my time."

"Oh? You're going to be on the mattress? And where will I be."

He grinned, "Right there beside me—for safety sake, you understand."

"Uh huh."

...

It took more trips than he liked through the laundry room, but soon they had a mattress and pillows and a couple of sheets. It was summer time with no air conditioning. They'd not need anything more than that. He'd also collected a couple of days worth of canned and bagged food from the pantry and jugs of water.

Then came a marathon job that left him exhausted. He transferred boxes from the garage and stacked them five or six feet high on the steps to the attic. As he'd said, under the steps was soon the place with the fewest clicks.

"I need a rest." He leaned up against the hot water heater, which had already cooled down to the tepid room temperature.

Ginger nodded and took one of the towels she'd brought and wet it. She began washing him down. "You're covered in sweat. If we're sleeping together, I'd rather you didn't stink quite so much."

He grinned at her choice of words. "When we headed out this morning, I had my hopes..."

"Don't go there, Buster."

He shut up. But he still grinned as he relished the feel of her washing his body.

...

When it grew dark, so did their thoughts.

"I'm worried about my folks."

He tried not to think about his.

"You live near that school. They probably went there for shelter."

"You think so?" she sounded hopeful.

"Probably. With a little common sense, they'd be okay. Thick walls, well stocked cafeteria. As long as there's someone to crack the whip and make everyone behave, it would be the best place to wait it out."

"What about your folks? And your uncle? I expected him to show up."

He was slow to answer. "They all went into Austin together. A baseball game."

"Oh. Maybe they found some place safe too."

"I hope so." He didn't really believe it. Downtown, close to the blast, with survivors suffering from burns as well as direct radiation, roads gridlocked—their chances were slim. He didn't want to think about it. If he was pleasantly surprised, he'd be grateful then. Until then, he wanted to keep his mind on keeping the two of them safe.

"Ah, Clark?"

"Yes."

"I think we forgot something."

"What's that?"

"I, ah. I need to go."

"I didn't forget. Outside the door, about five feet down, there's a five gallon can with a toilet seat sitting on it. Do your business and then tie off the plastic bag in the can with the rubber band. It'll keep us for a couple of days. After that, with the radiation lower, we can use the house toilets. We can fill the flush tanks with a bucket."

She reached over and kissed him. "You think of everything." She slipped out the door and after a bit, she was back, wiping her hands with a towel. "Toilet paper and everything. I think I love you."

...

He turned off the flashlight. "We need to save batteries. I'll go look for candles tomorrow. But for tonight, we'll just have to do without."

"That's okay. Do you want to be against the wall or closest to the door?"

"I'd like to be closest to the door, if you don't mind."

"I'm not claustrophobic. No problem."

He didn't want to mention his worry, that in spite of the fact that the radiation was deadly outside, there could be looters who just didn't know or care that they were killing themselves. He wanted to be ready, just in case.

Uncle Jerry had some guns, but he didn't know where they were, or even if there was any ammunition. He hadn't been a hunter. They were mostly antiques, hand-me-downs from his father and grandfather. Clark hadn't even looked for them.

If there were intruders, their best bet might be to close the door and hide.

"Okay, I'm in bed. Watch your head. That step is low."

Moving by feel, he found the thick lumber of the utility staircase and eased down on the mattress. She touched him as he settled in beside her. It was the most natural thing in the world to pull her into his arms. They kissed.

"You know, you've got me at your mercy," she whispered.

"I know." He kissed her forehead. They just held each other. She was shivering again, and he didn't think it was from the temperature. It was still over 90.

"Ginger?"

"Mmm?"

"I think I like taking care of you."

She gave him a squeeze.

In spite of the close quarters, and his strong suspicion that she was wearing nothing under that shirt, he was too exhausted. "I think you're probably safe for tonight."

"Oh?" she sounded a little disappointed.

"But tomorrow, I'm probably going to ask you to marry me."

She laughed. "Isn't that a little sudden?"

He pulled her closer. "Yeah, but still, give it some thought."

"Okay?"

The temperature separated them a few minutes later, and before he had a chance to change his mind about getting frisky, he dozed off.

...

Daylight, even allowing for the reflections it had to take to get to the cubby where they lay, was bright enough for him to admire her sleeping form beside him. The shirt she wore was not an adequate sleeping gown. She was curled around a pillow, and what he saw had his blood pumping. It took a strong will to stay put.

I've got to get up. Moving slowly and carefully, he rolled off the mattress and found the Geiger counter. He tiptoed out the door and sat on one of the storage boxes, just outside.

He checked the reading, more to get his mind off her than for any other reason.

It was slightly lower. The radioactive dust created in the blast had been burning off energy from the moment it came into being, but the dust was also settling out of the sky, building up on the ground, and on the roof, and on the porch outside. There was more of it now, but it was less energetic. If it rained, the equation could be scrambled again, but for now, it was safer than it had been when they had been building their nest.

But not safe enough. He should really be back inside.

Back inside with her.

Back inside her. No. Don't go there. He was her protector. He had to take care of her, and that meant more than just keeping her from being fried by radiation.

I wish I'd thought to bring my cell phone inside. The system was down, and might be down for good. But if the authorities were on top of things, the'd make an effort to bring up some kind of service. Maybe just SMS texting, since it had the simplest infrastructure. But he wouldn't know without his phone. And right now it was on the back porch in his pocket, getting irradiated. Semiconductors didn't like radiation either.

There were enough things to worry about that by the time Ginger stirred awake, he'd gotten his urges under control and came back into their cave for a breakfast of granola bars and cold pop-tarts.

...

With chores done, and nothing to do, Clark crept back onto the mattress. Ginger was there beside him a minute later. She'd managed to change into another shirt, and even combed her hair. He offered an arm and she snuggled close.

"Ah, Clark?"

"Yes."

"Mmm. Last night, right before you dozed off, we were talking." She paused.

"And I asked you to marry me."

"Yes. Sort of. You said you'd ask today."

"Yes. Well, will you?"

She turned over onto her stomach and elbows. She clicked on the flashlight so she could see him, but she stared down at her fingers and began picking dirt out from under her nails. "Before I say, I have to ask why. We weren't that close the day before yesterday. We'd dated and I like you and all, but marriage was way down the line."

He nodded. "And then the world changed. Even in the best case, it will be years before things are back to normal. Maybe I wasn't looking for a wife yesterday morning, but I was looking forward to spending some quality time with you. Yesterday and for many more days after that. Maybe I'd have gotten around to the flowers and chocolates and romantic evenings. Maybe I'd have gotten around to the kneeling proposal and the fancy words.

"But this past day has collapsed all those dates into one long hard stretch. I know much more about you than I would have learned in those dates. I know you can hold your own even when panic is clawing away at you. You can think of things I can't and we work well together. I know you still look fabulous even when you're face is dirty and dressed in an old man's shirt." He looked at her, trying to read her face.

"I know I like caring for you. I want to be here for you, even if things never get back to normal. And if they do, great. I'd still want you with me if we end up heading for college together next fall.

"And I don't want to wait. Look at us, two half-naked kids hiding under the staircase, side by side on a mattress. I want to go ahead and do the stuff we're supposed to be doing. You don't know how close you came to waking up this morning with me between your legs." She flushed and her lips compressed into a little smile.

"But I don't know your answer. I don't know what you want. I know you've been coming on to me a little more than usual, but I don't know if that's real, or just a girl in danger's reaction to the nearest male protector."

She shook her head. "That's just a guy fantasy. But as for us, you saw the swimsuit I wore yesterday?"

He grinned. "Yes."

She was angry, "Well, that's not the kind of suit a wear when I go out with my family! I bought that with you in mind. So if I've been a little, affectionate, it's not because I'd just latch onto the first guy who came around!"

"Sorry." He winced at her response. "If I'm not sure about your feelings, partly it's because I'm not sure about mine. I was thrilled by the way you looked yesterday. Now, I'm struggling real hard to keep from going... much...further."

She nodded, watching him. "The world changed. We've been running on adrenaline and bottling up all kinds of emotions. I didn't mean to yell at you just then."

They lay there in silence for a minute or so.

Then she asked, "Is it the sex? Do you want to marry me so we can have sex without feeling guilty?"

He shrugged. "I don't know. Partly, I'm sure. But when I look at the future, I'm not sure of anything—other than that I want to be with you. I can actually look forward to the future, with you. I mean, if my folks and yours are out of the picture, then we'll just claim this place and defend it and turn it into a little farm. With this place as a base, and if I can keep the Jeep running, we can go searching for your folks. Even if everyone survives, and we all have to live together, then this place is big enough to make it work.

"And with you and me, together, we can make anything work."

She smiled. "So, what exactly did you have in mind? The bridal shops aren't open, and it might be hard to scare up a preacher this morning."

He shrugged. "Legally, you have to get a license, but I doubt the county court house will be in business for a while. I just want to *be* married. I want to claim you as my wife with a clear conscience, if anyone asks. We can take care of the paperwork when things settle out. What do *you* think is necessary and sufficient?"

She rolled over on her back and scooted up close enough to feel him against her. She stared at the undersides of the steps above. "I'd like a ring." She thought some more. "We could make a certificate ourselves, and sign it. And I want a ceremony."

He whispered. "I can come up with a ring."

She looked him in the eyes. "I can do the paperwork." They breathed together for a tense moment.

"Clark, I do. I will marry you."

He pulled her into his arms and they kissed. When his hand started wandering across her hip, she snagged it. "Later. We've got some work to do."

...

Clark skipped through the laundry room without much thought. He was intent on scaring up the materials they needed. Soon, Ginger was working on the mattress on a drawing tablet. He retreated to just outside the doorway so he could fire up the torch.

Uncle Fred had been alone for a dozen years, and he spent his time tinkering with things. Thus the Geiger counter with his rock collection, and drafting materials for sketching out his projects. He also had a parts drawer for electronics. With one hand on the Geiger counter, monitoring his risk, he rummaged through the drawers until he found the parts and tools he needed—then he raced back safety.

Ginger had giggled as he carefully measured her ring finger with a piece of wire. From a little spool of braided, silver cable, he formed a loop, with the braid spread flat. The high temperature torch caused the silver solder to flow into the braid, changing it into a solid, if textured ring of metal. He checked the size several times, and buffed the result smooth. He could see every imperfection. It wasn't at all like he'd imagined, but it was the best he could do under the current constraints.

I wish I had a stone. He could probably make a setting, given his uncle's tools, but his rock collection was feldspar and quartz and mica, not rubies and diamonds.

...

"Are you okay, out there? I'm smelling smoke."

"It's okay. The torch is off." But as soon as he said it, he realized he could smell smoke as well. Wood smoke.

"Ginger, I'm going to check the house."

He made sure the torch was all the way off and the valves closed tight. He slipped the ring into his pocket.

She looked out. "Be careful."

"You. Stay put." He grabbed the Geiger counter and dashed from room to room, making sure that everything was as it was supposed to be.

But in the living room, the smell of smoke was pronounced. And he could see it, out the window. There was a grass fire sweeping through the area! He dashed from window to window, risking seconds of radiation to get a view of what was happening.

He raced back to the garage.

"Ginger!"

"What's happening?"

"It's a fire outside. We may be okay. The house is stone and if the trees don't catch, the house should be okay, but we need to be prepared."

"What do we do?"

He didn't know. The radiation outside was still terribly high. They couldn't stand more than an hour's exposure, and even less than that would leave them sick and susceptible to infection. Their only safety was inside, but not if the house was on fire.

"Ginger, can you tread water?"

"Yes. You want to get in the pool?"

"Only if the house starts to catch. Stay put and pray. But if I yell, we'll put on face masks again and get in the pool."

"What about the fallout?"

"The stuff that fell into the pool will be sitting on the bottom, so if we can just tread water in the deep end, and keep from stirring up any sediment on the bottom, the water will protect us from some of it."

He didn't go into what they would do if the house burned and left them with no shelter, because he had no idea.

He dashed into the main part of the house, quickly checking the windows and then retreating to the hallway. He pounded on the wall and yelled, "Still okay!"

He heard her faint reply. "Still praying!"

It was a long fifteen minutes, as the front rose bushes caught and flared high and hot. He checked the rooms closest and pulled the blinds, to keep the heat from catching anything on the inside.

But eventually, wide porches front and back, and no bushes on the end, left the limestone exterior walls untouched. The air inside was filled with smoke, and he had no idea how much of the fallout dust had piggy-backed indoors on the smoke. He checked with the meter, but the radiation from outside masked any readings from indoors.

"Ginger?"

She looked out.

"It's over. We don't have to move."

She sagged back inside, and he followed.

"You're sweating."

"So are you." He didn't tell her about the blaze in the front. He'd tell her later. "The house is okay, but it's been heated up. Thank goodness for stone walls and metal roofs."

"Come here," she patted the mattress.

He stretched out. She produced a rag and began washing him down. He closed his eyes and relished the cool feel.

"Shed that shirt and I'll do the same for you."

She swatted him with the rag. "Although it does sound like a good idea, for later."

...

He napped, while she finished some last minute preparations. She woke him, new clothes in hand.

"Put these on, outside. I'll call you when I'm ready."

He went out into the garage and changed into slacks and a white shirt, making sure the ring got moved into the new pockets.

"Okay, come on in."

She had a candle lit on the top of the hot water heater, and the soft glow made even their tiny, utilitarian shelter seem special. Fancy scissor work, cutting dozens of horizontal slits into a white shirt, made it into a white dress that when she pulled it lower, fit her figure and stretched to her knees.

"You look beautiful."

She glowed. He produced the ring. She was surprised and overjoyed at the craftwork.

"If it doesn't fit, I can..."

"It's perfect."

He slipped it onto her hand. "I take you to be my wife, to love, and to protect, 'til death do us part."

She could barely speak. Her eyes were filled with tears of joy as she kept looking from the ring on her finger to his eyes. "I take you to be my husband, to love, and to stand beside, and to make all your dreams come true, 'til death do us part."

She produced the paper. Fancy lettering proclaimed that they were married on that date, under the eyes of God. He signed and dated, and then she did the same. She carefully rolled it up and affixed a ribbon around it.

"You may now kiss the bride," she said.

He did.

...

After two days of serious honeymooning, Clark took the meter outside and determined that although the upholstery was singed in places from embers, the Jeep was still intact and started. They rinsed the porch with buckets of water from the pool and began the process of hunting down any radioactive hotspots and burying them.

Surviving neighbors recognized Clark from previous visits to his uncle, and when Fred didn't return, they upheld his claim of survivorship. A trip into town determined that both Clark's home and Ginger's had burned in the firestorm that followed the nuclear blast. No family members were located. It was a common story.

Clark and Ginger traded supplies and services with their neighbors—his Geiger counter surveys were particularly welcomed—and they had a fall garden going by the time that the Texas Recovery Census came around to register their existence. A photocopy of their wedding certificate went straight into the county records with no more comment than a congratulations. When Christmas rolled around, Ginger began chatting up her neighbors, hunting for a potential midwife just as Clark raised the sign advertising custom metal work. He never did get around to adding a stone to her ring. She was happy with it the way it was.

Maggie's Marbles

It occurred to me that many of the animals we have on Earth never look up—leopards in trees take advantage of that and so do hunters in their elevated deer blinds. What would an alien intelligence on another planet become, if they never looked at the stars?

Maggie perched on her favorite limb, watching him brush the loose dust off of the rippled, ceramic board. Dell Carver, in sandals and threadbare khaki shorts, looked up at her. "I don't suppose you want to tell me what this thing is, do you?"

"Brakk," the black bird replied, turning her head to the side, watching him with her left eye this time. For a native life form, she was remarkably similar in body shape to a magpie, if a bit larger. Even the black and white feathers were reminiscent of the Earth bird.

"I didn't think so. But if you do see anything you recognize, feel free to chime in."

He tossed a wafer of bread her way, and she dropped to the dirt in a flash to devour it.

A scrub board? A counting board? A work of art? He shook his head. No one even knew what the vanished natives of 24 Ceti Alpha 4 looked like. Their tools were plain and utilitarian—no decorations or markings. Diggers called them Goobers.

Maggie chose that moment to flutter down from her perch and land among his untagged collection of artifacts. She latched onto his new find.

"A good choice," Dell commented. "I found that in a rock slide next to a cliff a couple of kilometers west of here. It doesn't appear broken, except at the base. It was probably mounted on a longer pole. But I haven't any idea what it is."

He put his hand on the pole and Maggie fluttered her wings as he propped the broken pole up against a bench. She never let go of her grip.

"Maybe you're right, Maggie. It does look like a perch. Did the Goobers keep your kind as pets?" A fist-sized block of some hard material was mounted just below the perch. Dell fingered the thumb-sized dimple in the block. "If that's a feed dish, your ancestors certainly ate a lot lighter than you do."

"Klakk-kak." Maggie examined him, first with the right eye, and then her left.

"If that's a hint, you can just wait until later. I just fed you."

Abruptly she gave a loud shriek and fluttered off at high speed.

Startled, Dell looked around, scanning the nearly cloudless, blue sky. "Is it Sara's day?" Isolated as he was, he lost track of calendar dates.

He dashed to his tent and spent five seconds sniffing at his two shirts, before throwing on the old one and quick-walking to the clearing next to his dig site.

The saucer shaped craft was now visible, whistling as it descended. Dust kicked up as it settled onto hover skirts. Engine noise wound down to silence.

A smile came naturally when a light brown mop of hair poked out of the hatch. Sara jumped down to the ground and sauntered over towards him, looking very good in her wrinkled bush gear.

"You miss me?" she asked.

His smile said yes, but he shook his head. "You scared Maggie off again."

She waved at her craft. "Well, this time I even killed the life support blowers. I would like to meet this friend of yours."

"No telling how long it will take her to come back."

"I can wait. It will take hours to talk you out of your stash in any case."

He shook his head in sorrow and turned back towards his tent. "You know it makes no sense to give you any of my finds."

"But Dell, honey." She tripped lightly up beside him and intertwined her arm with his. "You know you can't sell them to anyone else. The Diggers Board has a contract with the corporation. Think of your stock options."

He laughed, and she joined in. It was all they could do about the situation.

"What is the stock price down to these days?" he asked.

"It was two and a tenth this morning."

"And what's the exercise price for the options the corporation is trying to tempt me with?"

She looked bashful. "Well, the director did drop it to five last week."

He sneered. "Down, down, down. I guess that reverse split didn't do the job. How long before the corporation goes bankrupt?"

"You aren't going to get out that easy, Dell. You know that the contract with Diggers will just be sold to one of the big archeology corporations if it goes belly up."

He led her over to his work table and pulled the drop cloth off an assortment of artifacts.

"Well, if that happens, maybe their stock options will be worth something. Until then, I can't see any advantage in giving up these."

She already had a viewer in hand, looking at the weathered collection of Goober objects. He kept behind her, so he could read the screen over her shoulder. He lusted after her toys.

"This one has a magnetic residue." She looked back at his face. "You see." He nodded. The false colors showed striations around the handle. He had it tagged as a watering pot, and it certainly looked like one—if the gardener had hands twice the size of his.

She shook her head at the readings, shifting scales. She sagged and slipped the viewer back into its holster.

"Oh, Dell, I'm about ready to give up on this place. All these hints, but no breakthrough. I have more worthless stock options than you do. All it would take is one good discovery, something to give the stockholders back on Earth hope that some lost alien scientific process is ripe for decoding—hope that with just a little more patience, they will all be richer than the investors in the Lambda Pegasus expedition."

He laughed. "We could fake something. All it has to do is last long enough to push the stock back up to make it worthwhile to cash out."

She slapped his hand. "You don't mean that!" She chewed her lip. "Although, it is a tempting idea."

"Ha. Sara, you know you love this stuff as much as I do."

She nodded, guiltily. "But I'm smart enough to ride around in air-conditioning and make you do the digging." She sat down on the bench and rested her clasped hands on one knee. "What else do you have for me?"

...

"Here comes Maggie." He pointed. Sara looked up from her portion of his supper. Negotiations had lasted most of the afternoon and he had talked her out of an extra ten options, tempting her with fresh grilled tallots. The fish he caught in the nearby stream were low in usable nutrients but tasted wonderful.

The options were worthless as stock derivatives, but they were the only currency on the planet. Diggers were incurably optimistic—it was an occupational hazard. There was always someone who would barter real goods for options. Dell knew that from long experience. He traded away too many critical supplies his first year here.

Sara watched as Maggie settled onto an overhead branch. "She doesn't want to get too close."

Dell smiled. "She likes me okay. She knows I won't bother her—and I won't try to sell her any options."

Sara pushed her hair back and looked at Dell with a smile. "Do I bother you?"

He grumbled low. "I would be bothered a lot less if I didn't know for a fact that you were just as friendly with every digger on your circuit."

"But Dell, Honey, I really mean it with you."

"Ha."

Maggie fluttered her wings and Dell reached for one of the dried wafers. He sailed it over towards her tree. She was down on it a second later.

"What's that?" Sara pointed.

Maggie had dropped a small gray object in her hurry to devour the wafer.

"Looks like a pebble, or a marble."

"Artifact?" She started to get up.

"Let me. You'll startle her." He rose slowly and stepped gently towards the fragments of the wafer that Maggie was hurriedly cleaning up. He rolled the marble between his fingers.

"A little more than a centimeter. Hard. Looks perfectly spherical." He set it down on the table. "Heavier than wood, but lighter than rock."

Sara picked it up and held it into the sunlight. "The surface looks textured, not metallic. Maybe with a polish over it." She looked at Dell's eyes. "Can I have this?"

He shook his head. "Sorry. My dig. I thought I had you trained. Nothing gets sold until I've logged it and tagged it. I'm not here for the money—I'm here to solve a puzzle."

Dell looked over at his feathered friend, now finished with her scavenging. "Besides, it's Maggie's marble. She might want it back." He set it on the table.

"I know some Earth birds collect shiny objects. Has Maggie brought you anything else?"

Dell shook his head. "No. This is a first for her. I've infected her. I talk to her all the time as I work."

He sighed. "Poor thing. To become a digger—what a curse. Sorry Maggie."

Sara laughed. "Well, I guess I'd better put her on my client list and see if she's easier to deal with than all the big smelly galoots I see every day."

"Smelly! I'll have you know I chose the cleanest shirt this time."

"But when did you wash it last?"

Dell sat back with a puzzled look on his face. "Wash?"

Sara slapped his arm and collapsed into quiet laughter. As she squeezed a tear from her eye, she started collecting her papers.

"I'd better get back. I'm losing the light, and if I stay here any longer, you'll own the corporation."

"Hmm. If I'm so wealthy, how come I can't buy a radio?" But he helped her carry the first tub toward her vehicle.

They topped the ridge and Sara stopped cold. She whispered, "Look over by the door. That's a tapig."

He looked, and in the dimming light, the large animal was suddenly visible in the shadows. Dell shrugged.

"Don't worry about it. Tapigs are big, but they scatter when they see men." He took a step toward the large grazer, half hippo and half tapir.

Sara grabbed his arm. "No, Dell. They're dangerous!"

"Since when? I've seen them since I settled this dig. They've never given me any trouble."

"But... surely you heard? The killings over at Blueman's dig?"

"What killings? Remember... no radio! I only know what you tell me."

"Oh. Well, tapigs are dangerous now! It started a month or so back. Two men were trapped in a pit and several tapigs went in after them and... well it was a gory mess from what I heard. There've been others. John Hall, on my circuit, for one. He's still in the hospital with cracked ribs and a useless left leg. There was a general alert!"

"Over the radio?"

"Yes, over the radio. Don't look at me like that."

They backed down behind the rise. The beast paced around below the saucer's open door. Sara hadn't lowered the ramp, and the opening was too high for the four-footed grazer.

"Look," Dell pointed. There was another, coming to join the first. Low-pitched snorts could be heard.

"What's changed them?" he asked. "People have been here for a dozen years or more. Tapigs have always been timid and avoid a dig area."

Across the clearing, one of the tapigs turned its snout in their direction and snorted. The others turned their way, too.

"Let's get out of sight." Sara whispered.

"You may be right." Two of the tapigs started moving their way.

Dell led the way back to camp, looking over his dig with a new eye. Where to hide? Tents were no help.

"Can you climb?" He boosted her into the largest tree in his camp. Neither of them were agile, but working together they made it up to the thick lower branches.

Tapigs came through the camp, snorting and pawing at the ground. Dell held his breath, expecting them to tear everything up and destroy his cache of artifacts. Instead, they quickly searched the area and although their heads weren't articulated to let them look up, they soon began circling the tree.

Sara and Dell sat quietly, sparing one hand each to hold on to each other. Maggie landed on a nearby branch and watched them. After fifteen minutes of snorting and pawing, the tapigs left together.

Dell whispered, "I'll go down and check."

"No, wait a minute." She reached into her pouch and pulled out one of her gadgets. She scanned the surrounding darkness. It showed a dozen heat signatures, behind the bushes.

Dell shivered. "They're hiding, waiting for us to come down."

"When do they expect you at the port?"

She sighed. "Not for a day or so. I knew you'd take a long time, so I planed to go half-way to Kreiger's dig and camp out for the night."

"Why? You could have stayed here."

Her lip wiggled slightly. "There's a pool at the office. I'm not supposed to know about it. People check my transponder to see where I spend the night."

"Really? They think you...?"

"Drop it, Dell." She stared off at the shadows below.

"Okay, but... Well what do we do now?"

"Emulate Maggie, I guess." On the next branch, a motionless ball of feathers waited out the dawn.

Dell nodded, and repositioned himself, trying to find comfort and a way to stay on his perch without keeping a death-grip on the branches. Soon, using their belts, they managed to settle in. He had his back to the main trunk, and Sara nestled her head against his chest.

"If I'd known what it took to get you to sleep with me..."

She poked him in the ribs. But she didn't move away.

Below, an occasional snort let them know their captors had not left.

...

Sara stirred, a mass of brown hair just below his chin. Dell put his hand on her shoulder to make sure she wouldn't lose her balance.

"Good morning." It was almost sunrise.

She grumbled, and began to cautiously extricate her self. "My back hurts."

"Not as bad as mine." As she moved off of him, he tried to stretch the kinks out of his leg.

"What're they up to?" she asked.

"Digging."

"Digging for what?"

"I think... digging up the roots of this tree."

Sara digested that. "I knew I should've started carrying a gun."

Dell nodded. "We have to get back to your saucer."

"Tapigs can run pretty fast, faster than I can, I think. On a good day, maybe, on flat land—but there are too many of them, Dell."

He watched the animals below. The torn earth had a dozen broken roots, gnawed through and dripping sap. With room for only two tapigs, they worked on the same side, digging a pit, tossing aside the dirt. After half an hour, another arrived and with some snorting, it took one's place and the tired one limped off into the brush.

"Dell, what's Maggie doing?"

He looked up. Maggie was shaking her head, with the feathers around her neck ruffled up.

"Maggie girl. What's wrong?"

The bird turned her head, trying to locate him, but her eyes didn't focus.

"Maggie, talk to me. Are you sick?" The bird shook some more, but paid him no attention. Sara looked a question his way, but Dell could only shrug.

There was a complicated snort from below.

Dell frowned. "I've never seen tapigs this intelligent before. They plan. They're acting together to dig up this tree. It's spooky."

"Brakk!" Maggie took to the air and fluttered down to the workbench and began sampling the remains of their evening meal.

Sara said, "Well, at least she has something to eat."

Maggie poked at the marble she'd brought to them last night, and then carefully picked it up in her beak. She tilted her head, watching the two humans up in the tree, and then sailed the few feet over to the ancient perch, still propped nearly upright. The morning sun broke through the trees and illuminated her.

"Brakk!"

Sara whispered. "Dell, what is she doing?"

"Oh nothing. She just likes perching on that artifact I discovered a day or so ago."

Maggie took the marble, and carefully dropped it into the recess on the perch.

"Brakk!" She pecked at the marble. In the early sun, it sparkled, giving off a rainbow of many colored reflections.

Maggie held her head back and in a clear voice, she began, "*Greetings my children.*"

"What!" Dell he had to reach out and grab the branch before he lost balance.

"Quiet! That's your voice, Dell."

"Maggie doesn't talk."

"She *is* talking, Dell."

He stared down at his feathered friend. She was rigid, as if in a trance. The marble was spinning in its recess. The voice sounded like his own, only higher in pitch, and spoken unevenly, as if it'd been composed of recordings spliced together.

...

"Your pain gives me sorrow, my children. Paradise calls to you. In Paradise you were born, and in Paradise you lived. But no more.

"Great danger has called you out. From your serenity, you now have puzzles. In Paradise, there was no puzzle, no pain.

"Pain is necessary, if you are to survive and your children are to survive."

...

Sara poked Dell in the ribs. "This'd better not be a joke."

"Shut up Sara."

...

Maggie's voice continued, *"You cry in pain, and your brothers listen. Danger has pulled you from Paradise. Speak to the birds and the wisdom of your ancestors will help.*

"Ask. We will help you. You are our children."

...

"Brakk!" Maggie shivered all over. Feathers stuck out untidily, and she began to groom, straightening and plucking.

Dell eased back against the trunk of the tree. He shot a glance down at the tapigs, but they kept working, as if they'd heard nothing.

"What was that all about?" asked Sara.

"It was a message." Dell's eyes were wide. "A message from the Goobers."

"In your voice?"

He blinked, and turned to her.

"Well... what else can it be? Maggie put a marble into that thing, a reader. She set it spinning in the sun and then spoke. The artifact is typical Goober style. The marble has to be, too. And Maggie..."

He shook his head. "I don't know where Maggie fits into the puzzle. Look her perch. It's just the right fit for her species."

"You don't think Maggie is a Goober, do you?"

"No. None of the artifacts matches her body, other than the perch. She couldn't lift that watering pot, for example.

"No, Maggie has to be a pet, a helper. She can obviously talk, but I'd bet she can only say what's imprinted on that marble."

Sara fumbled with her pockets and came out with a viewer and aimed it at the sparkle from Maggie's perch.

"There's a pattern reflected off of that marble. Not digital. Some kind of color code. I can't tell anything more from this distance."

She turned off the viewer. "Given what we know of Goober technology, I'd bet there is nothing more in that reader than some fancy magnetic fields. The bird started it spinning in the sunlight, and it's probably floating on a repelling field. No moving parts, no energy supply. Everything encoded into the surface of the marble, simple enough so a trained bird can operate it.

"But why did the Goobers want to send you a message?"

Dell shook his head. "That wasn't directed at me."

"But it was in your voice. Maggie listened and modeled the playback on you."

He nodded. "More than that. Goobers couldn't have known English. I've been talking to Maggie for more than a year. She's been listening, decoding my use of language. If we're correct that the Goober culture has long vanished, then that message had to have been composed fifty thousand years ago, or more. They sent a message off into their future, not knowing what language would be used—so they created a race of translator birds with just enough brain to recognize and digest what language they encountered.

"They couldn't have known English speaking archeologists would arrive. This message had to be directed at someone else."

Sara rubbed a finger next to her nose in thought. "Maggie noticed we were in danger and went to get the danger message from a library of marbles and brought it to us."

"No. She brought the marble before we noticed the tapigs, remember."

"A warning then?"

"The message was directed to the Goober's children. That's not us."

"It could be a figure of speech."

"Not when the message was so crudely translated. Figures of speech require layers upon layers of shared culture to allow them to be efficient literary shorthand. The writers of the message wouldn't use them.

"No, that message was literal—directed to the Goober's biological children. Maggie heard me use language and started training, not realizing I was the wrong recipient. It's probably just instinct with her. She's never used language for her own purposes."

Sara nodded, "And when the real Goober descendants died out, the messages just waited for any language-user to come along."

"Who said they died out?"

Sara frowned. "There are no tool-using native species on this planet. We've searched long enough to be sure of that."

Dell nodded, "And I believe you, but when two puzzles show up at the same time, I have to consider that they might be related.

"Consider this—Maggie has to be the result of careful genetic engineering. Just think of it, a translator bird able to piece together language by observation."

Sara smiled, intrigued by the thought, "Okay, if that is so, then the next question we should ask Maggie is how to use that technology. Let the company announce a breakthrough in genetic engineering, and our stock options will be worth fortunes."

Dell laughed. "I like you Sara."

"I like you too, Dell." She looked puzzled.

"Sara, where are you?"

She looked around. "In a tree."

"Why are you in a tree?"

"Okay, don't rub it in. I'm in a tree because murderous beasts are trying to kill me. You're right, maybe we can put Maggie's marbles on the back burner for a bit."

"Or maybe we should ask her a different question. Maybe our rescue is in one of those marbles."

"You think so? Why?"

Dell pointed down. "Those. The tapigs. I think *they* are the Goober's children."

...

Below, there were five. Two were working on the pit that completely exposed the roots on one side. The other three were arranged in a triangle, standing guard to keep them from escaping should they jump down from the tree and try to make a break for it.

"Dell, tapigs are herd animals! They aren't tool users either. Goobers built tools and shelters. How could these be their children?"

"Paradise and puzzles. The children of the Goober lived in paradise and now have to suffer through puzzles to survive. Think about it. Tapigs relaxed in the sun, with food always available. Predators don't bother them. Even the hard-wolves ignore them. Their meat is unpleasant—maybe their smell, too.

"Can you imagine a better nirvana?"

Sara laughed. "Not for an intelligent, tool-using species! Humans would go insane from the boredom. And you can't convince me that tapigs can handle your water pot, let alone make the full range of artifacts we've collected here. They don't have hands!"

Dell looked down at the tapigs. Two workers had their heads down in the soil, kicking dirt behind them. The guards appeared to be asleep, heads down, and motionless.

"Sara, look at the forepaws on that one."

She leaned over close to him, hanging on to another branch. "What am I looking at?"

"Don't they look swollen, inflamed? Some of them have been walking with a limp."

"You are right, both of them. Digging too hard?"

"I don't think so. Tapigs dig for roots all their lives. They are growing hands."

"Be serious."

"I am. Tapigs have a hoof and a pair of vestigial fingers, one on each side of the hoof. I think the fingers are growing. Two fingers with an opposable hoof could make a serviceable hand. Good enough for tool-users."

Sara was still looking down at them. "Maybe. But I've never heard of anything changing like this before."

"Oh, the genetics is common enough. Some genes can wait in an organism inactive, passive, waiting for some change in the chemical environment before 'waking up'. Single-cell species do it all the time. When bacteria crowd together, they 'smell' each other and whole sets of genes turn on and off as they switch from being free-floating individuals to being part of a bacterial sheet.

"Goobers could have engineered their own species to exist with limited brain capacity and no hands, but with the abilities still there in reserve, awaiting some environmental cue to re-activate.

"They lived peacefully in nirvana, until something we did triggered the change. All at once, the tapigs woke up.

"They invented language, turned aggressive, and started working together to get rid of us."

"Whoa! They invented language overnight? No way."

"I didn't say overnight. Who knows how long they've been at it. But if their brain expanded, simple grunts could quickly take on more meaning. Brain centers and vocal apparatus both have to develop. They'll get smarter, but the idea is already there—exchange information and work together."

Sara leaned back against the tree trunk. "Maggie talked about pain. How much pain? If you are right, and their bodies are changing on them day by day, enough to look inflamed, then they must be nearly mad with pain."

He nodded. "Don't expect talk them out of attacking us. We're the evil invaders from space, after all—killing them, pillaging their cities."

"I am not evil!"

Dell patted her on the shoulder, "Of course you aren't. I wonder how to say 'We come in peace' in tapig-ese."

She shrugged off his hand. "I can't believe the Goobers would do that to their children. What kind of monsters would modify their babies to be brain damaged and deformed?"

"Don't be ethnocentric. What parent wouldn't jump at the chance to have their children grow up in peace and happiness all their lives? Human cultures had their share of nirvana seekers, of various stripes.

"Think about it this way—imagine you could give your child grace and beauty and serenity, and all they had to do is give up pain and hate and worry."

Sara shook her head. "No. I don't buy it. We need our pain and suffering. We thrive on it."

"Humans thrive on it. Tapigs aren't human."

Dell waved his hand, "But that isn't our problem yet. We still have to get out of this tree. I don't know about you, but it'll be a race to see if I fall off of this branch before they uproot the tree. As it is, I am about ready to ask you to turn your back for a moment while I take care of a pressing issue."

She stifled a giggle. "I have the same problem."

Just then, there was a loud snap below, and the tree trunk shook.

Dell gripped the side branch tightly. "They severed one of the main roots. We don't have much time left. If you have any ideas, I'm listening."

Sara looked pale, hugging the main trunk. "I talked to John Hall, when I was ferrying him back to the hospital. They came at him from all directions, tearing at his legs. He had a gun, or he wouldn't have survived. We had to dig him out from beneath several tapig carcasses...

"Oh Dell! We hauled a couple of them back to the port for analysis. Do you think there might be a residual smell coming from my saucer? Maybe I started all this."

He thought for a moment. "No, a scent arriving just a few hours ago couldn't have triggered the language development and the body changes. It must've already been happening. My dig is small and my impact here has to have been minor. If these tapigs were affected too, then I'd bet it's a global thing. One modified tapig emits a scent that triggers the change in others.

"No, the scent of dead tapig in your saucer might have triggered this attack, but they'd already started developing."

Sara said, "The tapigs will get smarter—better organized. The attacks will get more widespread and the death count will rise."

"Starting with us, if we don't do something quickly." Dell looked at the surrounding branches. "Sara, I'm going to ask you to turn your back."

"Really?"

He nodded grimly. "Really." He reached for his zipper and she turned her head.

The urine scent and the sound of splashing on the tree trunk below made no mystery of what he was doing.

Dell explained, "Tapigs can't look up, so they aren't tracking us by sight. Maybe they can hear us, but unless you can make your viewer playback voices, a distracting scent will have to do."

The smell was definitely doing something to the tapigs. The guards squealed and tried to climb down into the pit with the diggers.

Dell put his finger to his lips and motioned Sara to follow him out on the limb. The main branch sagged as they moved farther from the trunk. It cracked, and they tumbled to the ground.

He grabbed Sara's arm and pulled her upright. She nodded and pointed in the direction of the saucer.

"Go!" he whispered, shoving her on. A few steps later, she realized he wasn't with her. He'd turned towards his camp. Her heart hammered, and her steps faltered.

The squeals changed, and shrill cries sent a shock through her spine. She was running again, and the only thought in her head was the memories of John Hall's horrible wounds. She crested the rise between the camp and her saucer, where three tapigs waited.

Behind her, tapigs squealed in chorus. The saucer guards halted their mock battles, turning their hefty bodies to scan the horizon. Sara tried to be motionless, as well as heaving lungs would allow, but she knew that was fruitless. Dell proved well enough that they tracked by scent.

One guard by the saucer shifted his fore body side to side with his legs, making up for an inflexible neck. His snout pointed directly at her. He snorted, and then squealed. He charged in her direction. Behind her, another call answered. She turned toward the nearest tree.

Tapigs saw her move, and began a full-throated charge. Panic rose in her throat.

"Heee! Yaw!" Dell shouted. Sara glanced to the side and saw him waving and shouting from the next rise.

Tapigs saw him too. As a herd, they turned from chasing her and charged him.

Sara turned in mid-step, racing back towards the saucer. Two broke off from the main herd and headed back her way. She leaned into the wind, her eyes focused on the door.

There were scrape marks all over the thick black flexible skirt that was used to keep in the air-pressure when the saucer acted as a hovercraft. Tapigs had attacked it, but a material designed to stand up to rough landings had been more than sturdy enough to resist hooves and teeth.

She sensed her pursuers on her heels as she raced up the side of the saucer and into the open door. She slammed it shut just seconds before the saucer shook with the impact of two large animals slamming into the skirt at full speed.

She didn't take any time to react. The control seat was her home—had been for five years. She slapped the switches without thought. Systems came on line. The view screen lit. Engines roared to life.

Her right arm fit into the yoke like a glove and she lifted the saucer on a pillow of air. The saucer rotated under her touch.

Dell was in a tree. More tapigs than she could count surrounded its base. He swung at the beasts below with a stick. *No, that's Maggie's perch. He'd gone back for it.* The fragmented lower end of the pole was a cluster of sharp splinters and he was using it to full effect.

The tree shook, and Dell was hard-pressed to hang on. The herd wasn't content to dig him out this time; they were going to topple the tree by brute force.

"Not if I have anything to say about it!"

Sara edged the saucer forward, closing on the tapigs a little better than a fast run. She expected them to scatter.

They didn't. The saucer's skirt slammed into the mass of bodies and was met by a mass cry of annoyance. *They are used to being rammed by others of their kind.*

Dell looked panicked, holding onto the trunk of the tree with all his strength.

Sara edged back from the tree, and opened the hatch remotely. She had to fly sideways, but she moved back in.

"I'm bigger than you! Get out of my way!" She put on more side thrust when she mashed up against the herd. They weren't taking her move tamely, shoving back. She raised the power again.

There was a crunching sound, wood against metal. *I'll mash Dell!* She was backing down the power when she heard him.

"I'm in Sara. Go!"

She eased away from the tapigs and made the jump in power that lifted them off of ground-effect and into free flight.

Dell slipped into the side chair.

"Oh, you're hurt!"

His leg was bleeding, and he still gripped the bird perch tightly in his hand.

He waved aside her concern. "Can you spot Maggie?"

"Maggie? I don't know."

"Look for her! She flies north when she hears your engines."

Sara changed her view angle. "We're still too close to the ground." She gestured toward the screen helplessly. "It's all a blur of treetops."

He moved the side chair closer. "Get some altitude then. We don't want her to panic. Head north, but slowly."

Sara took them higher, and then her arms started shaking. She closed her eyes and took a deep breath.

Dell looked up from the screen. "Problem?"

"I'm putting us in hover mode. Autopilot. Unless I take a break, I'll crash us. I'm a mess."

He nodded, gravely, but glanced back at the screen. He was clearly unable to give up his search for Maggie.

Sara sighed. "You can turn this ring to adjust the angle of the view. Don't touch any other control."

. . .

When she returned ten minutes later, cleaned and hydrated and caffeinated, she found Dell still staring at the wooded lands below, thumb and forefinger making tiny adjustments on the azimuth ring. His bleeding had stopped on its own, but she winced at the thought of the torn flesh below. This planet's microorganisms were close enough to Terran to inflame open wounds.

Dell looked up with a smile. "Maggie has cousins."

Sara slipped into her control seat. "You found her?"

"There's a whole flock of her species, all in flight, probably because of our engine noise. I watched them move, and they all congregated at this spot." He tapped the view screen. A peak rose sharply above the rest of the terrain.

Intrigued, Sara tapped a few controls, and a cross-hair centered on the peak. The lower half of the screen switched to a false-color magnified view.

"See this spot. I'm getting flickers of monochromatic light. I would guess there is a stash of marbles there. Good work Dell."

He sagged in his chair. "I guessed there would be a stash, and that would be where she would flee to when she felt danger, but I couldn't know."

Sara shook her head, "Right out in the open. I wouldn't have expected that."

"Tapigs don't look up. They can't climb. If the marbles are tough enough to stand up to direct sunlight and weather, then a nest on the top of a mountain would be the safest place the Goobers would think about."

"Good." Sara rubbed her hands. "All we have to do is warn everyone, collect the marbles and 24 Ceti Alpha 4 will have made our fortunes."

Dell shook his head. "Not quite. A warning is essential, but we need to phrase it right."

"Lock in our claim."

"That too." Dell's head was furrowed in thought.

"Tapigs are in the early stage of an intellectual chain reaction. How smart will they get, and how soon? There are rules against looting on inhabited planets."

She shivered. Their whole business was based on the finding that the native intelligences had died out. "We can't have that happen. What can we do?"

He tapped the screen. "Go down there and ask Maggie."

...

All of the translator birds fled the scene when they approached. Dell directed Sara to a small meadow nearby. They shut down the engines, opened the door and waited.

"This is on Maggie's flight path." He took the perch and clamped it to the open hatch.

Sara scanned the surrounding terrain with her hand held viewer. "I don't see any tapigs in the vicinity. A cache of marbles is just at the top of that peak. We could probably hike it in an hour or so."

Dell shook his head. "I'm not putting my feet on the ground here. We're stinking up the place with tapig battle scent already. I've learned my lesson. The marbles are easy to find, once you know what to look for. There are probably hundreds of nests. We don't have to collect them all. Let a trained scout with a personal hoverbelt go get them.

"No, what we need is Maggie, and one marble."

"One?"

"Yes. One to analyze and to determine if we can easily copy off the code. If the courts and the popular press get into this, we'll be in much better shape if we just take a copy of the data and leave the marbles in place for future generations of the Goober's children.

"But we need Maggie. She's the Rosetta Stone. As far as we know, she's the only one that's picked up English. Maybe we could train others, but that might take another year. Maggie is here, now. She's the proof when we make our claim."

They waited. Sara dug into her pantry for bread wafers. Dell called for Maggie out the open hatch.

"Here comes another one." Sara reached for her wafers.

"Hold off. That isn't Maggie."

"How can you tell?"

"The feathers are wrong. Scat. Go away. I need Maggie. Maggie, come here girl!"

Sara set a packing crate near the door and sat with him. "Don't you think we should send out our warning? This could take time."

He nodded. "I know. I just want to ask a couple of questions first. Once we go public, there's going to be a flood of questions coming our way. I want to say the right things."

"Can't some of that wait until we get better information later?"

"Perhaps. But how good are my guesses?"

"Brakk!"

Maggie landed on the perch with a flutter of wings. Dell gestured at the wafer box.

"Maggie. I'm glad to see you. Do you want a wafer?"

Sara tossed one on the deck, and the bird was on it in a flash.

"Are you sure it's Maggie?" Sara whispered.

He nodded, smiling at the bird. "Yes, you're my Maggie aren't you? I've got a question, Maggie. A question. How can the children stop the changes in their bodies? Maggie, how can the children stop the changes in their bodies? Answer my question, Maggie."

The bird didn't look up from her meal until the last fragment was tacked down and devoured. Then, she shivered and acted as if she were sensing the air. She shook her feathers down. Dell kept up his repetitive questioning. She fluttered over to the perch, and then off into the sunny sky.

"Stay put. If she is going for a marble, it won't take long."

Sara nodded. "Do you think the Goobers looked like the tapigs? Maybe they morphed from something bipedal, like us."

Dell relaxed into archeological speculation mode. "They probably changed very little. I'd guess they just regressed to what they were before they developed hands. It was the original fall from paradise for them. They developed hands to make them better at searching for roots and grubs. Once they made the jump to tool using, their brain expanded and their vocal range adapted to communication.

"But I'd guess they never looked up. They never looked at the stars. They never expected us."

...

Maggie returned with a blue-gray marble in her beak.

Sara started recording.

Maggie looked them over, and then dropped the marble carefully into the cavity. She pecked at the marble to start it spinning. She shivered and parted her beak.

> *"My children, you have asked how to stop the changes in your bodies. By now, you realize that you can talk with one another, and that you can pick up things. The pain of the changes will go away shortly. The changes will never go away.*
>
> *"Paradise is lost to you. Your children yet to be born can remain in paradise if you find the danger and remove it. The scent of one who dies strangely changes you. The scent will cause the change in your children.*
>
> *"Find out what causes strange death and stop it. Then, the changes stop in your children."*

...

When Dell was sure that Maggie was done, he took a couple of bread wafers and set them out. Maggie abandoned her marble in a flash and attacked her reward. Dell casually eased towards the door and pocketed the marble.

As soon as he removed the clamp that held the perch, he said, "Sara. Close the door."

She touched a control at her pilot's seat. With the faintest of noises, it sealed itself.

"Whew," Dell whispered. "I thought we were going to have trouble catching her." Maggie hadn't noticed, content to demolish the bread. It had been a very good day for her.

Sara asked, "Is that all you wanted to ask?"

He laughed, "No! But it's all we have time for. We have to get the warning out."

Dell composed it, and Sara's saucer had the transmitter and security codes for a planet-wide alert. It was brief but they made it sound official.

. . .

Alert! Alert! Alert!

There has been a tapig attack at the Dell Carver dig. No fatalities, but the site is now restricted due to tapig activity.

New guidelines: All sites be on the alert for any tapig activity. The aggressive behavior is triggered by the scent of dead tapig. Avoid killing tapig at all costs, as the scent travels widely. The last attack was triggered by the residual scent brought in by a company survey saucer. If attacked, evacuate the area or get above ground level and call for help. Tapigs do not climb, but they are persistent and clever. They will knock down or uproot trees. Tapigs do not fear humans and cannot be frightened away.

Important: All tapig bodies must be sealed off in airtight containers or removed from the planet. All transport vehicles carrying dead tapig must undergo standard quarantine fumigation before being returned to surface duty. No incineration to dispose of bodies.

It is unknown how long the effects of the scent will last. All sites need to review their evacuation procedures.

. . .

Sara winced as she sent the message out. "I'm not really supposed to use these codes. The company will be calling for me shortly."

Dell was attempting to feed a wafer to Maggie by hand, with intermediate results. "Better a warning now than later. And once they review our recordings, all will be forgiven.

"By the way, are there any other digs out there with no radio? We need to contact them as well!"

Sara wrinkled her nose. "Not on my route. You are the low man on my list."

"Thanks a lot."

"Oops. There's the recall beacon. I'd better answer it."

"Let's get in the air first."

She nodded and activated the engine systems.

Maggie shrieked and fluttered to the floor, a mass of twitching feathers.

"Kill the engines," Dell yelled, dropping to his knees. He reached out one hand, and pulled it back with a bleeding red stripe across his fingers.

The engine noise faded to nothingness in a few seconds.

"Maggie girl. I'm sorry girl. I won't let it happen again." He soothed the ruffled feathers and kept up a croon of comforting words.

"Sara, open the door."

"Are you sure?"

"Yes! Now! Do it." The door whispered open. Maggie launched herself out into the open air in an instant.

Dell watched her sail off into the woods. Sara had her fists on her hips.

"There goes our Rosetta bird!"

Dell nodded. "Don't worry." He reached into his pocket. "I still have the marble, and the perch. With our recording, it will be enough to get started."

Sara turned to her controls, and began lifting the saucer above the landscape. Out the hatchway, Dell could see hundreds of birds take flight.

He moved over to the side seat. He had a grin on his face. "I forgot that Maggie, and all of the translator birds are sensitive to engine noise. Maybe that's why no one ever mentioned them before in the reports. Only a dirt poor digger with no regular visitors could have made contact."

She looked at his face and frowned at his expression. "What's so funny? I don't relish having to report that we let the only English-speaking translator bird go free."

Dell spread his arms and leaned back. He looked at her fondly, "I think things are finally going my way."

"What do you mean by that?"

"The corporation will love us. We have strong evidence of extremely valuable genetic technology. Just the hint of that leaked in the right places will put all of our stock options well into the money. The whole planet will love us."

"Well, yes. But we still don't..."

"We still don't have all the translations, yes indeed. The corporation will want those dearly. And they can get them. All they have to do is fund my little project."

"What little project?"

"Oh, a little research lab at my dig site. Nice thick walls, maybe a nice elevated veranda among the trees. All the equipment needed to decode the marbles. Maggie lives there, you know. And she'll return to me. We have a good working relationship. Even the corporation will see that."

He sighed contentedly as he visualized his new camp. Sara sniffed, setting her saucer on autopilot and turning around to listen.

"I suppose you are fixed pretty well. Even with all the hints, it would take them a year get another translator bird listening to a human. All that time, the tapigs will be learning from their own birds, and who knows how smart they might turn out to be."

Dell nodded. "I thought of that. If I were a tapig, well versed in Goober technology, I think I could whip up a mutant flower whose scent could fumigate the alien invaders off the planet. It might be a real good idea to learn how to say 'We come in peace' in tapig-latin.

"Oh yes, there will be lots to do in my new place. I will need an assistant or two of course."

She nodded, "Of course."

"Yes, and an escape saucer docked right up to the building in case the attacks get too bad. A permanent pilot on hand, of course."

"Permanent?"

"Oh yes. It's a shame I only know one pilot in the whole system who I trust. Do you think I could convince the corporation to station her permanently at my place?"

Sara shook her head. "Not without a big pay raise, and an extra bonus for hazard duty."

"Hazard pay? I should think with strong walls, it shouldn't be too dangerous. The tapigs...."

She put her hand across his lips. "It's not the tapigs that are the danger."

Dell kissed her fingers. "It's a problem."

Sara smiled. "I'll risk it."

The Third Wish

After seeing all the botched three wishes stories, everyone thinks to themselves, "I would do a better job. I wouldn't waste the opportunity."

"You don't even try!" Beth's voice over the phone was so loud that Leon Neuman winced when he saw John in the next row of cubicles imperfectly try to ignore it. There was no privacy in this group. He picked up the next application and began to copy the hen-scratches into his screen. He couldn't stop working now, not even to talk to Beth.

"Are you listening to me?"

Leon nodded, then replied in a near whisper, "Yes. I didn't know you had asked a question."

"Well I did! What are you going to do about our house?"

Our house? Leon didn't recall making any of the two or three offers that would lead Beth Hannover to feel ownership. But now was not the time to point that out. He put the application in the 'Done' bin and picked up the next one.

"I told you I have written a letter..."

"In other words, you aren't going to do anything! You are going to let that bank 'droid lock you out of your own house and you are just going to stand there and smile."

"Well, it isn't quite like that. The contract clearly states..."

"You should march right into that bank and demand to see the president."

"I wish it were all that simple..."

"You are the simple one! That's it. No more. Don't call me again!" Click.

You called me. Leon let out a sigh and put the phone back on its cradle. He could type better with both hands anyway. He glanced at his 'In' basket. It was taller than it had ever been. Ferris had been quite clear. Get them all entered, perfectly, today, or find another job.

He could feel the other clerks watching him. He didn't need to look away from the screen. He was the boss's target. He was the one with the loud girlfriend. He was the pathetic one.

For just an instant, his mind went blank. His hands paused on the keyboard. The screen made no sense.

No. Keep cool. Think about one thing at a time. His hands resumed their rhythm. *Too many problems, all at once.*

The house–the bank was missing the payments he had sent it, and the man on the phone was quite abusive about it. They hadn't locked him out, yet, but it was on the agenda. He had made the payments. The checks had been cashed, but his account had been with the same bank, and he could not get any help ordering photocopies of the canceled checks. His own records were hardly conclusive. *F3, submit. Next form.*

His car had been old. It burned oil. AC worked when it felt like it. It badly needed a paint job. Now it was totaled. The guy who had rear-ended him hadn't even acted apologetic. There was no insurance from him.

Leon *thought* he was covered, but when he called, the policy wasn't on the computer. He had trusted that insurance agent. The broken windshield two years ago had been handled with pleasant efficiency. They had joked about boys with baseballs and he had been convinced that he would keep his policy with there forever. Now, his calls were never returned. The body shop had called to complain. He had to come up with money, or they would have it towed off the lot. *F3, submit. Next form.*

Money. The bills in his wallet might be all that he had, and the daily taxi ride to work was depleting that rapidly. Would he be working on this robotic, repetitive job if he had any other options?

At first, the job coming out of the blue like it did had seemed to the work of a guardian angel. The pay, while unspectacular, was steady. The work was undemanding. No one seemed concerned about his former work experience. No one even asked why he hadn't completed his degree. It was better than fast-food, or digging ditches.

Everything changed. His boss, Ferris, changed overnight from a pleasant good buddy to a strident monster. "This department is sloppy," he had declared. "Changes will be made."

Leon shook his head. All of those changes were focussed on him. He became the department scapegoat. *F3, submit. Next form.*

There was a noise, or maybe the lack of noise. He looked up from his work. A security guard strode through the maze of desks towards him.

Leon paused in his data entry midway through the next account name. *It can only be for me.*

"Get your hands away from the keyboard!" The stout man in the company guard uniform rested his hands on his equipment belt. His pistol was holstered, but plainly visible.

Leon sighed and lifted them away from his desk. He turned to the man at the next desk. "Bill..." he started.

"Get your mouth shut! Now stand up, slowly." The guard reached for the hand cuffs at his belt.

It was all too ridiculous. He had done nothing. It it had been possible, he would have laughed. As it was, all he could do was give the room full of his co-workers a rueful grimace and a shrug.

Bill didn't catch his eyes. He, as well as half the floor, had heard Ferris refuse to accept that the crashed hard disk yesterday was not his fault. The ultimatum wasn't likely to be met, even if Bill decided to drop his own work and try to help him out.

Leon felt the cold metal of the hand cuffs snap around his wrists. He couldn't even work up any more indignation. It was just one more calamity.

This morning had been a sign. The power had been cut off to his house, and he had overslept without the alarm clock. The cab company had been nearly an hour late in picking him up. Then, when he arrived at the office building, the elevator chose just the wrong time to lock up, with him stranded between floors.

He didn't blame Bill. It wasn't safe to even talk to him.

Once the guard marched him out into the hallway, Leon asked, "What...?"

"No talking." He poked him with his baton. He was pushed into the opening elevator.

Leon had a brief, very brief, surge of anger. If he had the slightest belief that outrage would do him any good, he would have blown his top. He didn't have that much optimism left.

Live through it. Something has to change.

The elevator door closed. The guard reached for the buttons then suddenly groaned. He fell with a floor shaking crash.

What now? Leon could only stare.

The heavy man looked unconscious. His arm was draped across Leon's shoe. He twitched his foot loose and stepped back.

What is wrong? He stayed motionless. Surely it was a trap. The instant he moved, the guard would open his eyes and shoot him.

But what if he is really sick? If he is having a heart attack he could die while I stand here.

The guard was motionless. Leon couldn't tell if the man was breathing. He found it hard to act.

...

Leon Neuman had always been fairly passive. He had been the third child of four. His place had always been to wait until his older brother and sister had their pick of seats in the car or their choice of TV shows. He had gone to his brother's college. He didn't recall giving the issue any thought. Such things were always decided before hand, for him. It had bothered him for years, but even now, on his own, he still moved through life step by step, checking his footing each time.

Leon shook off the paralysis, a man's life could be at stake. There were things to do. First things first. He pushed the call button. There was no response.

He yelled, "Hey! There is a sick man in here!" No answer.

He moved his bound hands up and pressed the door button. There was a lurch, as if the elevator car had dropped a foot, but the doors didn't respond.

Am I going to have to do this all myself? He kneeled down and put his hands on the man's chest.

He could see the man's gun, and the keys to the handcuffs.

There is something wrong here. He looked hard at the guard's head.

He stood up. *Definitely, something wrong.*

"Okay!" He spoke loudly, "You can get up now. I know you are faking it."

There was only the faintest of tensing in the guard's jaw, and he continued to lie as he had fallen. Leon was confident. He had taken enough first-aid courses in the past few years that he could plainly see that the man was in no real distress.

He leaned back against the wall, made himself as comfortable as possible, given the handcuffs, and started humming the repetitive melody of a song from the radio. He could out-wait them.

Twelve minutes passed. Leon tried his best to sleep. He would not rise to the bait.

"Okay Fred," came a man's voice over a hidden speaker. "You can bring him on up."

The guard opened his eyes and levered himself to his feet. He showed no sign of embarrassment when Leon looked him in the eyes. His perpetual scowl didn't change. He took out a set of keys and turned one of the locked switches on the strip that were labeled for fireman usage. The elevator started up.

Somewhere between the 22nd and 23rd floors, the elevator stopped and the door opened.

The guard grabbed his hands and removed the handcuffs.

"Get." He ordered. Apparently, the guard wasn't coming with him.

Leon rubbed his wrist where the metal had pinched, and stepped out into the elegant surroundings. The whole floor appeared to be someone's office.

The Old Man. It was a guess, but a reasonable one. Office rumor had it that the founder of the company, Edmund Tennery, had never really turned over the power to the current CEO and board of directors. Supposedly, he still pulled the strings from on high.

No one but the multi-billionaire recluse would likely have this office.

It was a very subdued decor. It you didn't pay attention, it looked nice, but if you examined the wood-paneled walls, and the comfortable furniture, you quickly realized that everything wasn't just 'nice'–it was perfect.

"Don't dawdle–come on in." It was the voice from the elevator.

Leon stepped silently across the carpet. As he entered the main area, he spotted the man putting up a book in a floor to ceiling bookshelf that stretched along the whole back wall..

Yes. He did look like the grainy black and white photo on the history plaque in the lobby. The old man waved to a chair. "Sit. We've got some things to talk about."

Leon did as he was told, but he was not too thrilled by this latest revelation. Anything new was likely bad news. The man sat at his desk and pulled some fat envelopes from a drawer.

"You are Leon Neuman, a data entry clerk. Why did you choose that job?"

"I didn't choose it," he answered abruptly. He throttled back on the anger that had jumped out. He continued, a little more civilly, "It was the last job on the list. You get hungry and any job starts to look good."

Tennery looked at the papers in his hands. "You didn't finish you doctorate. Why?"

"What do you have there? Have you been spying on me?"

For the first time the old man looked him straight in the eyes. He nodded, "Yes. Most of this is standard employment information, but I have been looking at you a little closer than that."

Leon felt a dark suspicion start to grow. It must have been reflected in his face.

Tennery read his expression and nodded, "Yes, I have been responsible for some of your recent troubles." He tossed one envelope his way.

"This is the corrected papers on your house. I have paid off the remainder of the loan. You now own it free and clear."

He tossed another envelope. It was smaller and contained something hard inside.

"This is a replacement car. It is parked in the garage below."

Leon glanced at the contents, ownership papers with his name filled out. The keys were fresh cut and shiny on a BMW ring.

"What is going on here? Was my boss...?"

"Yes. He was acting. He gets a nice new promotion out of it. You are already penciled in as his replacement."

"But," the old man held up his hand, "I didn't have anything to do with your girlfriend."

Leon sat back in his chair, holding the envelopes that were worth more than he had planned to make in many years.

"I don't understand."

"I don't expect you to. For the moment, just think of this as a job interview. Answer my questions and I will explain everything later.

"Now, you had begun work on your doctoral thesis, yet you dropped it and started job hunting. Why?"

Leon forced the whirl of questions to the back-burner and let his mind go back to that time, three years ago. It was painful.

"History isn't a science," he began. "I chose to explore the possibility of an alternate interpretation of Eisenhower's use of the CIA during the last few months of his term." He grimaced. "It just so happened that my idea was in direct conflict with a project my advisor was working on. He took it as a personal affront, and he had the reputation to make my project a non-starter. After that, every idea I brought up ended in a shouting match. My only choice was to move to a different school and start all over again, or go to work for a living. I didn't have the resources to start over."

Tennery nodded, "A tough call. But, if you had the money, would you have stuck it through? Was you interpretation right?"

Leon laughed. "This is history we are talking about—different interpretations on limited documentation. Without a smoking gun or a signed confession, it is all up to the best guess. I don't know if my idea was right. It seemed logical at the time."

The old man looked again at his papers. He glanced up at the clock on his desk and frowned. "Okay, next question. If you could make one change in history, what would that be?"

"Is this a serious question? I've got a million changes to make. For starters, I would like to have had rich parents."

"Yes, it is a serious question. As a historian, what would you have changed in world history? But you can make only one change."

Leon Neuman frowned. On impulse, he stood up and looked around the room. Okay, if this was a job interview, then he should at least try to make a good impression. But he had been run through the meat grinder, and he was not at all in a forgiving mood. If all the recent pain had been due to an old man's whim, he would make sure people heard about it. He would certainly take the house and the car, but forgiveness was something else.

Still, what was his mysterious job offer? The sunlight was streaming in through the large windows and he walked over to view the expanse of the city. There were millions of people out there. They each were moving on their personal track. Each one with a history. Change something in the past, and every one of those personal histories would be different. Some would vanish altogether.

Tennery walked over to look out the window with him.

Leon shook his head, "I wouldn't change anything. It is all just people, and people wouldn't change. Change who won a war, or who is president, and there would be just as many saints, and just as many sinners as before."

"You don't think big changes would do any good?"

"Oh, if I could tweak it—make a correction every day—then it would be tempting. To be honest, I don't think I am smart enough to make the one right choice the first time. That's what all the three wishes fables are about, isn't it? The first wish is wasted, the second one is disastrous, and the last one is used to put everything back like it was."

"I hope not."

"What?"

"How about small changes? If you could make a change in one person's history?"

"And still only one wish?"

"Yes."

"Oh sure, I know people who have messed up their lives. I'm one of them. I should have gone for engineering instead of history." He grinned. "And there are at least two girls who should have gone for the boy with the brains instead of the one with the good looks."

Tennery cracked a smile. "And which *one* of these mistakes would you correct?"

Leon turned to face him, "What is this job? Are you setting up some RAND-like think tank? Are you looking for deep-thinking historians? If so, I am not your first choice."

He nodded, "You weren't. I have been looking for the right person for several years now. Two others have been offered the job. One turned it down. The other... I had to withdraw the offer. He proved... unstable."

"What is this job? Surely you aren't going to all this trouble to replace a data entry supervisor?"

Edmund Tennery waited a moment, and then turned towards his desk. "Come here, I want to show you something."

They resumed their chairs, and the old man picked up a heavy glass ornament, a hollow globe, from the clutter of items on his desk. He shook it, and Leon could see a smaller sphere, like a marble, rolling around inside the sealed globe.

"It was a little before sundown on October 2, 1962. I was waiting for it to get dark before I hung myself."

Leon jerked in response. The old man had his eyes closed, remembering. He decided to wait and ask his questions later.

"It was a very bad day. My wife had gone into the city and I had watched my whole world burn to ashes when the first of the Russian A-bombs exploded over Manhattan. None of the explosions came close to me, but I was able to watch the flashes on the horizon. My neighbors panicked, rushing around, trying to prepare for the fallout.

"When the electricity went out, I sat in my car, listening to the only radio station that were still on the air. Of course, the announcer didn't know anything more than I did. The Cubans had shot down an American spy plane. Kennedy had ordered Havana bombed. The Russians retaliated–and New York was destroyed. I assume we also bombed Russia."

Leon ran the story against what he knew about the Cuban Missile Crisis, and there were was one glaring error—no nuclear war ever happened.

"Of course, not a lot of this meant anything to me then. I only knew that my wife and my little boy had died, and that I was likely to die from radiation poisoning within the next few days. My life was torn to shreds and I saw no real reason to continue. I didn't have a gun, and I knew that I would have trouble killing myself with a knife—I had a horror of doing it poorly and bleeding to death slowly.

"Hanging seemed a good choice, step off the second story balcony and snap my neck. It was just a matter of finding a good rope and tying a sturdy knot.

"It was while I was sitting in the living room, testing the knots, that the Wishes appeared."

"The what?" Leon asked.

Tennery shook the glass globe again. The marble-thing rolled around inside. "The Wishes. I received three wishes."

...

Leon already suspected the man was crazy. Of course, rich people were called 'eccentric', but with this last revelation, it appeared that 'crazy' might be the best term after all. He felt the urge to get up and leave, but he remembered where he was, on a secret floor of a building Tennery owned, with a security guard nearby that never cracked a smile.

"Of course I didn't know what they were," the old man continued. "I just knew that these three glowing marbles had appeared right in the middle of my coffee table."

Leon looked again at the marble. Was it glowing? In this light he couldn't tell.

"My first thought was that the radiation was already affecting my brain and that I was going crazy. I was using that table. I had dumped all the old magazines and had laid out the rope on it while I tried to remember how to tie a hangman's noose.

"I stared at them for a moment, and then picked up the closest."

Edmund Tennery's face changed, it was as if his age faded away. He was looking off into nothingness.

His voice was a whisper. "It was as if I touched God. Something like warm fire crawled up my arm, and as it reached my head, it seemed as if I were reaching into another place. It was like I had stuck my arm, and then my head through a hole in the world."

Tennery looked away from his vision and turned to Leon. "I can't explain what I saw. I have tried often enough, first to my wife, and then to several close friends."

"Your wife? But you said she was caught in the attack?"

He waved his hand, "Yes, I will get to that. I just need to explain, and I know I can't do it justice."

He paused a moment, gathering his thoughts.

"Imagine," he started up again, "that you opened up a large filing cabinet, packed with folders. As you run the tips of your fingers along the tabs of the files, you suddenly comprehend each and every nuance of every word in that file. You move your finger to the next one, and you are filled with it, while the first recedes to an old memory.

"Now imagine that each of these folders is a possible version of our world, and that there are millions of them. In a swipe of your hand, you can sample uncountable possibilities, from worlds of unimaginable advances where technology has accelerated far beyond our own, to worlds where life never began, and with another swipe, worlds of Eden-like pastoral simplicity or globe spanning tyranny.

"Uncountable worlds, and you have just enough omniscience to tell the differences.

"You can imagine what I searched for—a world very like my own, but one where this horrible attack never happened. I found my wife in many new worlds. I carefully searched for a minimum of side effects, and then when I found it, I grabbed it and pulled it out."

He was breathing hard as he related the tale. He paused, a timid expression on his face, as if fearing laughter.

"So this is the world you picked with your Wish?" Leon asked, willing to suspend any overt signs of disbelief, for now. If it were true, Leon didn't like the taste of it.

"Not exactly."

Tennery shook the globe with the ease of long practice, and the little marble raced around the inside. There was something odd about the marble, even when it was resting still at the bottom of the globe, but Leon couldn't put a finger on what it was that gave him that impression.

"The world I grabbed grew and swallowed me up, the feeling of fire faded, and I was once again sitting at my coffee table. The rope was gone. *I Love Lucy* was on the television, and there were two glowing marbles.

"I looked at the television shows, wandered through the neighborhood and sweated through the evening news. I didn't really believe it had all changed until my wife and son arrived at the end of a long shopping day with their horror tales of lost glasses and a drunk that shared their train back from the city.

"For nearly a month, I woke up each night and went into the kitchen to stare at the two remaining Wishes. I had hidden them at the back of a top shelf, in an old peanut-butter jar. I sweated through the new version of the Cuban Missile Crisis when it hit the news, and during its peak, I kept the jar with me at all times."

Tennery gave the globe in his hand another twist and watched the marble spin. "You see, I experienced the miracle. I watched my wife and son come back to life. I had solid memories. I could never convince myself it was a dream. I also had the two remaining Wishes where I could look at them.

"But in spite of all this, I didn't trust it. There was no explanation. Where did they come from? Why did they show up on my table? Why were there *three* Wishes? It frightened me.

"A year passed. The Kennedy assassination happened. By that time, I had moved the Wishes into a bank safety deposit box. As the world went into shock, I considered changing the world again."

He shook his head. "But I didn't do it. The people considered him a saint, but I had seen the world—my original world—destroyed by his mistakes. I became a judge. I let him die."

In the silence that followed, Leon asked, "What happened to the second Wish?"

There was a shrug. Tennery waved at the room. "I got greedy."

The storytelling was obviously having an effect on the old man. He was lapsing into silences. There was a hint of moisture around his eyes. Leon wondered if he was watching his collapse.

Finally, with a glance at the clock, Tennery sat back straighter into his chair.

"Of course," he resumed, "I didn't tell myself I was just being greedy. It was in the third year. I was having money problems. My son was having school problems. The Vietnam war was beginning to have its effect on the public, and every report of our soldiers being killed had a direct tug at my conscience.

"I knew I was weakening. My high-minded moral stand against bending history to save Kennedy was going to go out the window and I could see myself burning the remaining Wishes by rescuing a lost kitten or arranging for a sunny day for a picnic.

"Wrestling with the problem every day, and every night before I drifted off into sleep brought me to a plan. I would use the second Wish to choose a long and prosperous life here in New York. I would tie my fortunes directly into the fortunes of society. By wishing for this life, I would—as a side effect—be insuring no more nuclear wars or other great disasters during my lifetime. All this could be done with just one Wish. I could then save the last one for some great thing that I couldn't foresee.

"I pulled the dusty peanut-butter jar from the safety deposit box, half afraid that the Wishes would have evaporated or gone dark. Like two glowing eyes, they were still there, still waiting for me.

"This time, the fire of God's power in my hand was like euphoria, not at all like the terror of the unknown that I had felt the first time. Again there was this omniscience as I reviewed the potential worlds of my future. I took my time, savoring the possibilities.

"When I focused on my goal, however, I discovered that there were limits. I could get to nearly any end result, but not without consequences. If I wished to live to be a thousand, then all of human history had to change, back to the Babylonians, in order to advance the medical sciences enough to make it happen. If I wished for universal peace and prosperity, then something strange happened to humanity, some genetic twist back in pre-history, that allowed a more pallid version of the human race to come to be, a race that was content to live in a tightly controlled matriarchy in a prosperous hive city. If I looked for wide social justice, then America became a monarchy, and one that looked ready to collapse when the current King died.

"Again, I settled for finding a world with my original goal, but one with a minimum of side-effects. I had to settle for a shorter life than I had hoped. I had to settle for relative obscurity in spite of my wealth. I had to settle for protecting just my corner of humanity from disaster. In the end, this is the life I chose–knowing in the back of my head that there was always the third Wish."

Tennery rolled the globe across the table and Leon jerked from his chair to catch it. It was heavy, the glass was thick.

"Don't worry. I sealed that up long ago. It is tough. I have a big hammer in the desk if I really need to open it, but it is not likely to break open on its own."

Held close, the marble did glow. Leon tried to focus on its surface, but with no luck. Was he really looking into a million alternate realities?

Tennery's voice steadied. "So! This is the job I'm offering. Take the third Wish. Use it when it is needed."

Leon broke his eyes away from the globe. "What? Why would you do that?"

Tennery stood up. "Because I am going to die soon. I know the very instant when it will happen. Since I don't want to waste the Wish on extending my own pitiful existence, I needed to find someone to take over my place."

"Then why me?"

Tennery smiled, "Feeling the pinch already? Learn to live with it. But to answer your question: You are educated in history, so you won't panic when little things like depressions and brushfire wars happen. I also like the way you handled my tests—suffering in silence, but being smart and methodical.

"I read the checklist from your computer. You had the evidence. You filed the papers like clockwork. You could have convinced any judge, unless I bribed him. You didn't scream at the fates. You didn't threaten. You even listened to your girl-friend with more patience than she deserved."

Leon let the praise trickle off his back. He knew what kind of person he was. Methodical or dull, either term applied. What mattered this instant was understanding Tennery. Sane or not, right now the man was the most important influence over his own future.

"How do you know I won't waste your Wish?"

He shook his head. "I don't know. It is all a gamble."

The old man counted on his fingers.

"One, you can handle disappointments, even catastrophes.

"Two, you have no close family, no one you should feel compelled to rescue.

"Three, you can handle poverty. I have a trust set up to make sure you are eased into wealth with as little stress as possible. That shouldn't side-track you."

He spread his hands, "But I will be out of the picture soon and it won't make any difference what I think. But seriously, I don't have any choice."

Leon asked, "What about the old trick of using one wish to make more wishes?"

"Ha! How many times have I thought of that? There isn't any djinn to tell me the rules. What if it doesn't work that way? The omniscience vanishes as soon as the change is made. The only way to tell is to burn the Wish on the attempt.

"In any case, I am done with the responsibility. I didn't waste the Wish to bring my own son back to life. I didn't waste it to make my wife love me again, or to bring her back after her death. I won't *waste* the Wish!" He looked over at the clock on his desk.

"Anyway, my time is done."

Crash! The huge window shattered into a million white diamonds. *Crack. Crack. Crack.*

Leon dropped to the ground. He looked at his right arm–a thick numbness made it hard to recognize that the gushing red was his blood. He tried to clench his fingers together, but they didn't move. *Too much blood.* He gripped his good hand over the wound.

The door to the elevator came open and two guards in uniform came in crouched low.

"Get down," Leon called. "Someone is shooting at us."

The black guard waved him down. "It has to be Jennings." Fred, the other one, was scooting along the floor towards Tennery. *Crack!* There was another shot. There was a tight "Uhh" of pain from Fred.

Jennings? Was he the 'unstable' one?

Leon lifted his head slightly. He had to see what was going on.

Edmund Tennery was down, his head was covered with blood, and strangely misshapen. *He is dead, just like he expected.* The guard was bleeding—a large red patch growing on his side. *Why is he still shooting? Surely he could see his target go down. Unless I am the real target?* Fred's partner was already moving into the range of fire.

I have to stop this. Leon looked around for anything he could use.

Among the large glass fragments near his side, a glowing marble sat quietly in the thick carpet, freed from its prison.

Could I do it? Could I wish it away? I could bring back the old man. Keep the guard from being shot. Keep me from getting shot! Just make the shooter's gun jam or something.

It was tempting to reach down and pick it up–to start the magic. *But what if it is real—he wouldn't thank me to bring him back.*

There was another shot, and the other guard edged back to shelter. Fred was still pumping blood. *He is going to bleed to death. I have to do something.*

He looked around his limited shelter behind the desk. Glass fragments of the globe, shattered by the second bullet, and the Wish itself seemed to be his only tools.

Leon felt an ache creep up his whole right side. They were all locked down by the shooter. *I have to stop it.*

He let go of his wound and reached down with his good hand. With a scream of pain and effort from deep inside him, he shoved the massive wooden desk four feet over and toppled it.

The other guard was alert, and moved into the protected space and started pulling his partner to safety.

Leon leaned against the wood, until it jumped with the impact of a spatter of bullets as the frustrated gunman reacted to the barrier.

There was scattered debris everywhere. He picked up a decorative container and dumped the paperclips it held. Carefully he scooped up the Wish and closed the lid on it. His hand tingled in its proximity.

The body of the old man lay still. He looked at peace in spite of the violence of his death. *I'll think about it. I owe you at least that much. But I have to work it out, step by step.*

Step 1. Protect the Wish. He put the little box deep into his pocket.

Step 2. Stay Alive. His hand still tightly clamped over his own bleeding arm, he started his crawl out of the room.

Wildlife

Just after the birds waddled across the beach near our room in Traverse City on a trip with my nature photographer wife, this story came to life.

Greg Hammersmith frowned at the frozen image of a blue-winged teal tugging at the grass with its beak. *The keystone is off.* The deck-of-cards projector tracked his finger and corrected the frame.

"Off." The bird vanished, long enough for him to spray a fresh layer of Canvas on the wall where the image had been. "Calibrate and burn. Ten percent impressionist. Two inch frame, cinnamon."

After the projector did its thing, Greg picked the gadget up and stuffed it in his shirt pocket.

That gives the room some life!

But his smile faded. *I've already used up one bottle of Canvas already.*

In his pocket was every picture he had taken in his thirty years as a nature photographer back on Earth. There were many good shots, one blank space on the wall, and a nagging need to fill it.

One thing for sure, there would be no landscapes. Not with the scenery outside.

Greg's one-man habitat was sitting two kilometers to the west of Byrgius Crater, site number three in his year-long photo-shoot. It had taken eight years to get the funding and approval for his unique photo-essay on the lunar landscape. Twelve sites, one for each month, taking out time to relocate the habitat in the middle of each long lunar night.

The perfectionist in him wished he could set up his cameras and have a complete synodic period of twenty-nine and a half days to get every possibility of light and shadow on the craters and rills he had chosen, but some trade-off had to be made to keep the International Photo-Artistry Guild happy and the one-year job with an even dozen sites was the limit of what they could fund. As it was, his first site, with no Earth in the sky, had been terminally boring once the sun had set. At least on the earthward side, subtle changes in color reflected from the Earth's blue and white gave some variety to his shots.

He looked the bird in the eye. Greg remembered that teal. The duck had waddled ashore looking for crumbs left over from the tourists, alert for a handout, but still wild enough to keep his distance.

I miss wildlife. Luna is grand, but it's sterile.

Eighty percent of his photo library were animal shots—his official biographer had coaxed that admission out of him. He had only gotten into photography to capture the critters.

There are none here. He hadn't realized how much he missed animals until the tug relocated his habitat from Riccioli a couple of weeks ago, bringing fresh supplies, and two dozen fruit-flies along with the produce.

The infinitesimal insects died quickly, in spite of his precautions. In all his years, he hadn't really appreciated how short their lifespan was. Usually they reproduced so fast that they just appeared immortal.

These had survived Lift-Luna's food sterilization somehow, but not totally undamaged. His close-up macro photos of his guests had shown evidence of deformed wings and if he had been an entomologist, probably other mutations. Fascinating photos—but they weren't the kind that would sell.

Deedee dum, dedum. "Time for the photo of the day."

Greg nodded to the computer. "Okay. Give me a minute." He brought up the album and scanned through the last twenty-four hours worth of images.

Each new site took a couple of days to get the cameras positioned. About half of those he did himself, trudging around the landscape in a vacuum suit, riding a golf-cart. The others he put on tripods and sent them to position themselves. From then until the end of the month, he stayed indoors and rode herd on his remote eyes from the comfort of his desk.

At this sun angle, only three of the cameras were producing anything approaching artistic landscapes. Gigapixel frames were captured from each of the cameras every ten seconds. Of course he saved it all for later re-evaluation, but for now he scanned the day's worth as a high-speed movie, looking for some transient reflection or coloration that would make for an interesting....

"Ah, there it is."

He backed up the movie and located the best frame.

Three peaks on the nearby ridge had roughly the same surface angle and the sun outlined similar crests. "Three Kings" he typed in for the title. Cropping the image to center the peaks and tweaking the color balance for best effect, he let it sit on the side screen while he hunted for better candidates. After thirty minutes of searching and three other potential winners, "Three Kings" was still the best. So off to the L-4 relay station and then to Earth—in under ten seconds the day's tribute to IPAG was in place.

...

Deedee dum, dedum. "Review the Brazilian shoot proposal."

He frowned at the images from his easternmost camera. "Reschedule," he told the computer. It would nag him about it later.

The next shoot in Antarctica was already contracted. Perhaps that had been a mistake—two barren environments back to back—but it was only for two months. Was the boat trip up to the headwaters of the Amazon on over-reaction?

Still, the only way to survive in this business was to think ahead, find out what people want and be the first to give it to them.

It would be nice to be in a jungle shoot again, with wildlife appearing around every bend of the river.

But he could think about that later. Right now, there was a defect in Camera-8 that he had to resolve.

In the lower left of the frame, where the gray plains were just beginning to show shading as the sun crept across their rising elevation, there was a thin black line, straight as an arrow, where there had been nothing more than the random texture of microcratering.

Did I put it there? He had positioned the cameras during the lunar night, taking great care that none of the other cameras and none of his golf-cart tracks would be visible from any of the sites. But taking precautions never stopped him from making blunders before. Camera-8 was due to supply some great sunset shots in another week, and if he had ruined the frame, then he would have to take action quickly.

Or it could be a defect in the camera or the lens.

He looked at the site map photo he had taken.

"Camera-8, reposition yourself three meters to the south, facing the same direction."

A "Motion Jitter" warning appeared on the screen as the tripod took a few steps to the south. When it cleared, he captured the first frame. Visually it looked identical.

"Match and overlay. Zoom to pixels."

The frames were nearly identical, except at the edges where the errors caused by the re-pointing were visible.

So, it's not a camera defect. That line exists out there on the landscape.

"Position back one day on Camera-8, match and overlay."

The black line flickered on the screen.

So I didn't miss it. It appeared sometime today.

"Scan forward in time at 20 X." He would locate when it appeared. Maybe as it faded into view, he could see more irregularities. Straight lines weren't unknown in nature, but true ones were rare. Catch a horizon or the trunk of a tall pine in the right light and nature will show all her wrinkles. Greg's career had been built on nature's wrinkles.

He expected irregular dots to appear and then connect into a line. That's not what he got.

"Stop! Back that up and replay it."

As the line grew longer leading from the edge of the frame, he felt his remaining hair stand on edge. He wasn't alone. Someone was out there.

…

"This is Greg Hammersmith. Stop right where you are! You're messing up an important photo. Answer me."

Short range radio was line-of-sight only—it had to be with no atmosphere—but the idiot was in the line-of-sight. That was the problem!

With no answer, and with the line growing across the scene hour by hour, Greg kept looking over at the airlock.

Camera-8's frame is ruined already. If I don't take action soon, he may take out Camera-10 as well.

…

He kept one eye on the map as he wove the golf-cart across the rough landscape. The computer had sketched areas on the map that were hidden from all of the other cameras. It was zigzag at best, and seemed designed to cross the worst boulder fields in the area.

Greg was grinning, or maybe just clenching his teeth. It was good to get out of the house, but his schedule was wrecked for days. He rehearsed his greeting.

Do you have any idea what you've done? Taking nature photographs isn't anything like it was when I was young. Back then I'd think nothing of dropping an image into Photoshop and erasing an offending line, but photo ethics has changed. IPAG and all its brothers would blacklist anyone who faked any details in a nature photo. Even color balance has to be spelled out in detail.

These lunar landscapes are unique. Day by day more footprints are scarring up the dust—footprints that never fade.

Your tracks are destroying the only true record humanity will ever have of the primeval lunar landscape!

Greg caught himself weaving back and forth across his 'safe zone'. He grinned. *Not likely I'll be able to sustain the righteous indignation while leaving my own tracks across the dust.*

It was true he had to stop his unwanted guest. It was also true he was looking forward to meeting anyone with warm breath and a pulse.

The hunt was exciting too. *It's like the time Lisa spotted the grizzly from Mt. Washburn, and we raced down the old dirt road to be in place when the bear crossed near the highway.* He had gotten excellent photos of it by being in exactly the right place and the right time, but that was long before he had gone professional.

There had been so many good hunts, living on the road, or living in the field—on assignment, or to complete a book. And after her death, as painful as it was to live alone, the hunt for a reportedly-extinct finch across five states had been the only thing that kept him going.

Wildlife keeps me alive.

Every fresh encounter was a thrill, every cautious approach a refresher in humility, and every crisp image a triumph. Eye to eye with a non-human intelligence put a face on the universe for him.

Luna was a stretch. Yes, his "Canadian Rockies" had made his reputation, and his "Great Mountains of the World" book series gave him the freedom to travel anywhere. But for him, the centerpiece of the mountain pictures had been the cover of the Rockies book, a morning light image with a bull elk atop a sheer cliff, surveying his world. The theme was repeated throughout the photos—great animals living in great surroundings. Often the animal was imperceptibly small, and only he or perceptive critics could see them, but the stamp of life put soul in the scenery for him.

But there was no life in these lands. It was a mistake for an artist to forget his own passions. Mastery of the craft can only take you so far.

Greg shook off the feeling that he was stuck in a doomed, high-profile project. He could master the lighting and capture the sterile splinters of these peaks, but without life, there was no soul.

...

Deedee dum, dedum. The chime sounded in his helmet. "Approaching your destination."

The cart crested the rise and there was the track. Camera in hand, he stopped and snapped several shots. *It's not a wheeled vehicle.*

He stepped closer. There was a single continuous track in the lunar dust. *It's not footsteps either.*

Greg had expected a man, in a vehicle, or possibly on foot. This was neither.

The shutter click was inaudible and it bothered him. Even when cameras no longer had any moving parts that made noise, he always turned on the shutter sound. Without the feedback it threw him off.

He zoomed in for a closer shot of the tread marks. *Either a huge unicycle, or the grandfather of all pythons came through here.* The ridges across the direction of the track looked familiar.

Braced with the camera body against his helmet, he could hear the shutter faintly.

And the memory clicked.

Those are tripod tracks!

...

Everyone called them tripods, although they came with five to eight legs depending on how much weight they had to carry. The mobile robots with long legs were perfect for the dusty lunar surface. They had no moving parts, at least in the old gears and bearing sense. Legs moved by electrostriction. Dust could cling, at least until the tripod reversed its static charge, but there were no hinges or groves where grit could be trapped.

Greg had used the robotic tripods on Earth several times, once he had the budget to afford them. On Luna, they were essential.

He put the golf-cart in high gear and went bouncing across the landscape following the long patterns in the dust.

It can't be one of mine. All of my cameras are exactly where I left them.

A flicker of motion in the distance made him put on the brakes. His zoom lens brought his quarry into focus.

It was grayer than his tripods, shorter and wider. Instead of a camera, a fat instrument cluster rode on its 'head'. The gadget was plowing away in that spinning-top gait the tripods used for easy terrain. The whole device spun around and around, the legs laying down in sequence, leaving a track like a giant snake.

Greg snapped a long sequence. *I'll have to use the golf-cart. It's moving too fast for me to catch it on foot.*

As he drove over a rise, he scanned for escape routes a startled prey might take. *If it ducks into that boulder field, it could lose me.* He angled the cart towards the rocks. If it bolted, he wanted to force it towards open ground.

The thumbwheel on the camera let him set the shutter speed higher. Shooting with one hand while driving demanded it.

He came up even with the whirling tripod. *It looks like a fat gray octopus.* The device appeared to ignore him. It didn't bolt, but it didn't slow down either.

A familiar company logo was painted on it side, Mascon Mining.

But up close, he could see that it was damaged. The stub of an antenna caught the sun's reflection every rotation. There were other scrapes, but he couldn't see more while it was moving.

Get ahead of it. He darted ahead a few meters and pulled the golf-cart broadside across the tripod's path. His prey curved to one side. He edged the cart forward and blocked it again.

The tripod dropped out of spin mode and began crab-walking to one side. Greg hopped out and stabbed at the halt button on the top.

The tripod leveled itself and stood there, waiting.

…

Deedee dum, dedum. "Incoming call from Orin Lewis."

Greg leaned back from his desk and smiled at his publisher. "Hello, Orin. How have you been doing?"

There was the usual delay for the distance.

"Greetings there Greg. I just wanted to check in with you. Only a couple of days left before you leave Byrgius and I wanted to confirm your change of sites personally. We spent so much time choosing the original set, it surprised me to see you putting Tycho back on the list. You had been so adamant about staying far away from human settlement. Why the change?"

Greg smiled. "You know how it is, Orin. Once you get in the field, all your carefully laid plans go out the window. I could tell something was wrong at Riccioli but here it came into focus. I'm here to shoot the Moon as it is, not to make some statement about human footprints."

Orin nodded as he listened, and then commented, "I could see that something had changed a week or so ago. I forget when, sometime after that 'Three Kings' shot, your stuff started getting more lively, more like your Canada work."

"Yes. I saw a piece of mining equipment, and a realized that life was coming to Luna, even if it is just men and men's surrogates for now. With life the whole landscape came alive."

It had taken him hours to get the rogue tripod loaded onto the golf-cart and packed back to his habitat. Repairing its antenna and visual sensors was a job beyond his technical capabilities, but he was a photographer—he knew his way around computers.

Digging into its files he found that for over three years, the semi-autonomous device had struggled to follow its fallback programming: *If out of contact, return to base.*

The problem had been that the rock fall which took out its radio also blinded it. With no way radio or star fix to guide by, it had lapsed into a pattern of following the sun, which it could sense from its charging cells. The prospector-robot slept at night and traveled by day, only able to detect obstacles in its path with a flea-power radar and its neutron-emission detector. Cut off from its original duties it had gone wild—Lunar wildlife.

Orin accepted Greg's vague explanation. "You're the artist. If the rest of your stuff is up to last week's standard, we should have a best-seller when you get back.

"Judith and I would like you to come out to the cabin with us, once you get out of low-g rehab. There's a great trout-stream, just your style—I know you're a 'catch-and-release' kind of guy."

Greg grinned widely. Orin had a knack for knowing what he would do. 'Catch and release' was just the kind of guy he was. When he had reactivated the old tripod, turning it loose to find its own way across the enormous lunar surface, it had been as natural as breathing.

"It sounds great, Orin. Although I don't look forward to rehab.

"By the way, could you put in an order for three more tripods in the next supply run, there was a programming glitch and a couple seem to have wandered off."

Going Green

The Dr. Jenkins stories were to be a regular series of short, idea tales featuring this consultant to scientists. I only wrote two, and the other wasn't usable. I guess my idea stories tend to grow rather larger than Dr. Jenkins can solve.

Dr. Jenkins straightened his tie and opened the glass door to the windowless three-story office building. A lobby directory gave him the room number.

The gray-haired lady was pacing back and forth behind the conference room table, her suit conservative and expensive, her posture as straight as the English teacher who'd terrorized him in the sixth grade.

"There you are! For what I'm paying you, I'd expect you to be prompt."

"Yes, Mrs. Wilson." He didn't object to the drop-everything-and-come-immediately job. Those paid very well. "My service gave no information. What do you need?"

Her pacing stopped. She looked at him for the first time. "Um. Nothing. I don't need you. I just need your presence."

Dr. Jenkins said nothing. Consulting work often meant doing what was asked, rather than what was sensible. If she wanted to tell him what was going on, she would. If not, he'd still bill her.

She gripped the back of the nearest chair. "This is a closed medical research partnership. We have our own rules. Any of our doctors can seal his lab. Not even another partner can inspect it, except under special circumstances."

Her face was rigid. "Cyrus, my husband, is not letting anyone in. I'm not even a doctor. I'm the lawyer for the group. It's been ten days, and I want access."

"Have you spoken to him?"

She nodded. "He's hiding something." Her face tightened.

"But I can hire you, our designated Procedures Consultant, for legal protection. You have access. And you can bring in one assistant. That's me."

She headed for the door. He followed. Down the corridor, she produced documents and he proved his identity. The security guard was too well trained to show any emotions. He checked his notes and made a call on the phone into the lab.

"Ten minutes," he informed her.

...

The room was dark, barely lit. Dr. Cyrus Wilson was dressed casually, as if he were heading out for a game of golf. He came up to the glass and pressed the intercom button.

"Cin! What are you doing here? I told you I couldn't come out until this experiment was completed."

"Cyrus, what's happened to your arm?"

In the darkness, Dr. Jenkins hadn't noticed the man's discoloration, but the arm was covered in dark patches. It was less evident on the other arm, but even on his face, the researcher had discolored spots.

Wilson sighed. "Cin, I'm afraid that I've been infected by one of my own experiments." The room was obviously a quarantine cell. There was a bed, slept in. But there was also a computer terminal.

Motion in the darkness showed a nurse, dressed head to foot in contamination gear, stocking lab supplies on a counter. The doctor had made his cell into a workplace.

"Turn on the light. Let me see."

"Cin, I'm trying to keep the light low to keep it from spreading."

His wife shook her head. "I need to see."

He sighed. "Okay, for a minute. The light adjustment is on your side."

She glanced at her consultant. Jenkins found the knob and turned the brightness up. The skin patches were bright green.

"It's chlorophyll. The experiment was to take plants' ability to make food from sunlight and give it to livestock."

She put her hand to her mouth. "How did it happen?"

"Just a stupid mistake. A vial broke. Cut my hand. It was days before the symptoms appeared.

"Of course, I sealed the lab immediately. Anything like this would raise the specter of human genetic alteration. It's not, of course—just a chloroplast modified to take up residence in an animal cell as if it were a mitochondria. But if the media found out, it would be a disaster. I couldn't even tell you, Cin."

His wife didn't look mollified.

Jenkins looked over the control panel. For the first time, he spoke, "Dr. Wilson, are you concerned that this... green skin alteration, might be infectious?"

"Dr. Jenkins, is it? I just don't know yet. It would be unethical to risk it. Until we know more, or better yet, find a safe way to kill out all the chloroplasts, I'll have to stay locked in here." He explained how the carrier organism circulated through the blood stream, seeding the animal cells with the snip of DNA that formed the hybrid chloroplast. Only in the skin cells, exposed to light, did they develop and produce chlorophyll.

Jenkins watched the man carefully as he spoke. He watched the nurse, too. Something was off.

Turning to Mrs. Wilson, he whispered, "I'm unsure of one thing. Who is my client? You or the labs?"

She hesitated, glancing at her husband. She weighted her answer, and then said, "I hired you. Why do you ask?"

He turned to the glass. "Doctor? Could you send the nurse out? I need to ask her some questions."

"Um, I'm not sure if that's wise." He frowned and looked at his wrapped-up assistant.

"Oh, I'm sure there's no chance of any air-borne infection, Dr. Wilson. Not with the blood-borne organism you described. It's just a couple of questions, about your procedures."

Wilson was clearly, hesitant, but nodded. The nurse went out through the double-doors.

"I need to go through decontamination before I come out there with you."

Mrs. Wilson looked concerned.

Jenkins shook his head. "Nonsense. If you're worried, then we'll stay several feet away. Unless Dr. Wilson was misrepresenting the nature of the organism...."

Slowly, reluctantly, she came into the control room, still dressed in contamination gear.

"Hmm. The only thing I can see of you is your eyes. Why don't you take off that suit?"

She looked past him, towards Dr. Wilson behind the glass.

"Come on, it's hard for me to talk to someone when I can't see their face."

She still hesitated.

"Young lady!" Mrs. Wilson weighed in. "Do as you're told."

Behind the goggles, her eyes were wide with fright.

Jenkins pushed. "There's no reason not to open your suit. It's designed to keep the infection out, isn't it?"

She looked at Dr. Wilson. "Cyrus?"

There was a sigh through the intercom. "Go ahead, Janis."

"Your glove, please," ordered Jenkins.

She tugged off her right glove. The hand was solid green. Mrs. Wilson gasped and took a step back.

"The other one, too." To his employer he said, "Don't be alarmed. It's not contagious."

"How do you know? They both have it."

Jenkins looked at the stitches on her left hand and nodded. "See, she's the one with the cut on her hand. You husband said he had the accident, but he had no injury."

"Then, how did he get it?"

The nurse pulled off the goggles and head covering. She was a striking brunette, and even with a deep green complexion, she was beautiful.

Jenkins explained, "With this kind of organism, it's unlikely to be infectious through casual contact. As they say these days, it requires 'exchange of bodily fluids'."

Mrs. Wilson turned to the glass and shrieked, "Cyrus!"

...

"I could tell at once that the quarantine was just a fake, set up hurriedly when we arrived. The controls were dead. The air pressure system was turned off." Jenkins sat in one corner of the room. The others each took a corner of their own, as if seeing how far apart they get from each other.

Dr. Wilson, from the opposite corner, nodded. "We're working day and night trying to find a way to deactivate the chloroplasts. That much is true."

His wife glared at him, keeping her eyes off Janis Porter, glaringly green, except for her heavily made-up face, once she'd shed the suit. "Well, Cyrus, you've always said you wanted your name to go down in history. You've done it now. You've invented a venereal disease all your own. Only with this one, people can tell at a glance who's been doing who. You've ruined us all."

Jenkins held up his hand. It looked like he was going to have to be the voice of moderation. "Just a minute. Let's get all the facts before tossing our future to the fates. How does this disease progress? What are the symptoms?"

"Sunlight," offered Janis. "Light's the trigger. I was infected for three days before I noticed anything—but I was working night shift then. I never saw the sun.

"But came the weekend, I took off for the beach. I woke up from a nap in the sun and was like this—fully developed. No one was around. I wrapped myself in the towel and came straight here."

"Any other symptoms?"

"A slight itch for a day or so, but that's gone."

Dr. Wilson nodded. "My infection," he looked down, avoiding his wife's face, "happened a day before that, but I'd been outside, on and off. I'd noticed a few green freckles, and when Janis called in a panic, I knew instantly what had happened."

Jenkins nodded. "Now the critical question; who knows?"

"No one."

"The security guard? Ms. Porter? Who saw you arrive here?"

"Oh, he saw, but I'd done my face, like today." Her thick makeup was like a pink face mask on her otherwise green head. "As bundled up as I was, he didn't suspect anything."

"Dr. Wilson. Who knows the nature of this research? Who would suspect?"

"Hmm. Maybe Harris and Tarrant. But I've been pretty tight with it. How much noise did you cause Cin?"

She declined to answer.

Jenkins talked into the silence. "Okay, here is an option. Mrs. Wilson, how much would you pay to keep your husband's infidelity secret?"

"What are you saying? I don't like the sound of this."

"I'm not talking blackmail. I'm just doing my job. You're my client, not your husband, not the lab. That's my understanding. I may have a solution, but much of it will be up to you."

She looked at her husband, and frowned. She sighed. "I'd do anything to hush this up."

"Even turn green?" Jenkins held up his hand again to silence her outrage. "Consider this option. You and your husband hold a press conference. You're both visibly infected with the chloroplasts. You lay out everything about the research. Only two things change. Dr. Wilson had the accident, and you are the innocent victim. A loving husband is working night and day to find the cure for his wife.

"There'd be lots of press coverage. Some would be negative, but that can't be helped. Much would be sympathetic. If you, Mrs. Wilson, can show the world that the symptoms are mild and manageable, and that you aren't a dangerous Typhoid Mary, then your reputation would skyrocket, and the company would be in great shape.

"As I see it, you have a potential gold-mine here, if you can make it reversible, and there are no more side-effects."

Dr. Wilson frowned and asked, "What about Julie?"

"She has to stay out of sight, of course. Work at night; wear lots of clothes and makeup. See no one in person. There can be no hint, at this first stage, that a third person is infected."

His wife snarled, "Just forget her, Cyrus, if you know what's good for you! It was her mistake in the first place."

Jenkins turn his attention to the nurse. "Ms. Porter, there is definitely a future for you in this plan, if we can hold the secret together. After the cure is developed and announced to the world, and if the PR job is handled correctly, there'll be a flood of demand for this product, and not just for livestock.

"The company will need a media spokesperson. You'll need to spend every moment preparing. Be smart, sexy, idealistic, and very comfortable being green.

"Become a vegetarian, starting today. Read all the eco-fringe literature. Hit all the environmental web sites. Understand your audience. You have walk in their sandals and talk their language.

"But if you can pull it off, you'll be a celebrity forever."

Jenkins let each of them think about their roles in silence. He'd given them each a way to survive the disaster, and profit from it, but marital infidelity had torpedoed bigger conspiracies than this one. He gave them a 30% chance to pull it off.

In any case, he was billing Mrs. Wilson immediately.

The Manta

I've imagined the Manta for decades now. Variations of it were in my dreams as a way to freely explore the underwater realms. I've been pleased that every few years real world technology gets closer and closer to making it possible. Maybe someday my dream will come true. After my own experiences on Grand Cayman and in the eye of a hurricane, this story came together.

He was shoved sideways and almost fell out of his reading chair. His book slid across the floor. Angrily, he looked through the ceiling.

It's that girl, back again. What has she done now!

He checked to the side as the floor rocked under him. She'd snagged her anchor on the starboard wing.

The surface was churning above. The wind was strong. The pull could hurt the Manta.

Hurriedly, he slipped on his face mask and cycled through the airlock. The warm Caribbean waters were as familiar as air. He swam easily over to the wing, trailing the thin snorkel line that allowed him to breathe.

It's bad. The anchor had bent the aileron. A minute later he was back with a carborundum blade and sawed through the braided metal anchor line. He paddled back out the way as the last thread snapped, trailing bubbles from its cavitation through the water.

He could see the boat on the surface move.

But he could also see the girl in the water, swimming after it.

She'll never make it. The wind is pushing it too fast.

Stupid.

Stupid situation, or stupid girl—it was all her fault anyway.

They were thirty miles to the nearest shore. Unless she could catch her boat, and she couldn't, she would drown.

Serves her right. The Manta is down here on the bottom for peace and quiet. She had no right to come pester me.

She damaged my ship. I had every right to protect it.

It was hard to sigh into a face mask regulator. It lost some of its expressiveness. No matter, he'd have to rescue her.

But first, he had to repair the aileron or he'd get nowhere. In the airlock, he slapped at the big red button that used to be labeled, 'Stow Tail'. The markings were long worn away.

In the tool bin, he found a large rubber mallet. Not the best tool for underwater work, but it would have to do. With a piece of coral as an anvil, he bashed the aluminum reasonably flat. No telling what it would do to his flight path, but he needed to move fast before the girl wore herself to exhaustion.

Back inside, still dripping from the sea water, he checked that the tail was fully stowed. Familiar strokes on the control panel and the pumps began blowing the ballast water out of the wings. Before too long, the nose lifted abruptly from the silt and the Manta slipped silently free of her bed.

Using the wings and the slow rise of the ship, he steered in the direction he'd seen the boat, heading downwind.

How long had it been?

If she wasn't a good swimmer, there was no hope for it.

What will I do if she's already drowned?

His first impulse would be to leave her be and let the fish take care of her.

It's not like I'd killed her. She got herself into this mess.

The Manta had a variety of sun-shades on the inner surface of its transparent glass hull. He shifted the front ones back. He'd be flying this manually and he'd need the visibility.

On its own, the Manta sensed the surface and shifted ballast so the nose tilted downward. That was how she moved, in slow arcs through the water, using the rise and fall of the ship and its wings to propel it forward. He set a limit this time, keeping no deeper than thirty feet, rather than the deeper dives the ship normally used

There! He saw her. Her legs were kicking and she sculled with her hands, fighting the waves that threatened to knock her down below.

He adjusted the trim and eased under her. Slowly, so as not to drift out of position, he came up under her feet.

She must have thought he was a shark for an instant, the way she tried to swim straight up into the air, but she settled down once she saw the transparent central hull break the water beside her. She grabbed hold of one of the wing's ridges gratefully. Their eyes met, and it was hate at first sight.

...

He gestured her to go backward, toward the airlock, but she didn't get it, clinging to the trim fin like it was a life buoy. He sighed, tapped the control panel and went outside himself.

The wind was higher than he liked. Normally he just stayed below when there was any kind of weather. As soon as he stepped out onto the wing, he faced another kind of blow.

"You cut my anchor line! I might have drowned! And I lost my underwater camera!"

He chuckled inwardly at her priorities, but just pointed at the mangled aileron.

She didn't even look in that direction. "Are you some kind of maniac? Why did you do that to me?"

Inside his head, he was going to say, "Your anchor was damaging my ship!" But all that came out was "Ah. Look."

It had been so long since he'd actually talked to someone that his mouth felt wrong. The words sounded strange.

She frowned, glancing back but concentrating on him. She still was clamped on the fin like a barnacle in a dark blue bikini. Her wet, red hair obscured half her face.

He sighed and walked over, grasping her wrist and pulling her up to her feet.

She wobbled, and he realized she was exhausted from fighting the waves.

He held her upright and walked the both of them over to the aileron and pointed at the mangled mess. He wanted to push her nose in it like a misbehaved puppy, but perched on the edge of the wing like they were in unsettled waters, it was hard enough to keep them both upright without falling in.

She looked down at the bent metal and he guessed it was enough.

"Come on." He pulled her toward the airlock. She stumbled and he had to help her back up on her feet. Her eyes were on all the details as they went through the airlock, but he had no time to waste on a tour.

"There," he pointed to the couch. She gratefully collapsed on the seat, feeling the cushion gingerly, as if not knowing what it was.

"Sponge," he said, and she nodded, and leaned back, closing her eyes.

He looked her over, partly checking for any injuries. In salt water, even serious wounds could be washed clean and be undetectable from a cursory inspection, but they would need to be cared for. Luckily, he didn't see any injuries.

But he hadn't been this close to another human in years. He knew she was a girl, from the bikini, when she made her two trips overhead. The first time the Manta had been too deep for her to get any closer without breathing gear. This second time, because he'd been in the shallows charging the batteries, she had gotten closer, too close.

But at this range, the fact that she was mostly bare skin was kicking over some hormones that had laid dormant for a long time.

I can't have this.

He rummaged through his closet and although he had next to nothing, he found an old gray robe that was mostly threadbare.

"Here." He tossed it her way.

"Thanks." She pulled it on, keeping suspicious eyes on him. "My boat. We have to catch it."

He paused, thinking about it. He'd thought he'd just get her close enough to a shoreline and let her swim the rest of the way back to civilization.

I guess I might be able to catch it.

Without saying anything, he went over to the controls and manually cranked up the spine—an antenna pole that usually rode flat against the main hull.

The display screen came on with no problem, although he hadn't activated it in some time. Most of the electronics were sealed tightly behind the console, so that salt air that inevitably crept inside the cabin would not affect it. But they did take power, and he was always conscious of power usage.

Radar showed the blip.

"Moving fast. Try it."

He powered it off and cranked the spine down again. The girl was watching everything he did. Not that she'd be likely to make sense of it. All the controls were custom. The Manta was unlike any other submersible on the planet.

"What's happening?" She gripped the couch as the Manta began to sink.

"Chasing your boat."

She glanced up fearfully as the water level on the transparent sides crept up to cover up the sky. She looked over at the controls, but there were no fancy indicators, other than a ball bearing in a curved glass tube, a tilt meter, to show what was going on.

He went back to his chair, picking up the book where it had fallen. He settled in and thumbed the pages to find his spot. The light dimmed as they got deeper, but he was used to it, and they'd be swinging back shallower soon enough.

The floor tilted slowly, almost unnoticeably. The girl stood up, testing her balance.

He didn't look up from his book, but said, "The more you move about, the harder it'll be for the autopilot to stay on a straight course."

She nodded. "I need water. I'm dehydrated."

He sighed and put a bookmark in place. He rose and walked over to the water closet. He opened the door for her. "Faucet. Red is fresh water. Blue is salt."

She looked around. "Do you have a cup?"

He looked puzzled for a moment. "Stay put."

A moment later he walked back from the pantry with a washed out tin can that still held a scrap of label. It had probably been canned fruit. She took a drink.

"Desalination?"

"Yes." He walked back to his chair, but he kept an eye on her until she timidly closed the door. A moment later there was the sound of the power flush. And then came another noise.

He knew every pipe, every valve, and he could practically feel the change in ballast as she used the fresh water to rinse the salt off of her.

He sighed. It wasn't worth complaining about her use of his limited supplies. She'd be gone soon.

She walked out soon, drying her hair with the edge of the robe. She looked his way, but he concentrated on the text of a book he'd read dozens of times before. It did no good to look at her.

…

"My name is Brenda deMay, out of Miami."

He nodded his head to show that he heard her, but he made no reply.

After waiting she stretched out on the couch and adjusted the drape of the robe over her leg. He made no sign he was watching.

…

Brenda sat up abruptly when the Manta broke the surface and waves started splashing over the hull. He'd been expecting it. They had made several deep cycles and given the battery level, this was about the limit. He inserted the bookmark and went to the console.

"Can you see my boat?" she asked.

"Can you?" The walls were transparent glass. Why did she ask him?

She walked closer to the view. Water was still draining off the hull, and being replenished by wave splashes.

"Oh! I see it. I think. But it's much too far away. We missed it."

He nodded. "Drifted to starboard. It's the aileron you damaged."

She had her hands against the glass. "Can we get closer?"

"No. We have used up the batteries. I'll have to recharge. Your anchor interrupted my recharging cycle and it never got topped up.

"I'd recommend just waiting until the Manta is charged, and then I'll take you to the nearest inhabited island."

"Oh, no! That's a rental. I can't afford to lose it. Plus I've got all my camera gear on board. I *can't* lose that."

She turned to him and appealed, "Can't we charge it a little bit, or something. It's almost close enough."

It went against his better judgement. He knew what the Manta was capable of, and now with this leg of the chase completed, he had a much better idea of how fast the boat was traveling.

But he hadn't faced a woman's begging in a long time.

"I'll try it. Only once. If we can't get it after a ten minute charge, then we'll never get it."

He punched the deploy button and the tail uncurled from the spool. Normally he'd anchor in shallows while charging, but there wasn't time.

The long rubber tail extended out behind the Manta, much like the stinger of the great manta ray, only much longer. Since they weren't anchored, he went outside on the wing and tossed a sea anchor to slow their drift.

The tail rode with the waves, moving up and down. Inside the long tubes, the water they channeled spun little turbine blades, charging the batteries. Wave power had kept the Manta moving for a long time now.

He walked around outside the whole ten minutes, fretting about the girl. If they couldn't catch the boat, now even farther ahead of them, he would have to locate some place to dump her. Unfortunately, while he was well familiar with the undersea terrain, inhabited islands were places he'd avoided all these years. He was only dimly aware of which ones had which kinds of governments.

He might have to ask her which ones were friendly, and there was no guarantee she'd tell him the truth.

If she asks me to ferry her all the way to Miami, I'll make her swim from here.

He pulled in the sea anchor line and went back inside, slapping the stow tail button before sealing the door.

"Sit still." He pointed to the couch.

He adjusted the autopilot with a fudge factor based on his estimate of how much the bent aileron was affecting them, and then pressed go. He went back to his chair and picked up his book.

"What's you name?" she asked. "And what is it that you do out here, exactly?"

He shook his head.

...

Although there was no noise, he knew the instant the servos controlling the steering vanes ran out of juice.

He slapped the book together with a noise that made her jump.

"What's wrong?"

"Out of battery. This is it."

She looked up. The surface was still far above them. "What'll we do?"

He opened a hatch on the console and swiveled out a contraption that looked like a unicycle grafted with pipes to the control cabinet. He started pedaling. He could hear the air pushing into the ballast tanks. He supposed she could hear it too, but he didn't bother to explain.

They broke the surface, just like before, and he kept on pedaling until he was satisfied.

She was already at the windows, moving around, searching.

"There it is."

He looked over his shoulder. "That's still half a mile away. I'll take you to an island after we recharge."

"No." She dropped the robe and dashed to the airlock. She must have been watching, because she had the door open before he could get up from the pedals.

He followed as fast as he could, but she was already in the water, swimming away, before he could stop her.

Idiot. Cameras and a boat rental aren't worth your life.

He watched for a bit. She was swimming in the correct direction. They had surfaced cross-wind from its location. As long as she could make it before the wind pushed it out of range, she had a chance.

He had no illusions he could swim as fast as she could. He was in the water all the time and very comfortable swimming, but she was younger and more athletic. And the Manta was drained of juice. He turned and went back inside. He'd wait and listen. If her boat started, she was alive. If it didn't, she was dead.

He sat reading. He'd turned on the hydrophone so he could hear any noises through the water. He had enough juice for that at least.

Several pages later, he heard engine noises. He sighed, got to his feet and started pedaling, pumping water into the wing tanks. He wanted to be deep out of her range before she got some crazy idea to bother him again. He certainly didn't want the tail deployed where she could run her prop across it. Recharging could wait until she was gone.

...

He waited in the dark for a number of hours before surfacing and extending the tail. The air had gotten stuffy. Everything worked off the batteries, and without juice, he had no fresh air, no drinkable water, and certainly no heat for the grill. Raw fish was okay, but he preferred it cooked.

With that... disturbance... out of sight and mind, his brain slipped back into familiar grooves. He'd need to repair the aileron. And there was one source for the necessary parts. Shortly after dawn, with charged batteries and more tweaks to his autopilot, he set the destination to a familiar spot far from any of the islands.

It took more than a day, with several stops on the bottom to confirm landmarks, but as he drifted to a stop on the floor of the sea, the burned and sunken ship beside him looked just the same as it always had.

Normally, the snorkel tube gave him all the breathing range he needed, but not when crawling around inside sunken ships. An ordinary scuba tank took a while to fill with his under-powered pumps, but after reading another book, everything was ready. He suited up, and swam into the dark hold.

A few minutes later he came out, holding a piece of metal just the right size and composition to replace the aileron.

...

Editor Karl Hansen tapped his screen. "Are you sure you want to go with this? Everything in unsubstantiated. You don't even have pictures."

Brenda shrugged. "I have the aerial photo that started me off on this rabbit hunt, and some lovely beach scenery from Barbuda."

"But that's not even the location where you saw him. Nobody's going to take this mystery man story seriously."

"But I was there, I rode inside his winged submarine. He saved my life. It's a lovely story."

Karl shook his head. "On your own head, then. At least it's an interesting filler piece."

She beamed all the way back to her desk, although she felt a qualm. What if Mr. No-name discovered what she'd written?

...

The problem with cruising routes that he'd never mapped was that he needed to pay attention to where he was going. Just because there wasn't an island or a seamount on his old charts didn't mean someone hadn't parked an offshore oil drilling platform in his way.

Manta's autopilot used sonar to identify wave tops and sea bottom, as well as any obvious obstructions like coral reefs. It beeped. And then beeped again when no one came to change the settings. The beep got louder.

He startled awake. By that time the shriek was near continuous.

Barefooted as alway, he stubbed his toe on the control console as he dashed up to open the view and be ready to throw the wing plane into a stall position to kill his forward momentum.

The window opened to the four mighty pillars of a long established platform. He made a few tiny corrections, and drifted under the giant structure, careful to avoid the drill shaft and numerous chains and cross beams.

He was nearly at the floor level, and he could see debris that had collected there over time. Whether valuable lost tools, or trash, he couldn't tell. In either case, the operators hadn't considered them worth salvaging.

But his life was based on scavenging—whether scavenging energy from the waves or canned goods and repair parts from sunken ships. He had an eye for what might be valuable someday.

He banked around and made another pass below the platform. Even if he didn't want anything today, he might in the future. He'd see what was available, and mark the spot in his charts.

On the third pass, he frowned. *That's not right.*

...

The hatchway to the Operations Manager's office knocked.

"Come in."

A gruff face with a big grin said, "Burke, you've got to come see this."

He hurried down the walkway, high above the water. A cluster of a dozen men in hardhats were looking down at the surface.

"Get back to work, all of you!"

Down near the southeast pillar, a bearded man in faded blue shorts was standing on the deck of the strangest vehicle he'd ever seen, like an enormous manta ray, floating motionless.

Burke yelled, "Hello there! Can we be of assistance?"

The machinery made his voice difficult to hear, but he replied, "I've got to show the operator something. Something down below."

So it was a submersible? Something flickered through his memory. "Okay. I'll be down in a minute."

There was a rig for dropping a raft down to water level for the divers to work from. He held on with an appearance of fearlessness to the stabilizing line as he was winched down.

The submersible moved easily over to his raft. The man gestured, and Burke stepped onto the metal surface. When he started for the door to the interior, he asked, "How long will I be gone?"

The bearded man looked puzzled, then said, "Fifteen minutes? Something like that."

Burke relayed the information with a hand-held radio, and entered.

"My name is Joshua Burke." He held out his hand. The stranger took and shook, but didn't offer his name.

"I was passing through, and saw this."

They sailed down to near the sea bed, and saw that the pipeline was bubbling out oil from a four foot long crack. The current was sweeping it off to the north, so his crew hadn't seen the oil slick.

"I'll have to get a crew down to fix this." It was certainly true, but if this was some environmentalist, he wanted to be saying all the right words before things got ugly.

"Thought you might."

He adjusted the wings and began spiraling back up to the surface.

"This is quite a vehicle you have. How deep can it go?"

"Wrong question." He tapped the sides. "Compression glass. Gets stronger under pressure." He thought a moment, then said. "It'd be hard to blow ballast after about a thousand feet."

"So. Are you a scientist? Oceanographer? What are you doing in the area?"

He shrugged. "Neighbors. Just passing through."

When they were again level with the raft, Burke said, "If you'll wait a couple of minutes, I'd like to give you a gift, you know, for letting me know about the leak?"

He shrugged and nodded. Burke called up on the radio and a few minutes later, a small bag was lowered.

He pulled out a ragged newspaper. "These are some food staples. Just for variety's sake." He opened the paper. "I saw this article a few days ago. I think it's talking about you."

He nodded, and as if unfamiliar with the words, he said, "Thank you."

As Burke and his raft were lifted back up, the Manta sank back below the water.

First order of business, once the Manta was set in motion, was to inventory the food. The canned goods he placed in their proper positions along with others that had been salvaged from numerous ships he'd discovered. Certainly these were likely to all be good, which was more than he could say about the others.

The prizes were a box of saltine crackers, and a loaf of bread. He never found those in good shape from wrecks. While he couldn't gorge himself, they would need to be eaten before they spoiled.

Sitting in his comfortable chair, savoring a piece of whole wheat bread, he spread out the newspaper, uncomfortably wider than his books, and read the article.

There was a tiny little photo of Brenda on the page, and a bigger image of the Manta at something like a fifty foot depth, as taken from an airplane.

So, she was a reporter. I guess that makes sense.

"'A modern-day Captain Nemo cruises the waters of the Caribbean in his own version of the Nautilus. But this one is more interested in quietly reading his books and rescuing this reporter than stopping warships.'"

The story was a little bit reporting, along with more than a little fancy. She said little about the Manta, as if what he'd told her hadn't stuck. She was more interested in his missing life story than anything.

He shrugged and began reading the other articles in the paper. Much had changed since he'd last been on land. A lot of it appeared as bad as it was then.

...

"Hey, Brenda. When are you going to do a follow up report on Captain Nemo?"

Linda was always pestering her about her stories—partly to remind her that her science beat/human interest pieces weren't 'real reporting' like her political investigations.

Karl Hansen was close enough to hear. "She's not going to go galavanting across the Caribbean on a whim. Certainly not to chase down some pirate with a beard and an eye-patch."

Brenda said nothing, the 'eye-patch' dig was one she'd heard several times before. Her 'Nemo' had two eyes, but Brenda Starr, the classic comic strip girl reporter, had a one-eyed heroic lover, and her name was always inviting connections to the more famous Brenda. Karl was a little upset by the popularity of her Nemo story. He was happy with the readership interest, but like Linda, he had his own editorial standards to maintain.

But it wasn't ten minutes later when Karl waved her over to his office.

"Yes Boss?" she sat down as he waved her in and had her close the door.

"You remember Haiti?"

"The hurricane story?" She had been assigned to cover it, and spent a long week wandering through the tent cities, taking pictures and posting heartbreaking and heartwarming stories that the paper was happy to feed to the AP, UPI, and Reuters.

"Yes. I've been told to increase our coverage this season. If there's another disaster relief crisis like last time, or worse, like after the earthquake in 2010, we need to have someone there before it happens."

She smiled. It was never possible to be at the site of a disaster before it happened. Even when the storm path was predicted just right, it was always the little harbor town nobody'd ever heard of that was the hardest hit.

"So you want me in Port-au-Prince?"

"I want you to make plans. I want a folder I can open up at moment's notice that has the phone numbers for planes, hotels, government officials, everything. I want folders for all the hotspots. And if you can, it'd be great if you were on a first-name basis with the critical names."

She sat back, considering the magnitude of the task. "Just Haiti, or ..."

"Wherever the storm hits." He smiled. "Just think of the Caribbean as your own personal beat. Weather, earthquakes, volcanoes. If you're lucky, you might even get a revolution." He chuckled. "Just don't think of this as an excuse to chase pirates. Unless, they're real, of course."

...

"What is it that you do out here?" That's what she said.

He shook his head. He'd been minding his own business. He'd been tending his little bit of the sea bed, finding what little he needed to stay alive.

And now, what was he doing? He didn't even know. He'd been cruising an ever-widening circle, seeing places he hadn't known except from the charts.

Not that he could ever get too far away from... the center. But still, he hadn't put this many miles on the Manta since she was first launched.

He put the newspaper aside. He'd read it so many times it was falling apart. The paper stock was a lot worse than in his books. The pantry called to him.

He opened it and smelled the scent of bread. But that was gone. Just crumbs left to remind him. It was a shame that it was only available on land.

The Manta shook. He stumbled, grabbing the pantry door for stability.

What was that?

The water was shaking, churning, but he was nowhere near the surface.

Then it got worse, the Manta lurched and threw him off his feet. He scrambled on hands and knees to the control console.

There were vertical currents in the water, so strong he could see them. And the deck felt hot.

He wasted five long seconds looking around, before adjusting the vanes and steering off to port. The turbulence dropped away. In moments, the deck cooled back to normal.

It was a volcanic seamount, an active one. And a quick glance at his charts showed nothing like it at this location, so it had to be new.

Carefully steering around the red glow he could now see in the depths, he eased closer.

Lava was pouring out of a hundred yard long tear in the bottom of the sea. It squirted out like bright red toothpaste and turned dull and black before it had gone a few feet.

But not before boiling sea water to fierce temperatures and sending rushing plumes upward where they could eventually turn to steam. He had blindly sailed through one of those plumes.

From a safe distance at the side, he watched as the lava showed no slowdown. The black stone being created was building up as he watched.

Most of these Lower Antilles islands were volcano formed. I guess this is the start of a new one.

He visualized bright intelligent eyes and red hair. *I bet she'd like to see this.*

...

One thing no one would ever say about the Manta would be to marvel at her speed. She wasn't a motorboat, because she had no motor, and she wasn't a racing schooner because she had no sails.

Only her wings and the changes in her buoyancy worked to move her along. But normally, it was quite fast enough. He could watch the sea move by from his reading chair and be content.

But the trip back to the sunken ship where he'd repaired the aileron had taken him longer than he'd liked. Not that the undersea volcano was likely to abruptly stop, but for the first time in recent memory, he was in a hurry.

He put on the scuba tank and entered the sunken ship through the large access bay at the rear.

The black and blackened corridors screamed at him as he worked his way into the depths with his flashlight beaming a path of safety. He'd been to this ship many times, for tools and repair materials, but parts of the hull he'd avoided since....

There it is.

The doorway was wedged with silt and a few sea creatures that had started building homes in the protected cavity. A few kicks and tugs, and it came free.

This was the chart room, with paper charts and log books now turned to mush. But in the metal locker... He waved a fluttery storm of paper fragments aside. Floating at the top of the locker was a sealed plastic box, still apparently air tight.

Back in the Manta, swaying on the surface, he dried and then opened the box. Inside was a telephone with a long swivelable antenna. He checked the battery. Dead, but there was a charger. He tapped his fingers, staring at the winking led lights as it slowly came up to half-charge.

It was enough. He walked outside, and looked for a satellite.

...

Brenda rested with her head propped on her palm. It had been a long hard day. Her desk was strewn with maps and lists of phone numbers and post notes covering it all. On her computer, the screen was a mess of windows overlapped so deep she thought there was no end of it.

And then the phone started blinking. She glared at it, tempted to let it roll over to voicemail.

But that's not the way to clear out her todo list.

She picked it up.

"Hello, Caribbean desk." That's what she started calling her new job. Hopefully it would catch on.

"Ah. Brenda... deMay?"

The voice sounded familiar. "Yes. Hello there." Pretend she recognized them long enough to figure it out.

"Um. I saw this thing."

The hesitancy clicked.

"Nemo, is that you?"

"Ah. Well."

"Oh, yes, I know that's not your real name. How in the world did you find me?" Did this mean he was on land somewhere? Had he docked the Manta? And could she get a camera person there instantly to take a picture?

"The newspaper article. He... oil platform guy."

"Oh. So you've seen it. Are you mad at me?" She sounded contrite. Maybe she was, a little.

"No. Not that. It's the volcano."

She wanted to ask a million questions, but if he were taciturn face to face, it was three times worse over the phone. She did get a few facts. A new volcano was growing, with the co-ordinates. He was still cruising the sea on his own.

And he wanted to show her the volcano.

She promised she get there as soon as she could, although she had to confess that her job tied her down and it might take a while. She asked if she could tell the oceanographers about it.

"Ah. Yes. Fine." He did sound disappointed she wouldn't be with them.

But his battery gave out and the call died.

She rummaged through her contacts lists feverishly, and her fingers flew over the keypad.

"Charles! Yes, this is Brenda deMay again. How would you love to owe me a favor?"

Scientists alerted, she called out across the office, "Karl! You did say 'volcanoes' didn't you?"

...

The Manta anchored near the undersea volcano, carefully positioned to stay well out of the superheated water. He waited, tinkering with the phone.

The battery was damaged. He could charge it 75% according to the charger, but even then it only held the charge for a few minutes. He charged it several times, leaving the phone on, just on the remote chance she would call him back. But after trying that a few times, the battery showed no signs of recovery. He carefully stowed it back in its water-tight container, and went fishing.

A plane flew overhead and wagged its wings at him. He waved back, but there was a nibble on his line, and so he paid attention to lunch.

Fishing with a pole he did for variety. He also had a net. He used to have a spear gun, but one particularly large grouper took the spear in its side and kept on going, leaving him to more traditional methods of acquiring protein in his diet.

Engine noises on the hydrophone woke him the next morning. He surfaced as the fifty foot cruiser approached. The newcomers circled the waters, pointing at the upwelling and the occasional bursts of steam. After they anchored, a couple of men in a zodiac motored over.

"Hello, we're from the Rosenstiel School in Miami. This is Sam Jakes, and I'm Hank Eagleton. Are you Nemo?"

He frowned. "Ah. Newspaper name. But I called Brenda in Miami."

"Yes, I've read the stories. So this is the Manta?"

He smiled, with pride. "Yes. Winged submersible. I built it."

Sam asked, "We were wondering if you could show us the lava outflow?"

He nodded.

They all climbed inside, after he pulled the anchor.

The scientists were full of praise for the ship, and the room he had inside, compared to the submersibles that they used.

"Both Scripps and Woods Hole have submersibles on the way. We're just lucky enough to beat them here."

He sailed them along the rift and they took pictures for planning their investigations. The young men made an effort to include him in the conversation, but he mainly nodded. He understood what they were saying, but he just didn't have anything to contribute.

"So, are you going to claim the island, when it breaks the surface?"

He shrugged. "Why should I?"

"Yeah, I guess it would be pretty bleak and barren. No vegetation or fresh water. No soil even, until it collected some."

Hank added, "Yes. This is just the latest in this chain. There are three more in this series, probably from the same hot spot, off to the north."

"Where?" he asked. He pulled out his old charts. One was just an ink dot. The others weren't even marked.

"They're small. I only noticed them on the big charts when we were packing up to come here. Probably just rocks in the water."

Sam asked, as they chased down their zodiac and surfaced along side it, "Are you going to be staying here? We could certainly use your help."

He shook his head. "No, just passing through."

...

Curiosity was an old friend, and the tug of seeing unknown and unpopulated islands, was enough to turn him north. It was too crowded around the volcano, particularly since Brenda hadn't come.

Following the sea bed, and knowing a magma bed lurked below, he was more alert to volcanic features. There were lava features here and there, long cold now. Other rifts had occurred, but most had been smaller than the one he discovered.

And then, the sea shallowed out, and when he surfaced, there was a beach and a little cluster of trees.

I wonder if there are any dates or coconuts?

...

The straps on his long-unused sandals broke. He held them in his hand as he wiggled his toes in the sand. Ground felt funny.

But with a chore—fixing his shoes—and the different scents and textures of the very tiny island, he stayed for a bit, putting together a lean-to from fallen palm leaves. He caught crabs among the rocks and built an open pit fire. He watched the sunset and breathed the air until the stars came out.

But he went back to the Manta to get a good night sleep.

...

The hard glass hull of the ship took the rap of knuckles and hardly made a sound. But the shifting weight of someone pushing on the wings woke him out of a confused dream.

He looked at the hull and saw a smiling face surrounded by red hair waving in the currents as she knocked, holding her breath.

Luckily, he had settled only a few feet down below the waves for the night. He stumbled to the controls as she pushed off back to the surface for air.

"Hello." She looked like a drowned cat when he opened the airlock. But a happy drowned cat.

He nodded. He smiled.

"I got here as fast as I could." There was a seaplane rocking gently a hundred yards away.

"When I reached the volcano, they said you'd already gone. One of the researchers thought you'd gone hunting for this island, so I badgered my pilot into making a search pass. I was never so happy to see the outline of the Manta."

She waved over to the airplane. A tiny figure waved back, and the propellors started up.

"Your plane is leaving?"

"Yes. There's a storm in the area, and I could only get him to wait just a little bit."

"Why did you let yourself get stranded here?" He led her back inside. "You're wet. Let me get something."

"Wait a second. Help me with my bag." It was floating alongside, nearly as big as she was. He pulled it up on the wing and they brought it inside the airlock.

"I knew you wouldn't leave me stuck on the island. And if you won't take me back to get pictures of your volcano, at least you have a sat phone and I can call for another plane."

"How close is the storm?"

"I don't know, but the pilot was getting nervous. I've been tracking several tropical storm centers and one of them was heading this way."

"I'll take you to the volcano, but I need to check on that storm first." He paused to dig out the gray robe and handed it to her.

He cranked up the spine again.

"Nemo?"

He smiled and pointed to his shelf. "I've got that book."

"Sorry, but you never gave me a name, and I had to have one for my story."

He activated the VHS radio receiver and pulled a weather fax onto the display screen. He frowned.

"How bad is it? Will we be okay?"

"Once we get deeper. It's too shallow here."

He turned to the hull to get a better eyeball view.

"I should have noticed the signs last night. It was mostly clear, but those clouds—I've seen the like before. It's a hurricane." He pointed at the screen. "See this. That's the eye of the storm. And it's heading this way."

She pulled a camera from her bag and snapped photos of the sky, and then some at the interior of the Manta.

"Reporter."

"Well, yes. I thought you knew. You say you saw the story?"

He pointed over at his tilted bookshelf by the chair. It was designed so that the twenty or so books wouldn't fall out when the Manta banked and turned. None had even been disturbed during the turbulence over the volcano. A folded newspaper was poked into a gap between books. She snapped a picture of the shelf.

He winced at the click and flash.

"I just thought you were an ordinary pest, when you snagged your anchor on the Manta."

She gave a timid smile. "Several people had seen the Manta over the years. Some thought it was a sea monster, a giant manta ray. I was trying to get a picture, to prove or disprove the stories." She set the camera down and went to her bag.

He banked slightly, moving from the shallows near the island to slightly deeper waters where they could rest safely lower than the storm's churn zone.

"Did you?"

"What?"

"Prove or disprove."

She sighed. "Sort of. It was a popular story, and most people believed me. But then, there were no photos. Some people thought I made you up."

"So, you're back for pictures?"

She stopped trying to force a comb through her wet and tangled hair. She looked at his face, trying to read him.

"I think you've got the wrong idea. I'm not here to chase you down for a story. My boss told me not to waste time on the Manta. My job is to report science and human interest related stories in this area. Your report of the volcano was what brought me here. If I can get some pictures of the hurricane as well, that would be a bonus."

"So. No interest in me, then."

She took a step in his direction. "No, I don't think you understand..."

"Stay put there," he said firmly. "I can't have you walking around while I'm settling in."

She flushed in anger, and then took a deep breath, standing perfectly still as the Manta settled into a flat spot on the bottom. There was a shush sound as the hull came to a stop in the silt.

He smiled. "And now, we wait."

...

He could see that she was upset about something. "We'll be here a while, so get comfortable. I'd rather not try traveling with the storm passing overhead. I could do it, but I'd need to adjust the autopilot to keep it lower in the water."

She nodded. "Could I rinse off the salt?"

"Yes, but minimize fresh water use. The desalinator takes electricity and we can't recharge during heavy swells."

"Okay, thanks." She rummaged in her bag and went into the water closet. She poked her head out after a moment. "Is it okay if I rinse out my khakis?" She held her collar. "I'll be sparing of water."

He nodded. "Things dry slowly."

She thought, then nodded and ducked back inside.

He looked at her big bag. She'd certainly brought her baggage with her this time. Although it might be camera gear.

The door opened, and she came out in a white, lacy thing. He'd been expecting the bikini again. *Is that a nightgown?*

She was toweling her hair.

"I look a fright, I know. And sorry about the gown. It gets hot when you stay down here. I got a rash from last time and I didn't have time to shop for anything more suitable. I could wear the swimsuit if you prefer."

She looked innocent enough, trying to get her hair under control, but the lacy garment was as enticing in its own way as the bikini had been. He looked back at his control panel, although settled in, there was nothing more to do.

"It's fine." *I'll just not stare.*

"Come over here. I brought you some things."

She sat on the floor and opened the giant duffel.

Out came several large towels. "I noticed all of yours had worn all the fluff away. Here. These are nicer."

He fingered the thick fabric. He nodded. It was like he remembered.

"Now, these are vitamins. One a day. This is only about a year's worth, but I worry about your diet."

"Thank you." He stared at the bottle, wondering where to put it. He'd long exhausted his stock of pills. Occasionally he'd find a bottle of aspirin in a shipwreck, but he'd been lucky enough not to need much more than that.

"Now help me take these to the pantry." She had a little spice rack with a half-dozen little bottles. There were a dozen lemons, and several small bottles of jam.

"I know you live on fish, and here's no help for it, but it can't be healthy long term. You need more variety. I'd have brought more fresh fruit and vegetables, but I didn't think you had any refrigeration." She dug out several sealed bags. "These are dried fruits, but eat them slowly, so it won't upset your digestion."

Most of the bag was for him.

"It was all I could throw together on short notice. My boss said I couldn't go chasing after you, but this volcano was a special deal, so I had to move fast."

He was grateful, but he didn't know how to say the words. "Thanks."

She beamed, and he was suddenly aware that they were nearly head to head and that lace was distracting.

"Well." He moved back a step. "We're stuck here for at least a day or so. I'd better go hunt."

It occurred to him that he couldn't change clothes. More often than not, he just wore his shorts, and when there was no chance he'd be seen from topside, he'd go through the airlock to fish or work nude to save the washing salt from his clothes. He was well aware of how easy it was to chafe the skin wearing wet salty things.

There was no help for it. He'd just rinse them later.

"Can I help?"

He shook his head as he pulled a home-made spear from his tool locker. "Don't get your clothes wet again. I'll be back soon."

He went into the airlock and put on one of the two face masks. He'd seen lots of fish around, so maybe he could make do with the snorkel line.

Then he changed his mind and slipped on the tank. He needed a bigger fish for the two of them.

A few minutes later, he came up outside the hull and rapped the surface with the hilt of his knife. Because he was in the water and she was in the bubble of air, the optics were a little distorted. She had to come up to the glass before he could see her well.

He held out the fish, still on the spear. He gestured with his knife. He'd be gutting the fish outside and then come on in.

It was a familiar task and the scavengers were there to take care of the cast offs, and he made it back in without having his meal stolen.

"Here, take this." He handed her the meat, while he removed his swimming gear and took advantage of a rinse himself. His old robe was dry, so he put that on while his shorts were dripping.

She smiled as he came out.

"Teach me how to use this stove, and I'll do the cooking." She had already prepared the meat and had a lemon sliced.

"Okay." He turned on the heating element. "I sear the meat to save electricity."

"Fine by me."

The meat sizzled and they ate. She watched his expressions as he tasted the seasoning.

"Different," he mumbled.

"Different is good."

...

Dish washing was a matter of putting the dirty dishes in a chicken-wire cage in the airlock and checking on them later after the scavengers had picked them clean.

"I took pictures of you cleaning the fish."

"Just don't take pictures of me in the water closet, and I'll be fine."

She put her hand to cover a smile. "I'm not that bad, am I?"

He shrugged, but with a smile. She got to her feet and went to the counter top to clean up the spilled spices. Arranging everything with labels facing out, she began straightening everything within reach.

Nice feminine touches.

...

Scrubbing made her face facts. *I've upset his world. I have no right to come in here and demand to know his life story. He's not used to people, and I'm forcing this all on him.*

When she turned, to ask him whether to wash the cleaning rag on not, she saw him watching her every move. It was so different from the last time. He'd hidden behind that book the whole time.

But the expression on his face was sadness.

At least it's not anger. I've forced him to put up with me, at least until the storm passes. A guest. I'm a guest, and I shouldn't make my host angry.

When he went to sit in his chair, it was plain he wasn't really comfortable in that old worn out robe.

Next time, if there is a next time, I need to bring him a newer robe. Something that's comfortable damp. Something that washes well.

He was poking at the books, trying to choose one. He must have read them all a million times.

"You like to read."

He looked up. "I'm used to it."

"Did you always read a lot?"

He shook his head. "Read what I needed. Engineer, not a philosopher."

She moved a little closer to look at the titles. Yes, there was *20,000 Leagues Under the Sea* by Jules Verne. There were a dozen other science fiction titles, but mainly adventure tales, not deep sociological stories. There was a cookbook, a couple of marine biology text books, and three books that looked very waterlogged.

He watched where she was looking.

"I recovered those from a ship wreck. Got them out before they were too far gone. It took a lot of effort to separate and dry the pages without tearing them."

"What are they about?"

"I don't know."

"What?"

"Oh, I've read them, several times. But I don't speak French. Some of the words make sense, but not enough. Maybe someday." He looked pleased in anticipation of that far away event.

You poor, poor man.

...

"The storm is building." He pointed to the churning surf, like an active ceiling above their world. "It's only afternoon, but it's getting dark."

He liked the way her eyes lit up when she discovered something new about the world around her. Not so much when she tried to puzzle him out.

She went to the wall and leaned against it, peering out into the water.

I wish she were wearing this robe instead of me. To her, the nightgown was probably nothing strange, but it was exotic and enticing every time he looked at her. He'd harbored a suspicion that she was trying to seduce him, but if so, she was taking the long way around. Maybe she just honestly wanted to befriend him.

And take his picture for her newspaper.

In either case, he needed to stay out of touching range.

"What is your current project?"

"For the paper? I'm officially here to write a story about your volcano and hopefully to get some interesting pictures. But it looks like I'll have a chance to include pictures of the hurricane from the underside as well. Although, the way it's gotten darker, my shots will probably be blurred. I don't think my flash will reach that far."

"I can help. Come with me." He led her down a narrow passage.

"The Manta was designed to be a marine biologist's platform. There are a few features with that in mind."

"Marine biology. Swim with the whales?"

He nodded. "And the sharks, and pace migrating populations of fish and turtles and anything else that would benefit from long range operations without the necessity of a support ship."

He led her around to a platform on the other side of the water closet. "That's an optical flat port, perfect for taking pictures. I have flood lights, although I can only use them for a short period of time to avoid draining the batteries."

With a flip of the switch, the underside of the surf was angry and dramatic. He turned the light back off.

"I'll need my camera." She dashed back and returned a few seconds later, making settings changes. "How long to I have?"

He hesitated. "It will get worse. How about limit it to a minute, this time?"

"Great. Several stills and a video clip then. Help me get up there. I want to hold my camera up against the glass."

He took her hand and helped her up, then handed her the camera.

"You'll have to hold me steady."

"Okay. Ready?"

"Yes."

He flipped the switch, and then as the lights came on, he pushed up on her hip. She was intent on her shots, but he was mesmerized by the feel of her skin. He moved up the other hand to help.

"That's a great shot. How much more violent will the waves get?"

He released her and turned off the floodlight.

Mind on business. His blood was pounding. He carefully helped her down.

She put her hand on his chest. They were too close and he knew it.

She looked at his eyes and then asked, "Do you have a shirt?"

"What?"

"A shirt. You've been bare-chested the whole time except when you're in this robe. I'd love to take your picture, inside the Manta. But my co-workers have already been kidding me about my motives for tracking you down. I'd rather not show you in your robe, or looking too sexy."

He pulled away with an effort and went to rummage through his closet. There were tools and interesting shells, and several tennis ball sized manganese nodules. Nothing was on coat hangars anymore. The hangars had proved too valuable a source of wire for repairs. He pulled a khaki shirt from a drawer.

"I haven't worn this in a while." He held it out and she could see why.

She sighed. "I have a needle and thread. I can repair it."

She sat cross-legged on the floor with the torn shirt in hand, rebuilding the seam that had separated.

He watched her, concentrating on her fingers, to keep his mind off the way her nightgown was clinging to her skin. The humidity was very high, the air was stuffy, and even down here, he could feel the warm waters grabbing at the Manta's hull.

I guess I need a shirt. He'd hardly missed it. It was never cold. He spent his days away from the direct light of the sun most of the time. Luckily his shorts had held up, or he'd be walking around naked all the time.

Not in this robe. It's all ready too stuffy for it.

There had been other clothes. He remembered them. But they'd all turned to rags, and then lost over time.

But if I'm going to entertaining a girl... He smiled. There was a time, back in college, when that had a different meaning.

The smile faded and he concentrated on her fingers again.

...

Brenda was feeling slightly out of place, doing these domestic chores—woman's work. She was a working professional. She ate out, rarely cooking. If something tore, it took too much time to mend. She just bought new things, and retired the worn-out stuff to a box in her closet to fix someday.

I need to throw that box out. I'll never get back to it.

Nemo's eyes on her made her self-conscious. She was aware when he smiled and when his face dropped into that strange sadness.

"There. Try it on."

She held out the shirt and he took it. He hesitated and then went to the water closet.

Bashful. Men don't usually worry about dressing in front of me.

Not that she'd had a real boyfriend in quite some time. Linda had made a point of checking on her status from time to time. A couple of guys at the paper had expressed interest, but she gently shut them down. Luckily, her boss was totally married. Although she'd seen a certain look on Karl's face from time to time, she knew he was safe.

Nemo came back out wearing the shirt and his faded blue shorts. He put the robe back in the closet.

"It's too hot for that." He apologized.

She could see his shorts were still damp. He'd been right. With the humidity so high, things didn't dry.

"Did you want to take pictures now?"

She looked at the light. It was afternoon, but the storm had made it dark above. Nemo was avoiding turning on lights to save power, so it was dim inside even with all the window space. She'd stuck her fingers a couple of times while working, it was so dim.

"No. Let's wait until the light is better, after the storm passes."

"Good." He unbuttoned the shirt and carefully put it in the closet as well. "It's too hot for this thing as well."

She was jealous.

He asked, "Does your lace keep you cool?"

"No, it doesn't. Will it get any better?"

"Not until the storm passes. I have a snorkel that I can send to the surface so we can exchange this air for fresh, but not in this surf. The air system will keep what we have breathable, but I can't do anything about the heat and humidity."

She was really tempted to peel it off. He might not mind. But was she ready for the consequences if he took it as an invitation?

Brenda hesitated, and asked, "Would you mind if I changed to my swimsuit?"

He paused for a moment, and then said, "No. Go ahead."

She stood up and went to her bag.

The way he stares at everything I do, I feel like I'm naked already.

She blushed slightly as she ducked into the water closet to change.

...

It was too dark to read. It was too dark to do anything but sit, and wait.

He was conscious of her every move, as she stretched out on the couch. It was a different bikini from last time. Even in the dim light, he could tell that much. *Even smaller.*

"I'm not very good at this," she said.

"Good at what?"

"Doing nothing. Making time pass."

"Doing nothing makes it worse. Read, sleep, invent things in your head–those help."

She sighed. "It's too dark to read. I can't sleep, and I don't invent things, at least not like you do. Is that what you're doing? Inventing things?"

"Something like that." She didn't need to know what he was really thinking about. She talked with her hands, even in the dark. He could see her body move expressively. But maybe he should change the subject.

"What do you do? When you work, what is your brain thinking?"

"Me?" She paused for a moment. She shifted on the couch, obviously still uncomfortable with the heat and still, damp air.

"I've got a new job."

"You're still a reporter."

"Right. But I've been given a bigger responsibility. Before, I was just the girl who came up with human interest stories, and sometimes, science related stories in the Miami region.

"Chasing you down was something of a fluke. It happened because a couple who lived in Miami had gone on a sailing cruise that circled between Antigua, Montserrat, and St. Kitts. They'd flown into and out of Antigua and while they had been low over the water, they had taken a picture that showed the Manta. And it was obviously too large even for a manta ray. I had vacation time, so I talked my boss into letting me check it out, and you know the rest.

"But I'd done other stories that took me out of the city. The hurricane in Haiti was a big one, and I got lots of professional credit for my coverage of the refugees."

"I hadn't heard."

"You...Yes, I guess you don't follow the news do you? Haiti had a huge earthquake, and then came the hurricane. They have suffered."

"I'm sorry to hear that."

"Yes, but sometimes to a news organization, bad things are good for business. My stories from the Caribbean put me in a good position when the company decided to increase their regional reporting. I now have a job more focused on this area. So when your volcano happened, it was my job."

"So what do you do, between chasing after stories."

She sighed. "A lot of telephone calls. I am building a list of contacts—people I can call the instant something happens. Like when you reported the volcano, I had on my list a professor at the Rosenstiel School in Miami which was trying to increase its position in the world of oceanography. Giving them the scoop, and letting them take the lead notifying the rest of the scientific community made me some friends there, which might come in handy some time in the future."

He nodded. Not that she could see him. "Networking. I remember. Engineers do it too. Tell me more. Talk shop."

Maybe it was a mistake to urge her to talk more, because she did it so well, but it was better than brooding about the storm overhead, or about other things... long gone in the past.

She talked for hours, and all he had to do was to let her know he was listening.

But he must have dozed off, because a noise woke him. Her bikini top had dropped to the floor. He didn't look. It was dark. It was hot. He would have stripped off his shorts if she hadn't been there.

But he couldn't go back to sleep.

...

The light snapped on.

He was standing over her, shaking her arm. "Wake up."

On no. My top. She reached.

"No time for that." He pulled her toward the airlock. She stumbled, not quite awake.

"What's wrong?"

He pushed her in the tiny quarters with him.

"The eye of the hurricane. It's here." He threw some of the junk that had been riding there into the main chamber. "Here. Put this on."

It was a BC, a woman's model. She slipped the rubbery vest on. "I don't understand."

"Eye of the storm. Still water. May last an hour, may last three minutes. But we can raise the snorkel and get fresh air." He pressed a button that probably released it. She could hear something unspooling.

His eyes were bright and alive, and with a zip, the BC covered her breasts.

"You know how to use this?" he asked.

"Yes. Buoyancy Compensator. Inflate or deflate to balance a weight belt."

He nodded and wrapped the heavy weighted belt around her waist. It was already the correct size.

"We're going to climb up the main snorkel like a rope, all the way to the surface, and float there until the storm starts up again. Then we'll come back down. Got it?"

"Yes." She was finally beginning to understand. Floating on the sea, in the eye of a hurricane! It wasn't something to miss.

He started the air pump. The main snorkel must have been already at the surface. Then he pushed a button and water began spilling in around them. He fitted a face mask over her head, one with an air line attacked. Then he grabbed the other for himself.

"I have a waterproof camera."

"No time." And the water came up over their heads.

They were outside, and although warm, the water was so refreshing compared to the sticky air in the cabin.

He bent over her chest and blew into her BC's tube until he was confident that she was only slightly lighter than the water. Then he did the same to his.

He pointed up and they started up. He grabbed her belt and pushed her slightly ahead of him,

He's just wanting to watch my rear end, I bet.

But she climbed as she was told and they were soon at the surface.

She'd gone scuba diving before, and even some tether line swimming like this, but never in the dark. The main snorkel line was welcome in her hands.

Quickly, they were at the surface. His head came up beside hers.

He removed his mask and attached it to the buoy that sported a flag that marked the top of the snorkel line. "Now yours." She pulled it off and blinked her eyes to clear them.

The surf was hardly 'still', but up above, she could see a line of clouds moving off to the side, and the moonlight and stars shone down on them.

His arms were around her, and just for an instant, she thought he was being amorous, but again, he was adding air to her BC, making it more like a life jacket to keep her head above the water.

As his hands slipped free, she looked back up. There was enough moonlight to show both the near and far cloud walls. There was a hint of breeze, but she thought she could feel it getting softer.

"Stay close to me. And stay near the buoy." He reached over and pushed something, and it began a slow red blink.

She stretched out in the water. "This is marvelous. Have you done this before?"

"Not during the eye of a hurricane. It's just luck to be at the right place."

The swells were long and deep, and it was almost like a roller coaster.

"Enjoy it," he said. "It can vanish in minutes."

"I still wish I had a camera."

He laughed and grabbed her vest and kissed her long and hard. She was alive to the moment and returned it.

He paused, and in the moonlight she could see a wave of pain sweep over him. "I'm sorry."

"I'm not."

He clenched her tight. "I'm sorry! I'm sorry! I'm so sorry!"

She could feel him shake, and it swept over her like the wave that they rode. *Whose BC is this? And what is he sorry for?*

Things clicked. The Manta was slightly too large for one man, but it might have been the perfect size for a couple. The chair and the couch looked slightly 'after-market', like he'd remodeled things for his hermit-like existence. And the two face masks and two breathing lines, and now a female set of scuba gear.

He was still shaking, muttering, "I'm sorry" over and over.

"It's okay. It's okay." She held him gently. More than anything she wished she could call his name.

The mini-breakdown lasted only a couple of minutes.

"I'm okay. Sorry." He tried to push away, but she held his hand and wouldn't release it.

"It's all okay. Just relax in the water. Enjoy the moment."

He did as he was told.

The giant wall cloud that was coming their direction was lit constantly by lightning streaks, going from one part to the next.

As long as they don't come down on me.

The lightning scared her less that the idea of Nemo falling apart on her. She had no way to 'fly' the Manta, no idea of how to navigate. Likely as not, she'd make some mistake and leave them dead in the water, or worse, too deep to recover.

He mumbled, "I feel like I could just slip free and drift off forever."

"Don't you dare!"

He sighed. "I won't let you down. I'm just not used to emotions. Too many, too fast."

"Some emotions are good. I liked the kiss, by the way."

He didn't reply for a moment.

"I don't suppose you could let your company think you were just lost in the hurricane, do you?"

She was touched. "Sorry. They wouldn't believe it. They'd send someone to track me down, and they'd be looking for the Manta. It wasn't a big secret I was fascinated with you. And for all the features of the Manta, you didn't make it camouflaged."

"I'll put it on my todo list."

She smiled. He was coming back. *He can even be charming, at times.*

She pulled him closer and kissed his cheek. He fumbled a return kiss.

There was a wisp of breeze, and the moon began flickering behind the clouds.

"It's time." He pulled the both of them close to the buoy and handed her the face mask. "Get to the airlock. Don't panic, but don't dally." He pushed the release on her BC and vented the excess air. With things to do, he firmed up.

She nodded, with the regulator in her mouth, and began pulling herself down into the darkness, hand over hand.

He promised he wouldn't let me down.

Below, she could begin to see the light he left on in the airlock.

She felt him move up behind her almost the same time she got to the door. He was all business, getting their lines in, untangled, and closing the hatch. He could hear the main snorkel line being reeled back in as the water around them was being pushed out by the air.

"Ah! It's cooler inside now."

"We've refreshed the air. Go ahead and shower the salt off."

She almost forgot to grab up her bikini top as she did as she was told.

Would it be so bad if I did?

But with the BC in her hands, she couldn't help but remember that there was more to Nemo than just a lone inventor in a submarine. There was something broken about him. And she would have to tread gently.

...

He dropped his vest and weight belt in the corner and turned to the controls. He had to check battery levels and other consumables. He knew his own usage patterns by heart, but with the two of them, he needed to check.

When she leaves, it'll all go back to normal.

She came out of the water closet with a towel draped over her shoulders and a brush in her hand. She carried a large towel for him as well.

"You'll need to rinse off too."

He shook his head. "Thanks, but I'm going to conserve fresh water for now. We can't keep the lights on either."

She nodded. "Okay, but don't try to sleep in those wet shorts. I promise I won't peek."

After the lights went out, and he fingered his new towel for a while, he did exchange his shorts for a comfortable nearly dry wrap, although he felt her looking at him.

They needed to get some sleep.

"Nemo?" She sounded worried.

"Yes?"

"The Manta shook."

"No problem. We're safe, but the back half of the storm can be more violent than the front. It's just turbulence."

"Okay."

He waited for her to ask him to come hold her. *It's just a fantasy, but with a girl like her, she might.*

But she didn't.

"Brenda?"

"Um. Yes."

"Do I have it right that you came to me to get pictures of the volcano?"

"Yes. At least that's what I told my boss."

"But the volcano pictures is what they expected?"

"You'd be surprised what they expected. But work related—yes, the volcano, and hopefully more back story on you and the Manta. You've never explained where you came from, or even what your real name is."

"Okay. I can get us close enough to take all the volcano photos you want. We'll leave in the morning. With enough light to navigate by, I can keep us low enough to avoid the trailing edges of the storm."

The Manta shook again.

"Nemo?"

"It's safe."

"Promise?"

"Yes."

...

Brenda eyes came open, watching Nemo working away at his console. He'd gotten 'dressed' again, but she admired the muscles on his back.

Is this anything more than just a fantasy? Should we just take care of business and go our separate ways? I've dangled some lures, but he's not ready to bite.

And long term? I can't run a news desk from here, and he's not likely to dock the Manta in North Bay.

She asked, "What are you doing?"

He turned. She was pleased to see him give her a long look. But that was what bikinis were for.

"I've got the recharging tail extended. The winds are down, but the surf is still high. Not enough to be dangerous, but we need more juice before we start."

She got up and rummaged around in the pantry.

"This is like flour?"

"Yes. Kelp based, but it works in the same recipes."

"So I could make something like pancakes?"

He nodded. "Use the recipe on page 40, but make them thin. No butter, so expect it to be a little dry."

She found the little hand-written recipe book.

That's a woman's handwriting.

Page 40 had strike-throughs and alterations. Without most of the original ingredients, he'd made changes to make do.

She worked slowly, making her own changes, adding a dollop of jam where the old original had something called K-sugar. The stove was designed to heat the surface quickly, but it also cooled quickly. She rushed to lay the batter out and scoop it off as fast as she could. In the back of her mind, she was sure Nemo was growling about the electricity drain.

"Come here and eat, before it gets cold."

He walked over. No table, so they held their plates.

"Good. Strawberry?"

They had turned out like tortillas in shape and texture. "Right."

He opened his mouth to talk, but said nothing.

"What?"

"Oh, nothing. Maybe inappropriate."

"Say it. We'll both laugh and that'll be that."

He hesitated then said, "Why don't you stay and be my cook?"

She laughed. "You can come to Miami and answer my telephones for me."

They laughed again, but not very convincingly.

She put the dishes into the cage, a little sadly. Today was likely the last time they'd be together. She was a reporter, with responsibilities and deadlines.

…

The trip to the volcano was sedate. She had gotten cleaned up and dressed in her khakis.

"Get your shirt on. I'm going to take your picture when we get near the volcano."

As they approached the area, she looked for the other vessels, but saw nothing.

He shook his head, "Any surface craft would have likely made a run to avoid the hurricane. They'll be back in a week or so, I'm sure."

She took notes as he told her how he'd discovered it, and he flew the Manta through the same upwelling. She was giggly and excited when the craft bucked in the flow, and kissed him quickly on the cheek. He quietly determined to give her more excitement.

They made several passes over the glowing, churning pile of growing lava, with her camera clicking away.

Suddenly, the Manta heaved strongly to the side unexpectedly.

Brenda shrieked, "Nemo!"

The tilt kept increasing and the craft no longer responded to his control. The last thing he remembered doing was slapping at the emergency blow button. Then he fell, hitting his head against the thick glass hull.

...

Seconds or minutes later, he woke. The Manta was upside down, but she was on the surface.

"Brenda?" He found her laying unconscious against the glass not too far away. There was a discoloration on her temple. He made sure she was breathing, and resting securely, then walked across the curved ceiling to make sense of the controls.

"What happened?" She murmured a minute later. He went to her side and helped her sit against the wall.

"Another upwelling, stronger and closer than the first one. It tipped us over. We're like a turtle on its back."

"My camera!" He found it for her, and then checked for signs of concussion. She was a little disoriented. She wanted to make sure that the camera was okay, and then take a picture of the shambles inside, but he had to do it for her. He also took a few of her, and her bruised head.

"I need to right the Manta."

"Can you?"

"I've never done it, but I designed for it."

He started the pumps, emptying the tanks in the port wing and filling those in the starboard side. The 'floor' began to tilt, and all the loose items scattered over it started to slide.

"Nemo!"

"It's okay, Brenda. Here, let me help you."

He shifted her over to the wall, which was rapidly becoming the down direction.

"It's not enough."

She nodded, but he could tell she was still acting fuzzy.

"Brenda, I have to go outside and help turn the Manta over. You'll have to help. Are you up to that?"

She nodded. "What do I need to do?"

He tapped on the hull.

"When I signal you like this, push this red button." He helped her walk over to the control console. "No matter what, keep one hand on this railing, okay?"

"Okay."

He went to airlock, glancing back to make sure she hadn't drifted off. She smiled and waved.

He made sure the airlock door was securely closed and carried an anchor chain slung across his shoulder.

The vertical stabilizing fins made a giant-step ladder he could just barely navigate as he climbed up the port wing. He hooked the anchor chain to an eyelet at the tip of the wing and walked as if he were rappelling to the 'down' side of the wing. His weight tilted the wing slightly his way. Hopefully it was enough.

He kicked the wing.

Can she hear that? If not, he'd have to do it all over again.

Then, the pumps came on. He held his position until the wing began to come down. Shortly, the Manta righted itself, dropping him into the water.

He climbed up on the wing. He could see her through the glass.

"Brenda!"

But she didn't hear him. He turned toward the airlock.

...

The thumping in her head made it hard to think. She still wasn't quite sure what happened. Nemo was out and about and taking care of everything, just like he always did. But she wished he could get her an aspirin.

"Nemo?"

But there was no response. Did he hear her?

Did he fall off in the water? Her pounding heartbeat made the pain in her head ten times worse.

With her hand to her head, she looked around.

Everything was a mess. Things had fallen out of the pantry, the same with the closet. Tools and books and her jars of jam were all underfoot.

But where is Nemo?

There was a sound. *The airlock.*

She put her hand on the lever, and then hesitated. Would the water come in?

It took her so very long to think it through. No. They were right-side-up in the water, on the surface. It should be okay.

She pushed the lever and opened the door.

He was struggling with a huge spool of rubber tubing.

"Nemo?"

His face was dark and his jaw was clenched tight.

"Nemo, what's wrong?"

He let go of the tube he'd been struggling with. Then he kicked it.

"We... I got too close to the lava. Touching close. A big part of my charging system melted."

He looked up at her with pain written all over his face.

"I can't recharge the batteries. Once the current charge runs out, I'm dead in the water. Once there's no power, the Manta becomes unlivable. No way to move. No drinking water."

He got to his feet and went to the console and shut every power drain down.

She could feel his pain. This was his life, his baby.

"We can call for help."

"You can. And we need to, to take care of your concussion. If they take me, the Manta is done for." He took her hand. "I know they'd consider me incompetent. They won't leave me out here in the middle of the ocean with a stranded ship. You'll have to pretend I'm okay. The Manta is okay."

"But what will happen to you?"

He sat on the couch and made her sit too. He checked her out again. The bump on her head was as painful as ever.

He shrugged, "I know a sunken ship near here where I can get tools that I can use to work on the charging system. Maybe with repairs I can limp to the little island where the plane dropped you off. If I can get enough juice to keep the water desalinator running, I can live."

"You'd be like a castaway on the island, stranded."

"Maybe. With tools, maybe I could get things running again."

"Then let me stay with you and help."

"No." He touched her bruise and she winced. "If there are any complications, you're dead. I can't have that, even to save the Manta."

He stood up and dug out the sat phone.

"The battery is dead again. I'll have to recharge it." He made the connections to the charger. Then, when he cranked up the spine and turned on his navigation system, she could see him sag.

"Problem?"

He nodded. "The GPS receiver–everything on the radio spine is out. More damage from the accident." He checked some connections, then walked back and sat down beside her.

He took her hand, "Brenda, I can make the phone call for help, but I have no way to tell our current location. We were over the volcano, but you were knocked out, and so was I. The unstable winds related to the hurricane have pushed us somewhere, but I can't make a guess close enough to give co-ordinates to a rescue plane.

"I guess we could send out a general distress call, and let the Coast Guard or their like to determine our position from the radio signal, but then they'd know for sure that the Manta is disabled."

He stared at the floor. "I guess that's what I need to do."

"No. Don't. This is your freedom. You can't give that up. I am getting better. The fuzziness has gone away. Isn't there some other way to get a fixed location? Don't you have one of those sextants or something?"

He smiled and shook his head. "No. Sorry. I was always going to get around to it, but the GPS was always there for me.

"But I do know where some fixed locations are. If I could get to the island, or sunken ship—I've marked them on my maps, then we could tell your plane to go there."

"But how can you find those places, if you don't know where we are?"

"Oh, I can navigate by ocean floor landmarks. I do it all the time. The ocean may be featureless up here, but not down there."

Brenda leaned against him. "Then do that. Go to the sunken ship and get your repair parts."

...

"I'm going to turn nearly everything off. It's going to be a balancing act. I can travel using less energy for a slower pace, but navigating manually, I have to have sunlight strong enough to reach the sea bed. So, no crossing deeps, unless I know exactly where I am."

First order of business was getting her settled on the couch, with a pillow of folded towels, and a cup of water at hand.

"Stay still as much as possible. Rest for your concussion, and minimize motion to keep my course adjustments small."

"I can still talk."

He chuckled. "I couldn't stop you, could I?"

He checked his directions by the sky, and started them down.

Every now and then, he'd grunt or say, "Ah!"

She questioned everything. He'd see a bed of shells, or the edge of an old coral reef, and he'd recognize it from previous trips. Soon, he'd changed course and cut across an undersea valley, taking them deep enough that all the light changed color, and any fish out the window looked nearly monochrome.

"Every time I change tilt, up or down, I have to run the pumps to shift balance. So I'm taking deep swings to minimize the changes.

"You know, once, just to see if I could do it, I trimmed the Manta absolutely level, then turned the pumps all the way off and sailed by walking forward and backward in the cabin and compressing the ballast air with the foot pump. It worked, but I took a whole day to get a quarter mile. I'd have better luck just making little adjustments to move into and out of the currents—if I had a good map of them."

"It amazes me how much you do know about this world."

He shrugged. "I live here."

...

"There. I see it."

She sat up, only a little dizzy by her enforced idleness.

He blew ballast and they rose to the surface. As soon as he dropped an anchor line, he handed her the phone.

"The battery says it's charged, but the phone will die in about five minutes or so. Talk quickly."

She pulled out her note pad and called the air charter service. She sweated while they took her latitude and longitude and the description of what to look for.

She added a request for a portable generator and a hundred gallons of gasoline. Her boss might not cover that part, but she could afford it out of her own pocket.

The phone died, but after she had a confirmation.

She handed it back to him. "They'll arrive in about four hours."

"That gives me time to make a scavenging run. I'll take her down."

The Manta settled into a cleared spot on the floor only about a fifty yards from the strange looking derelict. There was another depression next to them, and she was positive the Manta had left that mark on a previous visit. She could see the name of the ship.

"The Ocean Ray. What do you know about it?"

He did that little shake of his head she'd come to recognize as shorthand for "don't bother me" or "I'm never going to tell you".

The burned hull was of a peculiar design, like one of those research vehicles with a split hull at the rear with cranes to raise and lower buoys and shuttle craft.

And submersibles.

Nemo was already in the airlock, getting on his scuba gear. Brenda looked around the Manta, with all the debris from their accident still on the floor. She walked over and picked up some of the diving gear. She began collecting them to tidy up the place, but she turned each item over in her hands, looking for any clues.

On three of the hand tools, someone had etched OCEAN RAY. On the BC she had used, there was a very faded label, written in pen, "Sally Gerber". On one of the unused scuba tanks, there was the marking "Oscar Gerber".

She looked outside and was surprised to see Nemo off to the side of the Ocean Ray, near a pile of rocks. She rapidly dug out her camera gear and snapped the telephoto lens on it. Zooming in, she could see him hovering near the top of the pile—obviously built by hand—where there rested an isolated round port-hole that he must have cut free from the hull of the ship.

She'd have given anything to see if there was some kind of inscription. But she knew what was under that pile, and who authored all the feminine traces she'd found in the Manta. *Sally Gerber.*

But does Nemo know? Can he remember it?

She'd read a story long ago about a man who lost his wife and unable to deal with it, lost his memory. Just how broken was her Nemo?

...

Right on time, the seaplane came down, throwing up rooster tails of water until it slowed, and then taxied over to the Manta.

Getting the generator unloaded an onto the Manta's wing without dunking it was a little difficult. The gasoline tanks just floated.

"It's a project of his," she explained to the pilot. "He's going to set up a home base on a tiny little island near here." They said nothing about the Manta's damage.

He gave the pilot instructions about her head injury and insisted he ignore anything she said about feeling fine. She had to get to a doctor.

Brenda got onto the plane with her camera and the clothes on her back.

He stared off to the northwest long after the plane had shrunk to nothing in the sky. He might have done so for days, if his repair work hadn't been so urgent.

...

The trip to the island was slow going. Soon he ran out of battery and had to surface, haul out the generator onto the wing in the open air, run cables through the airlock and burn gasoline. The weather had to be perfect, so for three days he had to drift before he could get a charge.

Finally he arrived at the island and secured the Manta for an extended stay.

He anchored her in the shallows, and he hated that. Getting well below the churning surf was rule number one in keeping the Manta safe. But he needed to access the damage in the air to make repairs.

He'd need to watch the sky very carefully.

Wednesday noon, he turned on the sat phone.

"Before you ask, Nemo, the doctor gave me some pills, and I have to go back next week for another checkup, but she says I look fine. But she did say you did the right thing getting me checked out."

"I'm glad. I was worried."

"Well don't worry. I'm back on the job. The photos of the volcano and the hurricane from the underside are already on the company's website and I'm getting emails from girls all over the place telling me how sexy you look."

"Hmm. Don't tell them where I am."

"Your secret is safe with me. How are you doing?"

"I've disassembled the charging spool. It'll take some work, but some parts can be salvaged."

"That's great. Will there be any problem, keeping the same call schedule?"

"No. Wednesday is fine."

There was no answer. The battery had gone dead.

He turned off the phone. He went inside and put it aside, hoping to get it charged again before the next call.

I need to get back to work.

Instead, he went to the closet and opened the drawer where he'd put her washed and folded nightgown. He felt the lace and remembered the texture when she wore it.

"Enough of this."

But in the airlock, he paused and ran the tips of his fingers over the name "Sally" written on the edge of one of the face masks hanging there.

On the shore he had built a platform above the high tide line where he was cutting the charger spool apart and separating the segments that could be salvaged from the burned and ruined ones. With luck he could splice the good parts together to make a smaller charger. It would produce less than half the power of the original, but it was enough to keep the Manta alive, if he used little artificial light, bathed infrequently, and traveled very slowly. It would also be fragile. If it broke in use, he could lose it all, far from any shore.

I'll lose her. In spite of her best intentions, there's nothing to bring her back.

...

Frank Hancock, president of Green Wavepower, in Jacksonville, Florida picked up his phone.

"Sir, there is a Ms. deMay asking to see you."

"She's here? With no appointment?"

"That's correct, sir."

"Hang on."

He hit the mute button and hit the button for his Chief of Research.

"Jerry, she found us. And she's here, now."

They conferred. He put his secretary back on line. "Send her in."

...

Brenda had learned that sometimes, pretending to know the whole story would shake out more details than she could ever ask for.

It looks like this is one of those lucky breaks.

She only came here because she found references to the company by tracking down a very sketchy list of Oscar Gerber's work history. But from the moment she walked in the front door, it was plain that practically everyone at the small company had a guilty conscience. Without asking, she had been directed higher and higher on the org chart. Clearly no one wanted to be fall guy.

She walked into the president's office with a confident smile and shook his hand.

"Have a seat Ms. deMay. I must say, I've enjoyed your work."

She looked at his face, and the way that he was struggling to look her straight in the eye.

"My Haiti stories or my... more recent work."

He actually flushed. He spread his hands.

"I'm not going to try to stonewall you, Ms. deMay."

"Brenda. Call me Brenda."

"Ah, yes. Brenda. The thing is, from the first article showing the photo of the Manta—copies spread like wildfire around the factory—we knew that Oscar's submersible had been found. We just weren't sure that Nemo was Oscar."

He went to a file cabinet and pulled out a large leather bound folder. He opened it up and handed it to her.

"The Manta was built here in the large building you passed when you arrived here."

She flipped through photos and blueprints, progress reports and material work sheets. It looked very different, a machine up on stilts surrounded by cranes, not like the creature of the depths it seemed to her before.

There was a photo of Oscar, clean shaven and in a business suit, standing beside a woman in a white lab smock.

Mr. Hancock said, "Of course, when the photos came out, 'Nemo' was obviously Oscar Gerber. I suppose you have questions about why we didn't contact you?"

She looked up at him, as he hovered around where she sat. "In a bit. But first, I have a few questions about Sally."

He nodded, sadly. "I gather she didn't survive."

"She's buried under a rock cairn right beside the burned hull of the Ocean Ray, sitting on the sea bottom."

Frank sighed. "It's rather ironic."

"How so?"

He gestured, pacing. "Sally was a gifted scientist. She came to us originally for custom aquarium tanks and fittings. She was a bit of an odd duck, a marine biologist who was much more comfortable in a lab coat than in a swimsuit, if you get my meaning. She loved sea life, but she didn't like getting wet.

"When Oscar fell in love with her, he fell all the way. Marriage wasn't enough. He sunk practically everything he owned into the Manta."

"He told me that it had been built as a marine biologist's platform."

"He built to be Sally's lab! A place she could work, in her lab coat, if you will, but out there close to the animals she loved."

He gave up pacing and pulled another chair close where he could sit down. "It's a small company. We all pitched in. When they sailed away with the Manta loaded aboard the Ocean Ray, everyone thought it was like the last curtain of Snow White, with the loving couple heading off to live happily ever after."

He stared at his hands, shaking his head. "It was two months out when the word came. The cook washed up in Antigua with the story. Something in the engine room blew, starting a massive diesel fire. The Ocean Ray went down fast. He saw bodies, but he was the only one out alive."

She nodded. It certainly matched what she'd seen. But Oscar had been spared, perhaps out in the Manta. He came out alive, but broken inside.

But it didn't explain Frank Hancock's guilt.

She tapped the folder. "And Oscar Gerber's relationship with the company?"

She could tell she was close. He hesitated a moment, and then got to his feet and dug out another folder.

"Oscar was our Chief of Design. We were so supportive of the Manta because he was churning out new inventions almost daily, it seemed. He had the vision, you see. And when problems came up, he invented a solution. He invented a lot of solutions.

"We changed the name of the company because of one of them."

She rummaged through the patents, stopping when she came to the wave charging system. She held it up. "You sell many of these."

He nodded, solemnly, "More and more. And that's what happened.

"Oscar left with little money. He sold his house, his car, and cashed in his life insurance policy to get the Ocean Ray launched. But he had some shares of the company and these patents. He left us a power of attorney, just until he returned. And then he never returned.

"The money?" she prompted, guessing.

He nodded. "We leased some of the patents, and manufactured some other things." He looked out the window. "I suppose someone should have moved to declare Oscar dead, and then we would have had to turn it all over to his estate."

"But you didn't."

"No. We didn't." He sighed. "We pretended he was still sailing away, and that the power of attorney was still perfectly valid. The company needed to grow, and we were managing this fat trust fund.

"So we traded shares for cash. All legal. I think. It's just, what with the green energy surge, Oscar now owns a controlling interest in the company."

...

He sweated in the sun, using a hot knife to seal segments of the rubber tube together. It was slow work, and then he had to test his welds. The wave power system had to flex, and his repairs left the rubber much weaker than it had been originally. The repaired version was only fifteen feet long, which was barely enough to span the distance between wave crests, and it had to be at least that long to even work.

The power from the spinning blades was just a trickle charge to the batteries. His repairs were working, in theory, but in practice, he needed to change out the rubber tubes to make them stronger.

He looked up at the palm trees. *I don't think I can make rubber from that.*

A stick jammed into the sand cast a shadow that was creeping closer and closer to a conch shell.

Time.

He went over to the waterproof case and turned the sat phone on.

It buzzed. He grabbed.

"Hello."

"Nemo, are you still at the island?"

"Yes."

"If I air-dropped a package offshore, could your retrieve it?"

"If it is close. The Manta doesn't have much power."

"Be ready tomorrow at noon."

"What is it?"

"I'll explain when I get there."

...

He prepared the Manta, burning all but two gallons of his fuel to bring it up to half-charge.

I hope she knows what she's doing.

He pushed the Manta out of the shallows by hand and climbed on. Without a clear idea of where the drop zone was going to be, all he could do was be ready to move.

Two specks appeared from the west. He waited until a parachute appeared out of the back of one. The plane banked and headed away.

That's my package.

He ignored the other plane and tilted the Manta's nose down, banking to port. In a couple of minutes, he surfaced next to the floating package, about the size of three refrigerators, side by side. He hooked a line to it and pulled the parachute in. *That could be useful someday.*

The seaplane was landing. With a splash of spray, it turned towards the island.

The Manta was never made to tow packages, but a force is force. It was like trying to sail while anchored, but the package moved. Ten minutes into the struggle, he was close enough for Brenda and the pilot to wade out into the shallows to help.

The three of them dragged the package to ground. He dropped an anchor line for the Manta and waded ashore himself.

Brenda was smiling, but she was worried.

"Are you okay?" he asked.

She hugged him, and they kissed. It was a little dazzling.

"Okay. I'll take that as a yes."

Brenda still looked worried. She turned to the pilot. "Joe, we're going to need some time to talk."

"Sure." He turned back toward the plane.

She grabbed a satchel from the beach. "Come on, let's talk in the Manta."

He helped her up, and they went inside.

"Okay, what's the big secret?"

She sat on the couch and patted beside her. When he sat, she opened her satchel and pulled out a printed booklet.

"The package outside is a charging system very similar to the one you built for the Manta. This is the technical description."

He opened his mouth, but nothing made sense. He opened the pages, and flipped through the numbers.

"Where... where did you get this?"

"Frank Hancock gave it to me. To you really. I need you to sign this."

She held out a sheet. His eyes glazed. Down at the bottom, there was a place for Oscar Gerber to sign.

"It's important, Nemo. I really didn't want to have to confront you with this just yet, but it's worth a lot of money and they wouldn't let me take it without promising to get your signature."

He... couldn't think. Brenda put a pen in his hand and set the paper on top of the booklet.

"Nemo. My Nemo, we need to have a nice long talk together, someplace quiet and safe and away from all the pressures and deadlines. I hate this, but you're going to have to do it. This is the only way to keep the Manta, your Manta, alive. You know it. This is life for the Manta.

"Don't really think about it. Just put the pen on the line and let your hand take over."

She had her hands on his and moved it to the paper.

"Nemo?"

He looked at her, looked at her eyes.

"Nemo, do this for me? Okay?"

He blinked. His eyes blurred. He looked down at the paper again.

"You did it! I'm so glad." She hugged him and took the pen from his hand. There was a scribble there, but he couldn't focus to see what it said.

She put the paper away in her satchel.

"Come here." She put his head on her shoulder and rocked him. "It's okay. Everything is okay."

...

Brenda latched the airlock door behind her. It twisted her up that he was still asleep and couldn't say goodbye. She paused long enough to check the rope that tied the Manta and the charging station together.

It wasn't a perfect match for the one he built for the Manta, but she had a couple of Green Wavepower technicians cross check between the Manta designs and their current products to find one that would work.

It was a devil's bargain. She had promised to hold off reporting this part of the story until Oscar Gerber could talk with Frank Hancock personally. But it was a million dollar part that had been pulled out of their shipping department, delaying their delivery to some town in Maine. He demanded Oscar's signature on the delivery notice, and it would be charged against Oscar's fund.

She wanted nothing more than to stay here, to be by his side when he woke up.

But he's a survivor. If it had been me, stranded alone in the middle of the ocean with my one true love dead in a burned ship, the victim of my own grand plan, I'd probably have curled up and died. He did the next best thing, but that didn't keep him from surviving.

Joe was twiddling his fingers with a leer on his face. "We're going to have a hard time making it on to your destination. Have a nice... talk?"

"Get your mind out of the gutter, Joe. It was just business. I had to explain the delivery and get his signature. It was complicated."

...

He woke with a headache, and trouble remembering where he was.

The island. Yes. Now, I remember. Brenda came to visit.

"Brenda?"

He got up to look around, but there was a letter resting on the control console.

Nemo,

I have to go to the Cayman Islands for a news special (on turtles) and I apologize for leaving you alone. I'll be back as soon as I can. Check your phone at noon, and I'll call when I can.

Until then, I hope you can repair the Manta with the new power unit. I also left you a couple of other presents. We really need to find more time together.

Brenda

New power unit?

"New power unit!"

Suddenly, he remembered the air drop and the planes.

He snatched up the technical data that rested beside the letter, ignoring the fresh sat phone batteries and the laptop computer.

It was all too good to be true.

He hurried out to crack open the shipping crate.

He caressed the brand new black tubes wound tightly into the crate.

I can make this work.

...

Frank Hancock examined the papers that had been faxed to his office from a hotel in Grand Cayman.

"Yes, that's Oscar's signature. So he's in the Caymans? I thought he was in Antigua?"

The attorney shook his head. "I don't care where he is, as long as I don't see a lawsuit with his name on it."

"Amen."

...

He worked until the light faded. His power miserly instincts wouldn't let him turn the floodlights on to work during the night.

He stumbled back the Manta. But even in the faint twilight, he could see the items on the console.

Fresh phone batteries. Great.

He opened up the laptop. There was a note covering the keyboard:

Nemo, computers may have changed just a bit. Here's a quick cheat sheet.

It was basically a list of icons and what they represented. About two-thirds were familiar, not that the email or web browser did him a bit of good out here in the middle of the ocean, but the word processor and spread sheet would come in handy. Shortly, he'd have enough electricity to afford it.

The last computer he had was lost when....

He blinked and shut it down. More things to deal with tomorrow.

...

Noon, the phone buzzed. With batteries that held a charge, he could afford to turn it on beforehand and not have to watch the 'clock'.

"Hello, Brenda."

"I'm so glad to hear your voice! Did you find everything?"

"Yes, I've got the power system mostly in pieces—in a good way. I'm using a spreadsheet, and I'm using the new batteries. Do you have time to talk?"

"Unfortunately, not today. I've got an interview with some turtle-breeders in a couple of minutes."

"Turtle-breeders?"

"Long story. I'll get you a copy of the article when I'm done. I just wanted to make sure you were okay."

"I'm okay. Getting sunburned, but okay."

"Great. Talk tomorrow?"

"Yes."

...

The next day, noon passed with no call. But he was deep in recalibrating the power system and didn't notice it until later. He was sad she hadn't called, but the new system had given him fresh batteries for the Manta and he was thrilled at how much better performance he was getting from his systems. The previous batteries had been aging, and he hadn't really noticed.

The day after that, he had installed the new system and was on a test cruise, seeing how well he could recharge in open water with a sea-anchor. He forgot to recharge the phone battery.

...

He was back on the island, treating himself to a nice grilled grouper with jam glaze when he suddenly remembered that she hadn't called in days.

He checked the phone and put it back on the charger.

I can afford to do that now.

The next project was to take the leftover pieces and put together a secondary power system for the island—something to have packed up and ready, just in case.

It was a shame Brenda wasn't calling, but perhaps he'd done something to offend her.

Food stocks were getting low, so he returned to his regular kelp beds and harvested enough to make a batch of his staple flour he used for breakfast and the times when fishing was poor. There were also salvaged canned goods from recent shipwrecks and her gifts, but as Brenda said, his diet was poor.

He shredded the kelp and followed a finger stained recipe written in a feminine hand that he'd been using forever.

For some reason he paused when he pulled out the fragile sheet. By this time, he knew the steps by heart anyway, so he carefully put the page back in a safe place.

Wednesday again. Why am I paying so much attention to the calendar? Maybe it's that computer. I should turn off its calendar display.

Then it occurred to him, hadn't Brenda called on Wednesdays?

But noon came and there was no call.

I've got it wrong. There's something I'm supposed to remember. What is it?

Maybe Brenda would know.

He had written down her office number when he tracked her down the first time to report the volcano. He punched the buttons.

"Hello, is Miss deMay there?"

There was a silence. "Who is calling?"

He had a moment of panic. "Uh... Nemo?"

"Oh, you mean she isn't with you?"

"No. I haven't seen her since..." He strained to remember. "She was going to interview turtle-breeders."

"That was a week or more ago. She turned in that report and then went missing. I just thought she'd gone to spend time with you. I was about getting ready to track her down and threaten to fire her. Are you sure you don't know anything more?"

"No. Sorry. I'd thought she was just busy at her job. Now I'm worried."

"Me too. Call this number if you find out anything. I'll check my sources as well. Can I call this number and get you?"

"I'm underwater most of the time, but you can try. I'll check in when I can."

...

I need more information. He looked at the laptop. *Where can I get a network connection?*

He stowed the island project just well enough so it wouldn't be ruined by rain and made a run for the oil platform.

He was pushing it, but he was surprised at how much faster the Manta could travel when he had enough energy to push the ballast pumps faster. Faster rise and sink times meant more thrust on the wing.

He surfaced near the platform, intending to call for the man he talked to the other time. But the laptop flickered an icon. There was a wireless connection coming from the platform. The computer automatically connected, and there were suddenly a dozen alerts, warnings of various systems coming awake that hadn't bothered when there was no network.

Frustrated, he clicked the little boxes until everything settled down.

Okay, Brenda said there was a website.

He pulled the old newspaper and found the highlighted box that advertised the paper's companion on the web. He connected and began reading every article that had her name.

He was coming up to speed, when he made the mistake of reading the article that had pictures of him. There were comments, several of them, that claimed to identify him.

His eyes blurred.

"No! No time for that."

He forced the noise growing in his head off to the side.

I have to find out what happened to Brenda. That's the only thing that matters.

The memory of signing a paper forced its way back.

There was a scribble.

"You did it! I'm so glad." The signature said Oscar Gerber. It was his.

No time. Deal with that later.

Brenda got the power system for him from Frank Hancock.

...

Frank picked up the phone.

"Sir, there's a call for you, from Oscar. Oscar Gerber."

"Put him on."

"Hello, Oscar! I'm glad to hear from you."

"Um, Frank. When did you last see Brenda deMay?"

The voice was Oscar's, but he sounded different. A lot of years and a lot of miles, he guessed.

"It was over a week ago, when she picked up that power system for you. How is that working out for you, by the way?"

"Fine, Frank. But she's missing. What can you tell me?"

"Oscar, I have no idea. I don't know what she told you about the stocks, but certainly we wouldn't do anything illegal."

"Huh? No, Frank. I'm not saying that. I just want to know everything about Brenda."

"Oscar, I'm afraid it's very little. She came here, asked about Sally, haggled for the power system. She delivered it to you, and then faxed me the document from some hotel on Grand Cayman."

Sally. It hit him like a brick to the head. He staggered, but he didn't drop the phone.

Stay focused.

"What hotel?" It was almost a whisper.

"I can look it up. Hang on." There was the sound of a file cabinet being opened.

"It was the Meridian Grand Cayman."

"Thanks Frank."

Before he began the next step, the phone buzzed.

"Hello?"

"This is Karl Hansen, Brenda's boss. She took a chartered plane from Jacksonville Florida, two of them in fact, to a spot near Antigua."

"That was me."

"Good because she didn't charge those to the paper. But she did charge one part of the flight. She stopped in Antigua, apparently to refuel, and then turned around to go to Grand Cayman, which is where I told her to go to research stories of turtle poaching."

"Turtle poaching. Really?"

He could hear the man shrug. "It's news. That's what we do. Grand Cayman has a big sea turtle breeding facility. Reports were that a lot of the turtles that were being released to the wild were going missing—more than normal losses. She went to do a little research, and turned in a story about the turtle farm and such as background.

"And that's the last I heard of her."

"So, did she go off to do another story?"

"She didn't charge a flight to the paper. As far as I can tell from her expense account, she's still on Grand Cayman. That's why I thought she went back to you. She's pretty good about paying for personal things."

"She stayed at the Meridian."

"Hmm. I don't see that. I'll call and check. Can you stay by the phone?"

"Yes."

It was unbearable to wait. His memory played back her voice complaining about waiting.

He pulled out his charts and estimated how long it would take for him to get to Grand Cayman with the Manta. It was days, at best. Even at his new best speed, he'd still have to take breaks to recharge. And this would be over unfamiliar waters. Deeper waters than he was used to. No settling down on the bottom to anchor for the night. Not unless he wanted to do so in Cuban waters.

Is the US still hostile towards Cuba? Maybe it's all changed. Who knows?

How much time could he afford to waste by the oil platform to find out simple common knowledge that he'd skipped over these past... how many years?

He checked the calendar, and felt the weight of lost years.

I've been like a man in a coma. All because of... Sally.

There was a flash of memory. Racing back to the Ocean Ray, trying to dock with the ship while it was still sinking. Seeing the flames running over the surface of the water. Pushing into dead corridors in scuba gear. Finding her. She'd barricaded the door to keep the fire out. She'd drowned instead.

Oh, my dear Sally. So afraid of drowning that you couldn't go into the water. What did I do? Why did I make you go?

He remembered a noise. A strange wailing noise. His own screams of madness into his scuba mouthpiece.

...

The phone buzzed, shaking him out of the nightmare.

"Hello."

"Nemo, or is it Oscar? The hotel didn't have a record of her checking out. They sent someone up with a key. It looks like her place was ransacked. Some of her luggage was still there, but her papers, her computer, and her camera are all gone."

"She wouldn't have left her camera."

"I'd agree with you there. I'll get the local police on it. I don't know what else to do right now."

...

He remembered Grand Cayman. A fancy place. *I won't fit in there. But I have to go.*

He rubbed his beard. Maybe he needed a trim.

She called the pilot 'Joe'. The airport at Antigua might have information on him. It's worth a shot.

...

The dark haired boy saw a snorkeler coming ashore and raced across the sand, conch shell in hand to try to get him to buy it.

But Leon's run faltered when the swimmer shifted his load. It was a huge shell, nearly four times the size of his conch. Still, he might want to buy something else.

"Hey mister. Where did you get that shell?"

He looked scruffy and his beard looked like it had been roughly cut.

"Out in the water—deeper than usual." He nodded to the conch. "Do you sell shells to the tourists?"

"I'll sell anything. Beads, shells, coconuts. I can get you a map of the shipwrecks or a taxi."

He shifted his load as he hooked his snorkel, mask and fins to his belt.

"I'm short on money. Take me to someone who'll buy my shell for a good price, and I'll give you a percentage."

Leon hesitated as he balanced the idea of trying to buy it himself, versus taking the percentage.

"I'll take it for twenty, American."

He chuckled. "I can get much better than that. What do you say, twenty percent?"

Now he was talking real money. Faces flickered through his head. Who would pay the most?

"Come with me. I know a man."

"I thought you might."

...

The shopkeeper looked like an island version of Abraham Lincoln, tall and angular, rather than one of the seedy types in a Humphrey Bogart movie, but it was the latter image that came to Nemo's mind as the merchant examined the shell.

"Where did you get this?"

He waved his hand in a general direction. "Oh a few miles that way. It wasn't the largest shell in the bed, but I hesitated to take one that was still growing."

He was a little giddy from moving around among all these people. It took practice to ignore all the individual movements, and he wasn't used to it. He fought the urge to turn and watch people pass by on the street.

Experienced hands scratched at worm holes that testified to his story.

"I would pay 2000."

Nemo was watching Leon's face. "Is that US or East Caribbean?"

"Um. Perhaps 700 US."

He frowned. "I really need more than that."

"Don't we all?" the merchant smiled. "Do you have anything else to sell?"

"Oh, lots. I just grabbed the first thing handy."

"What kinds of things?"

"More shells, of course. Mollusks and sea turtle."

The man frowned. "You do know that any trade in sea turtle products is forbidden."

"Except in the Caymans."

"Well, yes, of course." That government had rejected the sea turtle ban and instead had aggressively farmed them, allowing turtle products internally as a way to make the turtles pay their way out of endangered status. As a result, the turtles they released to the wild had boosted the overall population.

But any export of sea turtle products from the Caymans was strictly forbidden.

Nemo shrugged, dismissing the idea. "I've always had the idea that when the critter no longer needed its shell, there's nothing wrong with making something of it."

The merchant sighed. "Yes, I know. I have seen turtle-shell items and they are quite exquisite. But to be caught making such a transaction is not worth it to me."

Nemo nodded. "Then how about these things." He pulled a couple of manganese nodules from his bag. "You know what they are?"

Eager hands fingered them and hefted them to test their weight. "Whose water's?"

"A n' B." There had been a lot of interest in the metal balls that grew on the ocean bottom, mainly for the nickel in them. But what with the cost of deep sea mining, and the payoffs to the international community for harvesting in international waters, the big mining operations bailed out. "The bed is in pretty shallow waters, too.

"Tell you what. I'll throw in these, you pay me 1000 US for the shell, and maybe we can do more business in the future."

As they walked away, Nemo counted Leon's share of the cash. "I cut your in for a bigger deal. You point me to a barber shop and a place where I can buy some decent clothes."

...

"No, Saul. I told you not to do that!"

King slapped the big man's hands away from her and examined Brenda's face. The bruise ran down the left side of her face from a cut near her eye down to her jaw. She glared at him.

"Someone called in the police. We'll either have to get rid of her or move her."

"She called me stupid."

"Well, so do I! Now we can't sell her until her face heals up. I had a buyer, now I'll have to cancel."

He locked eyes with his captive. "You know, you're not helping yourself by taunting Saul. It's all your own fault for sticking your nose into other people's business."

He could tell that she was thinking up something particular clever to say, but he didn't have the time.

"Saul, get Woody on the line. I think we'd better use Miss Girl Reporter here to feed the turtles."

. . .

Bathed, beard trimmed to a shorter length, and in a white suit with a matching hat, Nemo walked onto the grounds of VC Bird airport. From Karl's report, this was where Joe the pilot refueled before taking Brenda to the Caymans. It was a long shot, but if he could find out anything about Brenda's plans, it would be some light in a very dark tunnel.

He had the urge to race to rescue her, but without some knowledge it would all be a waste of effort.

The little charter companies had ticket offices and he located the one she took easily.

"Hello, sir." The attendant in her uniform and tilted cap was cheerful and pleasant. Not that she distracted him from Brenda in any way, but today had been a revelation. There were so many pretty girls in the world.

"Hello, I was told a friend of mine was chartered between here and the Caymans by a pilot named Joe."

"That must be Joe Tomlinson. He runs banking charters and ferry runs to many of the smaller islands that don't support long landing strips."

"Banking charters?"

"Oh, yes. Some of our clients are Americans who fly here and to the Caymans to take advantage of our favorable tax laws."

After a long chat, he came away with the impression that Joe was a favorite of a number of businessmen who liked to move cash off shore without necessarily filing all the paperwork that would be required taking a regular commercial airline out of Miami International.

He'd seen the seaplane. It would he handy to pick up a 'businessman' with a suitcase full of undeclared cash and ferry him to a place where a suitcase full of cash was business as usual. He had no solid proof the man was crooked, just a feeling.

A second stop by the shell vendor's shop led to a mention of a couple of names that just might be interested in good quality sea turtle shells. There was a bigger market for the stuff than he had originally been led to believe.

...

"Leon, can you take me on a little boat ride?"

"Yes, sir. How far?"

He changed back into his shorts and packed his new clothes in tightly sealed, collapsed plastic bags and met Leon at the beach.

As they motored out into Fort Bay, Leon looked puzzled as Nemo strapped on his swim fins and prepared his snorkel. "Are you taking your new clothes under water?"

"Right over there. See the buoy flag?"

The boat slowed to a stop. "Sir, how long will you be down?"

"Oh, I'm leaving. Thanks for your assistance. He handed Leon a few bills and then went over the side. From nowhere, he pulled a net out of the water and Leon helped him stuff the clothes bag into the net, and then he and his purchases went out of sight into the water.

Just a moment later, Leon jerked when the buoy slipped below the water as well.

"What is going on?"

He hurriedly dug into the gear that came with the rented boat and strapped on goggles. Leaning far over the edge, he dunked his head, just in time to see a giant devilfish sail silently away.

...

The Manta's new batteries went flat right when he'd expected. It was so nice to have a power system at the peak of its performance.

But right now, he had to keep from tumbling.

With the water pumped out of the ballast tank, the Manta was rising from the dark depths at an uncomfortable pace. He made tiny adjustments to the ailerons to dampen out some instability.

He dared not shift his own position either. Climbing so fast air bubbles were created from nothing in his wake, he had to stay right on the edge of stability. Those vertical fins had been an extra, when he designed the Manta. They distracted from the elegant look of the wing. Certainly the real manta ray had no little fins sprouting from its back. But without them, he'd never be able to climb at this speed.

The darkness was dropping away like a sunrise in fast-forward. He gripped the railing tighter.

Like a whale breaching, the Manta popped through the surface, and even cleared air for a heart-pounding instant, before slapping the surface and skidding along like an unmanned surfboard.

Finally, the slush and sway told him that he'd come to a stop. The windows were still seeing spray splash down.

Nemo dashed to deploy a sea anchor so he could extend the tail.

He was dead in the water until the batteries recharged.

Residual juice was enough to give him a GPS reading. Over two hundred and eighty miles on that last charge. It was still going to be a very slow crossing from the East Caribbean to the West, but he couldn't go any faster.

He's considered all options.

He had no money, and even if he could talk resources out of Frank as he suspected he could, his passport was long gone. Likely he'd dropped totally off the radar—a dead man. He had no visas, no official presence. Other than swimming ashore like he did last time, he'd be lucky if they let him on any of the islands.

But suppose he could cross that legal barrier. Taking an airplane, without the Manta, would mean he was just a homeless traveler. He could never air-ship the Manta without disassembly, it was too wide.

Much the same applied to catching a ride on a ship. The Ocean Ray had a special rig to handle the Manta. That didn't exist any more.

Besides a commercial liner wasn't all that much faster than the Manta.

He smiled.

No, making his own way across let him arrive unannounced, like he did on Antigua. With clothes, he could move around incognito. With the Manta, he could investigate off-shore locations, hoping the Royal Cayman Islands Police Service would do all they could on land.

Like Brenda said, the Manta was his freedom. And he had to have freedom to act.

...

"I should never have let this happen."

"What do you mean?" he asked the editor.

"I sent her into a potential active crime scene, and she'd not a crime reporter. Science and human-interest, that's her job, not dealing directly with people who might pull a gun on her. And I let her go alone."

"Is that usual? A reporter on assignment as an individual?"

He hesitated, "Well, actually yes. I mean, it's not uncommon for a photographer and an investigator to work as a team, but normally, a reporter works alone."

"Karl, if you made Brenda take a bodyguard, she'd freak on you."

He sighed. "I know. It's second guessing. It's an editor's hazard. But she was always right on top of everything, and I fell down on my side of the job. We should have had a solid check-in schedule, and I should have acted the instant she went silent."

"I did have a phone schedule with her, and I got distracted. My fault as much as yours."

The editor didn't let himself wallow more than a couple of minutes. In spite of everything, and Brenda's priority, he had dozens of other tasks demanding his time.

Nemo claimed his charging was done and he had to go.

But some of the details the man revealed were disturbing. The RCIPS were not hopeful they would find her. There were a huge number of people leaving Grand Cayman every day—air liners, cruise ships, private charters and just individual travelers. It was a small island with a large tourist presence.

There were regular missing persons reports, not all of them unplanned. It was a usual story for someone to drop out of sight, and Grand Cayman was nice place to do it.

But there was a hint that there were more women going missing than was usual.

...

A hundred gallons of fish guts came splattering down into the trough, and Brenda immediately stuck her hands to the elbows in it. With wooden paddles, she pushed the stinking, gagging mess down the metal channel, trying to keep the feeding channels from clogging. There were a dozen large tanks filled with all sizes of sea turtles, and she had to do her best to see that all were fed, and none were poisoned by an over abundance.

It was a nightmare sweatshop version of the feeding tanks she'd seen in the official turtle farms. Theirs were bright and sunny, these were dark and dank. Theirs were spacious and had plenty of room to walk about and see all stages of the turtles' development in clean water ponds, she had to wedge herself between the wall and the tanks, with barely room to breathe. Theirs fed the turtles a carefully designed food in tidy dried pellets, Brenda recalled them fondly as she shoveled the fish guts.

The official turtle farm was right next to a lovely restaurant where she'd watched the sunset. Brenda was so hungry the fish guts were tempting. Almost. And she collapsed between feedings on a metal bench.

But there was one advantage. None of the other crew were the least bit interested in feeling her up. They couldn't get close enough without gagging.

She sagged on the bench. The turtles' future was bleak. Grow big enough to harvest for meat or shell in the dark tanks, and then face the knife.

Hers wasn't much better. She'd overheard their plans. When her face healed, they'd rinse her off, paint some cosmetics on her, and put her on a plane to meet her new owner. She suspected she'd be learning a new language soon, if her owner allowed her to talk.

...

Nemo circled Grand Cayman at a respectful distance. Close to shore, the waters were full of scuba divers and snorkelers, and kayakers. And around the Georgetown port, there were even tourist submarines to look out for.

But one thing he had discovered as he recharged off the coast of Jamaica—with an appropriate antenna on the spine, he could pull WiFi signals from the land. It took some hunting to find ones with no password, but he could hover about three feet below the surface with the spine up like a periscope and browse the net.

He pulled detailed maps and identified places Brenda's article mentioned. He'd be retracing her steps.

At least that was the plan.

But the first step was to find a place to hide the Manta close enough so he could get ashore. That was going to be a tough one.

Rounding West End, he saw a southern stingray bury itself in the sand. It was an idea. The problem was to avoid all the enticing dive spots he saw marked on the chart he'd downloaded.

Waiting until dark, he found a particularly dull stretch of sand 'downhill' from the inner bay and settled in. The hull color and the white coral sand weren't too different, but he spent some time shoveling sand all over the wing area. He couldn't risk the snorkel this time, as it was practically identical to a dive buoy and would likely attract others to see what was interesting below.

He swam ashore with nothing but his change of clothes, snorkel, mask and fins. For all the bad things that could be said about his hermit lifestyle, he was an excellent swimmer.

Taking advantage of a tourist shower on a pole, he found a changing booth and was soon walking the road toward the restaurant Brenda had mentioned.

No one thought it odd when a man in a white suit and carrying snorkel gear came in for dinner. His server was friendly, and when he mentioned coming because of the article by Brenda deMay, he found out that he wasn't the only one.

"Is it true that she's gone missing?" asked his waiter.

"So I've heard. The police are looking for her. So is her newspaper. I hope she didn't get caught up in the turtle scandal."

At first the waiter disclaimed any idea that there was a problem with the turtles. But it was after sunset, and the crowd had thinned out considerably. When Nemo appeared to be content to let his prime rib settle until the place closed, the man dropped by again and pulled up a chair.

"You talked like you knew her."

"Oh yes, I do. She's a friend. And she's done me a big favor. I'm looking for her."

"Are you a reporter too?"

"Not a reporter, not a policeman, not anything official. I'm just a friend, seriously worried about her."

The waiter leaned a little closer. "I liked her too, and I'd hate to think she was caught up in anything seedy."

"If you know anything, I'd treat it as a personal favor if you'd tell me."

...

"The Caymans have a good thing going with the sea turtles. We thumb our noses at the endangered species requirements, within our own island.

We grow them like a domestic animal, and turn a large number of them back to the wild. We harvest some—you've seen the braised turtle on our menu. With the local sales and the tourists able to see them at the farm, it's enough to keep it going. It's good for the turtles, it's good for us. It's crazy the rest of the world doesn't get on board and let us export.

"But there are rumors, just rumors, that some drug dealers or someone like that has set up an operation somewhere offshore that traps the turtles we release and harvest them for the shells, outside the export controls we have in place at the harbor and the airport."

He shrugged. "If you have something valuable that's illegal, someone will try to find a way."

"Did you tell this to Brenda?"

He looked uncomfortable. "Maybe. A bit of it." He shrugged. "She's pretty."

"I know."

...

A clue in hand was worth more than a day's walking aimlessly around the island, hunting tips the police had already discovered.

But I'll have to wait until morning. I won't be able to find the Manta in the dark.

He found a secluded spot on the beach where he could hear the waves. He made a pillow of his suit and watched the occasional cloud move past the stars.

It had hurt, every time the waiter mentioned Brenda in the past tense. It was like he knew something even worse, but feared to tell him.

Of course I could just be imagining it.

I lost Sally. I don't want to lose Brenda.

The two women were not much alike. Brenda was a red-haired adventurer, not like gentle dark-haired Sally, always quiet, always ready to retreat behind her clipboard.

He dozed off, dreaming of better times.

...

Gulls and itchy skin woke him. It was already later than he'd planned. The morning sun was a couple of hours high.

He brushed the sand off and took his bundle of clothes down to the water and tied the water-tight bundle around a rock, testing it to make sure it would sink. He'd hate to lose his new clothes because he couldn't pull the bag down with him.

The water was crystal clear, and that certainly was one of the magnets that drew the divers out in droves.

But as he approached the place where he expected to find the Manta, he was worried to find a boat anchored nearby. He took a deep cleansing breath, and went straight down.

There were two divers in tanks circling around the ship. One was brushing sand away from the window to peer inside. He was nearly at the airlock before they saw him.

Not attackers. Just divers.

One of them saw him fumble with his package and moved closer and pulled his regulator from his mouth and offered him air.

Nemo shook his head and did the OK hand sign before he pulled out the little cylinder that worked for him as a key. He fitted it into the hole and opened the airlock outer door.

The friendly one obviously wanted to be invited in, but he had no time. He grabbed his own snorkel line mouthpiece for air as the airlock purged the water.

Inside, the divers watched him through the window as he set down his package and went to the control console.

Tap, tap, tap.

He looked. One was holding a slate board. On it was written NEMO?

He smiled and nodded with a thumbs up. He opened the laptop and typed in huge letters, STAND BACK, TAKING OFF. He showed it to them.

They moved back a few feet. He carefully blew some air into the ballast tanks and the Manta lurched up in a haze of sand. He moved off, banking toward deeper water.

If I thought I could remain secret, this kills it. They've got a story for their buddies now.

It made it even more urgent that he find Brenda fast.

...

An offshore place to collect turtles—that meant somewhere off the West End. If they were still there, they'd probably be far enough from the shoal waters to avoid divers for the same reason—to keep their actions secret.

He began moving in widening arcs. He tried to keep low, so surface boaters wouldn't see him. He also tried to steer wide of divers, but there was no guarantee that they wouldn't notice. The Manta was never designed to be hidden. No camouflage. Brenda had mentioned that.

He didn't really think the small dive boats were likely worth a look, but what *did* constitute a likely place to collect turtles?

He walked over to the book shelf and pulled out one of the marine biology texts.

Sally wrote this. How did I keep myself from thinking about her all the times I read it? The name was plain to see on the cover. She had rejected the idea of putting an author's photo on the cover.

He quickly found the section on sea turtles. She had sections on diet and behavior, and many photos. He'd read it like a robot, how many times? This time he couldn't read the words without hearing her voice.

Setting it down, he went back and turned on the hydrophones and turned up the sensitivity until the system was on the verge of feedback. He adjusted the frequency shift.

Parrot fish were clattering away, eating algae from the coral. Motors from boats rumbled. The cabin was alive with the sounds of the sea.

While cruising five miles out, he heard a metallic thumping, and under it, the clicking of hundreds or thousands of turtle beaks.

...

He crept in slowly, staying deep. It was them, he was sure of it. Secured in three hundred foot waters were a pair of aqua scooters and a large folded net. When the turtles were released to the wild, divers could sweep the area and snag hundreds. This was likely the best turtle netting area in the world.

What do I do now?

He could move off, and call in their location on sat phone.

But could the local police do anything. Was this in their jurisdiction? And what were the chances they had a local contact with the police? Could he risk it?

Even if the police moved, the turtle-nappers likely had some kind of early warning system. They could move off, or dump the turtles well before a ship could arrive.

What are the chances Brenda is aboard?

She couldn't be shut up. If police were coming, her fate was a bullet and a weighted chain over the side.

So, first order of business—find out if she was there.

...

The criminals had divers, but they weren't in the water. If they had some kind of detection system below, he hadn't triggered it.

He drifted higher. He cranked the hydrophone system up higher, listening for any other sounds among the turtles.

There were footsteps, even the sounds that had to be voices, but muffled and distorted by the system, he couldn't make out any words.

What if I put a microphone directly in contact with the hull?

It would be risky.

He moved gently under the hull of the ship. He went outside and attached a fishing line between their anchor chain and the Manta. He could snap it easily if he had to make a dash for it, but it would keep the Manta from drifting away.

He found a diver's headset gathering dust in the closet—a project he'd been working on for Sally years ago. With a hydrophone microphone, he had a system he could use manually.

He drifted to the hull and like a doctor with a stethoscope, he listened. He moved a few feet and listened again.

Near the waterline he heard men talking, mostly English, but with a heavy island patois. They were talking food, and cards. He listened as well as he could.

It took him a moment to realize one of them had mentioned 'da stinky girl' and her scar. His heartbeat was so loud the hydrophone was picking it up.

In a little bit, he was sure she was on board. Now, how to find her.

With a little more guessing and a little more listening, he identified the hold where they said she was hiding and feeding the turtles.

There was a shifting noise. Someone was moving.

Brenda is right on the other side of this metal.

His heart pounded.

...

She'd tried to make a pet of one of the turtles, one with a bite out of his foot, but they churned so much in the tank that she only saw him for a moment and then he was gone.

She sighed and plopped back down on her bench. She'd need to refresh their water in another twenty minutes or so. She was surprised they'd survived as long as they had without her. She guessed her arrival had relieved one of the goons of the babysitting task.

Tap, tap.

She frowned. That sounded close. What could it be? The anchor chain?

She listened.

Tap.

Tap tap.

Tap tap tap.

That was no random noise. Someone was tapping. She moved her head. It was louder. She stepped a few paces down the walkway and listened, but it was much softer. It had to be just outside.

Hesitantly, she went back to the place it was loudest and tapped 'shave and a hair cut'. A couple of seconds later, the person outside repeated it.

A person, outside. One of their divers?

I tiny voice in her head screamed that it was Nemo, but she couldn't let her believe it. He was over a thousand miles away, near Antigua. What would he be doing here?

Chasing me?

Has he come to rescue me?

If so, how?

"Nemo," she said.

Tap, tap, tap, tap.

He would have his hydrophone thingy. Wouldn't he? Could he actually hear her through the hull?

"Okay. One tap for yes. Two for no. Is this Nemo?"

Tap.

She gripped the railing as all the strength drained out of her.

"Are you come to rescue me?"

Tap.

"How?"

There was no response.

"Do you have a plan?"

Tap tap.

She swallowed as tears threatened to overcome her, just from the idea that he was out there for her. Romantic Nemo, king of the sea, was one of those ideas she had to force out of her head. It was plain she'd gotten herself trapped so far from hope of rescue that she had to face facts. Drown in the tank with her turtles or allow herself to be carted off a life she dare not dwell on.

But she was a survivor. She'd considered escape. She'd made plans. Unfortunately none of them had a chance of working.

Not until now.

"Nemo, don't think of coming on board. There are about five men with guns."

Tap.

"If I can get to the deck, I could jump into the water. Could you rescue me then?"

Tap.

They had locked her down here, but they told her not to even think of trying to escape. They were far from land, far from any other boat. She'd drown, if the sharks didn't get her first.

She had to make them leave the hatch unlocked. The latch was simple, but the handle was on the other side. It moved a metal tab to grip the edge of the portal.

Can I wedge it? She circled her limited domain. There was a pair of work gloves.

If they were distracted...

She went back to the Nemo spot.

"Are you there?"

Tap.

"Can you make some kind of distraction? And I don't mean one that gets them shooting at you!"

There was a long delay. He was thinking. Then came, Tap.

"Good. How quickly can you put it into action?"

Tap Tap Tap

"Sorry. Is it greater than one hour?"

Tap.

"Two hours?"

Tap Tap.

"Okay, come tapping when you're ready."

...

He swam back away from the hull. It had taken nearly the full two hours to get everything set up, and he was sick to his stomach. It was complex, and depended far too much on the turtle poachers making mistakes.

But they had to be nervous, this close to shore.

Now he had to wait, counting in his head, while Brenda did her part.

...

"Help!" she shouted, banging on the locked hatch. "Help! I'm drowning."

There was no response, she banged harder, until her hands were bloody.

The hatch gears moved.

"What's going on!"

She screamed, clearly in panic. "The fill valve is stuck. The hold is filling with water! I'm trapped."

He swore and came down the hatch, knocking her aside. "Get of the way!"

He pushed by her, nose wrinkled at the smell. He found the water valve, and it was indeed stuck. Sea water was pouring in and the turtle tanks were sloshing over their sides. Some were moving around on the deck.

He put his weight behind the valve, and with a twist, it released, as a scrap of cloth caught in the mechanism came loose.

"Get this cleaned up. And get all those turtles back in their tanks." He struck her on the side of the head and she fell to the ground.

He was half way up the ladder when he heard a huge bang, metal on metal, as if something had rammed the ship.

Voices cried out in the distance. He was out and slammed the hatch shut. He gave the wheel a tug, but he was so distracted he didn't notice that it hadn't spun.

Brenda saw the gears grip the jammed glove, and then release.

It worked.

Her head still rang from the blow she'd received, but there was no time for babying herself. She edged the hatchway open an inch. There was no one in the corridor. Hopefully they were all outside looking to see what had caused the impact.

She just hoped they were all on the starboard side as planned. She raced out the port side.

"Hey! The girl's making a run for it."

Brenda had played this scene in her mind a dozen times. If there was a quick shot on deck, she'd crumple at the railing and never see Nemo, or anyone again.

She banged her knee on the railing, but it was just spice for the adrenaline in her blood.

Bang! There was a shot, but it missed.

And then she was over the side.

Splash!

The man with the gun looked over the railing. He couldn't see her.

"The sharks'll finish her."

He waved his arm in a circle up to the man in the pilot house. "Let's get out of here." Something was going on, and he didn't like the smell of it.

The anchor chain rumbled to life.

...

She looked dazed. Nemo grabbed her and jammed a regulator in her mouth. She gripped it and breathed hungrily.

She's bleeding! A cloud of red surrounded her and he couldn't see where the wound was.

He looked around. He had seen sharks, big ones, in the area as he made his preparations. Blood in the water would call them.

He pulled her along, swimming as hard as he could.

Brenda's eyes widened and she fought him for an instant. Then he saw, there was a shark coming.

He said, "Blood!" in a splash of bubbles before he took the regulator back to get a breath for himself.

Brenda ripped her blouse wide open. Buttons drifted down.

What?

She stripped it off, and he saw it. The blood was coming from the fabric.

He helped. Jeans, underwear, everything, they left it staining the water red as they swam quickly to the airlock.

A swimming set of teeth tore into the clothes, shaking them, frustrated.

Another shark came to join the party, but they were inside.

They collapsed on the deck when the airlock was clear. He had left towels out for her. She clutched them to her.

"Just stay put. I need to get us clear."

He snapped the fishing line and banked the Manta clear of the ship, and the collection of sharks swirling below it.

"They'll get away," she said.

"No they won't."

The anchor chain was rumbling. Down below, tied to the chain were the poacher's fishing net and his own airdrop parachute, both filled with a collection of rocks and shells and sand, and even the remaining aqua scooter he hadn't used to ram the ship's hull with. Slowly, it was all being hauled up into the propellers. By the time the anchor rose, with bottom silt and sand still washing free of it, the net snapped.

There was a rumble in the water and the propellers started to turn, wrapping the parachute and net and debris tightly around the shaft, jamming it so tight the propeller couldn't move.

"Let's get some distance. They could still send down divers."

Brenda smiled, staring at the swirling sharks. "Let them."

...

They surfaced, far enough to be out of gunshot range. He handed her the sat phone and the list of numbers.

"This is the Royal Cayman Islands Police Service. How may I help you?"

"This is Brenda deMay. I have just escaped the turtle poachers who have kidnapped me. Their ship is disabled at..."

She gave the GPS co-ordinates and told them to hurry.

Explanations could wait.

She handed back the phone. "Can we get back closer?"

"Why?"

"They know they're trapped. As soon as they get word from their spy in the police department, they'll dump all the turtles—try to get rid of the evidence."

He took them down and she was right. Turtles were being tossed by the bucketful overboard into the shark infested waters. Some were instantly gobbled up, but there were so many, fleeing in all directions, that most were escaping.

Nemo frowned. "I wish you had a camera."

She looked up. "We do have a camera."

He looked puzzled, "We do?"

She grabbed the laptop and fired up a program. A tiny light appeared above the screen, and she was staring at her bruised and damaged face.

She shifted her position, and the towels draping over her shoulder to look reasonably decent, and then clicked the record button.

"This is Brenda deMay reporting. I have just escaped a crew of sea-going poachers that have been collecting and killing the endangered sea turtle. Just moments ago, they realized that their ship has been disabled and have begun dumping the turtles as the Cayman Islands police race to my rescue."

She turned the laptop around so the built-in webcam could pick up the carnage. Letting the camera run for several minutes, there were some dramatic shots—some of the sharks crunching the turtles in their teeth. Many of turtles swam close to the Manta in their race to escape.

Finally, she turned it off.

"I can't watch this any more."

"I'll move us away again."

As they started to move, there were bullets zipping into the water. A couple even got close enough to bounce off the hull, but by the time they reached that depth, the shells had spent their energy.

"Is turtle poaching even illegal here?"

She nodded. "Yep. Fines, imprisonment, the whole thing. Besides, I claimed kidnapping. That should get a response even if there is some problem with the turtles."

He put his hand on her shoulder. "When I Karl and I were tracking you down..."

"You were working with Karl?"

"Yes. Neither of us knew you were missing for several days, until I called your office. He though you'd come to visit me."

She frowned. "I guess I'd better put in a call to him as well, before he fires me."

...

She made the call. He was greatly relieved to hear from her.

"I'll be sending video, once we get network. And Karl, although I will be taking a break, don't you dare give my job away to someone else."

Nemo put the Manta on a slow autopilot course for Grand Cayman as soon as the shooting between the police and the poachers was captured on the laptop video. The poacher's ship would have to be towed to harbor.

"Lie down on the couch."

"Oh?"

"Just do it."

He checked her out from toenails to split ends. He had no bandages other than what he made himself, but he got her various wounds cleaned and sacrificed the edge of one of the blankets to bind the worst of them. The bruises would have to heal by themselves.

"This is just to get me naked."

"Hmm. Stay put." He dabbed at the cut by her eye. "Without cosmetic surgery, this will definitely scar."

"Maybe I'll leave it. Make me fierce."

He asked, "Do you want to be fierce?"

"I..." she paused, and tears started flowing. "I was so scared."

He held her tight. "Do we have to go back to the land yet? I could just coast out here and take care of you."

...

He made a call. He explained the situation.

"She's been traumatized—kidnapped, beat up, threatened with rape, trapped in a dark hold, with people who would kill her without a thought. She's perfectly willing to give a statement and by trial date, she'll be ready to spit in the eye of a dragon, but right now, she needs to stay with me, calm and protected.

"I can't come ashore—I'm a US citizen, but my passport is in the bottom of the sea off Antigua. If we could arrange to meet a boat..."

. . .

It was a spectacle. The Manta coasted to a stop in the shallow waters dubbed 'Stingray City' where dozens of tourist boats were already there so that people could swim with the stingrays.

The Manta was like the creatures' giant-sized brother, almost too big for waters.

Brenda, dressed in Nemo's old clothes, while he wore his white suit, stepped out on the wing as a RCIPS officer in uniform stepped over from her boat to join them. Nemo apologized for the lack of chairs, but they got down to business. Brenda made her statement before the police camera and signed papers. With thumb drives, they made copies of the videos and swore oaths they were true copies.

By the time the police were done, the TV crew from channel 27 appeared.

Brenda and Nemo were both star attractions, and he was glad to be able to say, "Enough" after a few brief statements. The cameras followed them inside and kept rolling as the Manta slipped away.

. . .

"Where are we going?" she asked, as she changed out of his clothes and into the lacy nightgown he had kept ready for her.

"I thought Miami? Although we could go by way of China if you wish."

"Jacksonville. Definitely Jacksonville. You need to have a serious talk with Frank Hancock, and I need to be there to make sure he doesn't take advantage of you."

She described the situation, and although he was willing to let it ride, she insisted.

"You need me to take care of you."

"I thought you wanted to get back to your job."

She stretched out, with her head in his lap. He straightened her curls.

"Well both, actually. I'll be all over the Caribbean, and so will you. We work well together. I can help you and you can help me.

"I want us together. Maybe not every day, but why can't we be partners and lovers and friends?"

He smiled. "You know, there's a word for that. There's even a ceremony that goes with it."

She felt a wave of confusion and panic. He stroked her good cheek and held her hand.

He pressed his case. "It won't be traditional. Neither of us could fit into that lifestyle. You can keep your professional name, and I'll probably do the same."

"Nemo?"

"Yeah. I've gotten used to it."

"You know they've named your volcano Nemo's Seamount on the charts?"

"No, really?"

"What else could they call it?"

She put her hand to her bruised face. "You know I'm a mess. Are you really sure you want marriage?"

"You know my history. Do you think I could settle for anything less? I'd love it."

He kissed both cheeks. "I love you, Brenda, Girl Reporter."

"And I love you, Captain Nemo."

A long while later, she asked, "How long will it take to get to Jacksonville?"

"Several days. It's over a thousand miles. We have to go around Cuba and then up the Florida coast."

"We could stop by Key West and visit a county clerk, couldn't we?"

"Yes, we could."

"Any way we could make the Manta go faster."

He chuckled, "Yes. How do you feel about roller coaster rides?"

"Life with you is a roller coaster, Nemo. Let's go!"

Turkey Dinner

I wrote this piece of whimsy before the giant feral hogs became the local monsters here in Central Texas. Maybe the vacuum is getting the last say after all.

"Evolution is like a turkey dinner," said Bud with satisfaction, nudging his buddy with the butt of his rifle.

"Huh?" asked Jeb.

"How long has Mark been? I'm not going to haul this thing all the way back to the break in the fence without the pickup."

"Okay," Jeb sighed, "tell me this great insight of yours." He leaned back against the still warm 600 pound feathered bulk of their night's work.

Bud patted his prize, "You've got to admit we have evolution-in-action working here. This jumbo turkey and his brothers never existed before. And it's because all the ingredients came together, just like a turkey dinner.

"Forget all that millions-of-years noise you got in school. Look at the charts in the encyclopedia sometime. The dinosaurs died off, and overnight, there were a million mammals. It was the vacuum that did it. The land has room for only so many big herbivores, only so many big carnivores. Kill off those and new ones *have* to pop up.

"Now look at what we did. Humans are the top of the food chain! We spent thousands of years killing off the big shag-nasties. There used to be woolly mammoths, saber-toothed tigers, and giant cave-bears roaming these hills. Once we made them into barbecue, and hat-racks and nice winter coats for the Missus, the place was empty. The vacuum started calling out for big critters.

Jeb shook his head. "Okay. If you say so. I just wish Mark was back. We are breaking some kind of law being here in the refuge. But you could be right."

"I know I'm right... " Bud looked up at the sound of a tree branch breaking in the distance. "Did you hear that? Mark must be coming down the ravine."

The two of them got to their feet and looked expectantly in the direction of the noise. The branches shook and parted with a squeal as the head poked into the clearing. Bird eyes the size of cantaloupes looked at the two men with a quizzical stare, first from one side of the massive beak, and then the other.

Jeb poked Bud with his rifle. Bud seemed frozen as the head started rising, breaking free of the low trees until it towered thirty feet over them. *Meleagris Rex* watched as the two former top predators started running. "Gobble-gobble" it rumbled as it started after them.

Milemarkers

I'm not going to try to explain this story. Read it—it's short. The idea came in a flash as I was driving through Monterrey County in California and saw the MON on the milemarker beside the road.

DAN

Black arrows on the yellow warning signs shook Dan from his driver's daze. He downshifted the Jeep with practiced ease, bringing him into the zone, edging the yellow stripe through the curve. A white mile marker flickered by, the text a blur.

He had been driving five years now, and it seemed as if he had been doing it his whole life. The Jeep seemed perfect for him—fast enough on the highway, but when the mountains called, there was always four-wheel-low and high clearance to get him through.

He glanced at the girl beside him—still not used to having Julie riding shotgun. She returned his grin, her black close-cropped hair whipping in the breeze.

There! Another mile marker. He frowned. It was hard to read them. Someone had put a lot of information on the small sign, no more than six inches wide. *Did that say Monday?* He shrugged.

Dan was ready for the next one. *Friday - April 7 1989.* He nodded. He was making good time.

There was a sweet scent in the air, and the trees were decked out in white blossoms, but that passed quickly. He started to make a comment to Julie, but she was asleep, her long black hair tied back in a bun.

Wednesday - October 16 1996. He was getting better at reading them, now that he knew the format. The trees were brilliant in fall foliage, as the road passed through a protected valley. He rolled down the window on the Chevy pickup, to catch a whiff of the crisp cool air. In the rear view mirror, he could see a low slung Corvette advancing rapidly. The two-lane blacktop had far too many curves for easy passing, so he accelerated a little. By the time *Saturday - February 2 2002* flickered off the side of the road, the guy behind him pushed his luck and passed on a blind curve. Luck was with him.

"Idiot," Julie muttered. He saw from the way she shook her blond hair that Mr. Sports Car was now in her Little Black Book of Permanent Grudges. He had made up that name as a joke, but he wouldn't be surprised if she hadn't gone out and bought one.

When Dan crested the summit pass, and their Volvo passed the sign declaring *Tuesday - June 28 2011,* he absently reached for the gear shift that was no longer there. *Old habits die slowly* he thought, but the Volvo was smart enough to shift gears anyway.

"What is it?" Juliana asked.

He gave her a shake of the head. "Nothing. Just thinking of old times."

She made no comment, sitting upright, her pinstriped suit and careful makeup making an impressive picture. These days he didn't know whether her silence was the same as disapproval or not.

He turned his mind back to the road. Out of the valley now, the road divided and he could inform the Suprim's cruise control to pay attention to the guide strip. Three higher powered cruisers whipped past in the fast lane, tired of riding behind him on the narrow road.

He didn't mind. The speed limit was fine with him.

Up ahead, he saw another mile marker, and watched until it came into focus–*Monday - September 8 2025.*

Still making plenty good time.

Juliana was staring straight ahead. He would have called it a glare, but he knew it was just her natural expression. When the gray started in her hair, she had gone with a streaked look, and it gave her the appearance of an hawk on the lookout for an unwary rabbit.

"Can't you go any faster? That was the Jacobsons who passed us."

He put more pressure on the accelerator. "I don't think we need to get there any sooner." He felt her response rather than heard it. She would never be happy unless they were doing the passing.

A Lexus Grande swept past so fast he hadn't realized it was approaching. Juliana was silent again.

He gave their Lexus more power, but there was nothing he could do. They were already well over the speed limit and still the slowest car on the road.

Saturday - January 29 2033.

Dan gritted his teeth, and tried to ignore the ache in his back. *We are still going too fast. I don't know why we have to get there in a hurry.*

Another mile marker flickered by, and for the first time in a while, it blurred past too fast to read. He let off some speed.

"What are you doing?"

"Slowing down."

"You idiot, we can't do that."

He turned to her, noting that the hunch in her back was getting worse. With her hair gone gray and wiry, she looked like a crone.

There was a honk from behind, and a blink of headlights. Even with two lanes, he was becoming an obstruction to traffic.

Sunday - May 13 2040. The cars in the fast lane were whipping by bunching up the ones behind, making it impossible for them to pass him.

I'll have to speed back up. But he didn't want to. *Where am I going anyway? Why am I driving?* He blinked his eyes shut for a long second—anything to get a moment's peace to think.

Another sign appeared, off to the left in the center lane. It was a crossover. *Authorized vehicles only.*

A flicker of motion in the rearview mirror. He took a breath, gritted his teeth, held the horn down, and with a shriek of rubber on the road, jumped across the fast lane and skidded sideways onto the gravel crossover lane.

"Daniel! What are you doing?"

"Going back!" He struggled to turn the massive vehicle onto the opposite lane. With a sigh of relief that the lane was empty, he pulled out and gained speed.

"Stop it this instant, Mister! This is illegal, and we are going the wrong way!"

Dan ignored her, as he ignored the chorus of honks from the vehicles he had barely missed. At least those were receding into the distance.

"Juliana, bear with me. This is something I have to do."

She was glowing with rage. She slapped at his arm. "Stop this. Stop at once!"

"No." Dan kept his eyes on the road. He put the accelerator all the way to the floor. There was no traffic, and with two lanes he could flatten the curves.

Opposite the divider, there was an endless stream of cars. They flickered as day and night passed several times a second.

How fast am I going? The speedometer was stuck, trying to read a negative speed and failing. He looked for mile markers. Strangely, there were none on this side of the highway. He could see them pass on the other side, but he couldn't make them out in the rear view mirror.

Oh well, I know the road.

"Now you've done it!" Juliana declared. He saw she was back in her pinstripes. It was good to see her sitting straight again. The pain in his back had vanished as well.

"What do you mean?"

She looked behind them. "The cops are after you."

He saw that she was right. Far back in the distance, a familiar flickering light was following them.

Whether it was the illegal crossover, or their speed, or even just going back the wrong way on the highway, Dan knew that if they caught him, he would be in serious trouble.

Up ahead, he could see the merge signs as the road narrowed to a two-lane highway again. He could still make good speed on the twisty lanes, but he would have to be careful. He let off the accelerator and whipped by the speed warnings and curve signs.

The first curve almost took him as the car shifted from the Suprim to the Volvo and he wasn't prepared for the weight change.

"Let me out!"

"I can't. The cops are still coming."

"More the reason not to be here in this car with you when they catch you."

The blinking lights were gaining on him fast. He couldn't maintain speed on these curves. He looked at Julie carefully, taking in the length of her black hair and the style of her clothes.

It was the expression on her face that gave him the clue where they were on the road. It was concerned, angry but not hateful.

"Hang on." She gripped the safety handle.

He remembered bridge on the way up and sure enough over the next rise, he saw it. He braked heavily and rumbled off the shoulder into the grass. The pickup bounced over the rough terrain, but he jerked it around out of sight of the road.

Seconds later, he could see the reflection of the cop's lights on the trees as it passed with a whoosh, and the eerie shriek of its siren.

The door slammed shut. Julie was out.

"Julie! Come back here."

"Not on your life, Dan. You've gone crazy. I'm not going to go down with you."

There was a tightness in his chest, along with the racing of his heartbeat.

"Julie, you have to stay with me." It was a simple statement of fact, an emotional truth.

"No." He could hear the pain in her words. "You have to go, now! They will be back for you. You will have to get off the road."

He still sat paralyzed.

Quietly, she repeated, "Dan, you have to go now." And then she was gone, clambering up the rocks and out of sight.

What did I do? Why is she leaving? The memories up the road were rapidly becoming indistinct.

Dan couldn't take it in, but his hand moved on the gear shift and he backed the pickup around and back on the road. He glanced at the traffic moving on the far lane, but the determination to go the other way remained. He pulled into the vacant lane.

The police car had gone ahead of him, but Julie was right, it would turn back for him soon. He had to backtrack on the highway as fast as he could before there was the glimmer of cop-lights coming his way.

He felt the gear shift morph back to the old Jeep's knob in his hand. The wind whipped at his face, smearing and drying the tears.

"You have to get off the road." Julie was right, and he had a vague memory of where to go.

The two-lane highway passed an old dirt road, and he almost missed it. He smoked to a stop, in the middle of the lane, catching the sight of the passing travelers gawking at him. He backed up the two hundred yards and turned through a gap in the traffic.

The rutted lane turned quickly uphill. He paused long enough to shift to four-speed-low and kept on as the road became little more than a trail.

The siren echoed across the mountain. He killed the engine and watched from an overlook as three police cars passed by. The first one hadn't turned. It just called for reinforcements.

He sat on the rock, taking a moment to breathe and to think.

They would not give up the chase. No one was allowed to cross over. He would have to give up the road altogether. He ached inside—feeling a loss, although he couldn't put a name to it. Fear was driving him now.

He walked back to the Jeep and scavenged an old backpack that he tossed into the back seat the day he had started driving. He turned the steering wheel to the side and with a great reluctance, he released the hand brake and slipped the gearshift into neutral.

It gained speed, rolling back and off the trail, crashing noisily into the trees. Satisfied it was out of sight, he slipped on the backpack and set off across the ridge line, leaving even the trail behind.

JULIE

The trail turned uphill again, the "M" blazed in the bark of the tree leading her on. Julie cupped water from the mountain stream and drank before picking up her walking stick and moving on. She could feel her hair dragging across the back of her neck. It had been too long since she had last cropped it back.

An eagle shrieked across the mountain valley, and a sudden movement caught her eye. Off in the distance, far up the pass where her trail led, she could see someone move quickly across the ridge. *Who is that?*

Her heartbeat picked up. The trail she was following was a lonely one. What were the chances she would meet someone up here, so far from the main road?

She leaned into her walking stick. The stranger had been moving fast—could she catch up?

A "T" marked ancient gnarled juniper, pointing the way past the pass, but she paused and looked back up where the trees thinned out near the peak. There was definitely a trail there, well worn among the rocks, circling the peak like a dusty halo. She couldn't tell where it went, but it appeared flat on this side.

She grit her teeth, and stepped off her trail.

Stepping from rock to rock, occasionally feeling the mush of high altitude tundra, she approached the spot where she had seen the other hiker.

Footprints, man-sized in the dust. Lots of them. It looked like a hundred men, all wearing the same size and style of shoe had passed this way.

She looked off to the west, in the direction the toes pointed. Something was definitely wrong here. *Where are the trail markers?* Her own route just a few hundred feet down the hill called to her. Could she dare follow this rut? Was it that important to see another person?

A noise snapped her around. Back the other way, just coming around a bend in the trail, another man approached.

He looks the same. At least the jacket was the same color. Maybe he had just looped the peak.

"Hello!" she called.

He paused in his steps, just now noticing her in his path. "Hi." He closed the distance, a smile on his face.

Julie couldn't help smiling back. Other than the beard, she thought he looked good.

"My name is Dan." He held out a hand and she shook it.

"Julie. I didn't expect to see anyone out here."

He nodded. "Me neither. I've never seen another soul on these ridges."

She pointed down hill. "My trail goes that way. Where are your markers? I can't see any."

He looked puzzled. "Markers? I just follow the footprints."

Julie knew that was wrong. "How long have you been here?"

"How long?" The glaze in Dan's eyes told her the answer before he said, "I dunno. Forever I guess."

The dusty trail, with endlessly repeating footprints unnerved her. "Come with me. My trail is marked."

He followed, trusting her, even as he had a hard time stepping outside the boundaries of the dusty path. He stumbled on the rocks, and she had to help him maintain his balance on the uneven terrain at first.

She spotted the "T" with relief, afraid that it might have vanished. He noticed it too and pointed it out, to her relief. He wasn't stupid—just dulled by being caught in an endless loop.

They passed "W" and "Th" before he pointed out the Jeep.

"Hey, look at this." He ran over and examined the vehicle caught among a cluster of pines.

Dan cautiously wedged his way though the door, and after a labored crank, and a cloud of black smoke sputtering out the tail pipe, the engine finally started.

"Stand back."

Dan shifted the gears and tried to move it. The rear tires smoked on the rocks. He shifted into four wheel drive, and with a squeal of rubber, he edged cautiously out of its trap.

"Get in. I can make out an old trail here. It heads down. I bet it joins the highway before too long." He tossed his backpack into the back seat. "I've always wanted a Jeep."

Julie was amazed at the find. It would be nice to get back to civilization, and it would be pleasant to ride along with Dan for a while.

She reached for the door latch and sat down on the cushioned chair. Dan closed his door and revved the engine.

Julie shouted, "Wait!"

"What?"

She was shaking her head. "I can't do this."

"What do you mean?"

"Something is wrong here." With a turn, she was out on her feet again. Her arms were shaking. Less than a memory, it was a conviction that driving off would cost her soul. "I feel... *twisted* in there."

Dan shook his head. "There is nothing wrong with a car. Millions of people drive them every day. Do you want to drive? I'll let you drive."

"It's not that. I can't go that way. I don't know why, but I can't." She pointed over to the footpath. "That's the way I must go."

Dan sat there, his foot on the pedal, hands on the wheel. The Jeep was his dream car. The road ahead was clear.

Julie stepped back, and turned toward her trail. A feeling of wrongness lanced through his chest. A whisper—*not this time*—echoed in his head.

"Hey, wait up." He turned off the key, pulled the hand brake, and grabbed his backpack. "We'd better stick together."

It's a Wonderful Morning

In the old days when I commuted thirty miles to work every day, I passed through Manor Texas and those water towers stretched high, reaching for the sky.

When the water pressure dropped to nothing in the middle of his shower, it set the course of the whole day. Ken Leighton, held his breath, and when the water started coming slowly back up to pressure, he let out his breath in a noisy sigh. He stood motionless until the suds from his shampoo started dripping down into his eyes. Rinsing off quickly, he psyched himself up for a day to remember.

He glanced in the bedroom for Ruth, then headed down to the kitchen.

At least the kids were where he expected them to be. Billy was already on the computer, hiding the screen when he walked by. Molly was finishing her hair and applying more make-up than he liked to see.

"Would the younger generation come here for a moment," he called. Molly stuck her head out of the bathroom and waved. Billy was almost a minute before he appeared, it probably took that long to close his game.

"Do any of you know where your mother is?"

Billy shook his head. Molly frowned in thought, and said, "Maybe out in the garden. She was talking about grasshoppers eating the roses."

He nodded. "Okay, good enough. But the real reason I called you two was that I am feeling very good this morning, and I want you two to play hooky from school."

There were two open mouths, staring at him. Molly glanced at the old pendulum clock over the fireplace. He hoped he wouldn't have any problems with her.

He turned to his son, "Billy, I think you should hit the cable modem and see how many points you can rack up blasting your Commander buddies."

The boy still looked frozen, but he said, "It's a school day."

"And you don't think there will be anyone on the Net, is that it?"

"Well no... Are you okay?"

"Fine. It's a wonderful morning. You would really rather go take that math test of yours?"

"No!"

"Then get at it. The Internet is waiting."

Billy shelved the question of his father's sanity and turned towards the computer. He walked quickstep, as if running would break the spell.

"Molly." His daughter was waiting for some clue as to what was going on. He tried to keep his own face calm, although his insides threatened to bubble up into his voice at a moments notice. "I think you should take advantage of the time zone difference and rack up some long distance charges with that friend you made last summer on your Student Ambassador trip."

"Jean Louis?"

He nodded. "Yes, that boy in Leon, France."

Her face paled, and then she straightened. She set her hair-brush on the table and turned toward her room. He was proud of her.

"And Molly?" She looked back. "Keep an eye on Billy. Make sure he stays on the computer. Playing Commander."

She nodded.

Ruth was indeed working with her roses. She glanced up at his approach, and read his expression from years of practice. She set down her tools. "Problem?"

"The water pressure dropped. I'm keeping the kids home from school today. And I suspect that you will get a call from the Band Boosters about fund raising."

She nodded gravely, "I think you are probably right." She started peeling off her gardening gloves, letting them drop to the ground. "You are still going to work as usual?"

He nodded. "Somebody has to drive the car pool."

"Be careful. The traffic can be murder."

He gave her a kiss. "Don't I know it."

...

He edged the large SUV out of the driveway. It was so huge he got a few comments about it from the people at the office. He just smiled and repeated his story about how great the Surburbanator was for long vacation trips with the kids, and how he really didn't mind the gas consumption.

It also made a great commuting vehicle, now that he had Perry and Hugh to ride in a car pool with him the thirty miles to the plant.

He picked up Hugh first, and they rode together in the front seat without much chit-chat. They arrived soon enough at the Blackhawk housing development where Perry lived next to the twelfth hole.

"Hey, Perry. Lose any more windows?" Hugh asked, as Perry slid into the rear.

"Seatbelt," Ken reminded, as he always did. It was one of his unwavering rules.

Perry clicked into place. "No, not since you clued me in on that armored glass. I still get startled out of my chair by the noise, but at least no more glass to sweep up."

"Your own fault for living in a golf course. Did you call Foreman?"

"No, " Perry admitted, wiping a perpetual sweat from his forehead, "I haven't had the time."

"You can't play without clubs, and Larry will fix you up with a set."

There was silence for a while, as Ken drove the back roads towards the plant. The roads were bumpy. The county hadn't gotten all of the roads repaired from the spring flooding. For the past few years, the climate seemed to alternate between floods and drought, and rural two lane blacktop's seemed to be the prime victims.

But the back route was at least as fast as the interstate, and there was a lot less traffic.

Just outside of Manor, with the town's new single-pillar white water tower on the horizon, emblazoned with the galloping mustang emblem of the local high school, Perry asked, "Hey, did either of you guys notice a water pressure problem this morning?"

Ken and Hugh exchanged a quick, grim, look. Ken replied, lightly, "Yep. It caught me in the shower and I was afraid I was going to have to towel the shampoo off my head. Luckily, it came back on."

"Strange."

"No, not really," Hugh commented. "Utilities out in the country are a lot more likely to go out. Perils of rural living."

Perry nodded, satisfied.

...

They were past Manor, near the Decker power plant dam, when the car shuddered.

"Uh, oh." Was all Ken said when the engine died. He had to concentrate on guiding the heavy vehicle safely to the side of the road with no help from power steering.

Perry had leaned over to stare up at the sky. "Can we get the window open?"

Hugh shook his head. "Power windows." He followed Perry's gaze, and saw it.

There was a second sun in the sky, a little bright ball rivaling the sun, but fading rapidly in brightness.

Ken asked, "What is that?" He slowed, finally, to a stop.

"A hydrogen bomb, I would guess," said Hugh. "First step in an attack. A high altitude blast to knock out all the enemy's electronics with an electromagnetic pulse before the real attack happens."

Perry asked, "You don't think it is the terrorists do you?"

Ken pulled the key out of the ignition and inserted it into a special switch on the console, marked as a way to disable the passenger-side air-bags when small children were riding in the front seat. He turned it. The whir of the air-conditioning came back on, as well as the dashboard instruments.

Perry struggled with his seat belt. "Hey, this thing won't unlatch."

Hugh spoke calmly. "Now don't be silly Perry. You know it wasn't the terrorists. It was your attack. Your people have started the invasion."

Perry's face went blank, literally unreadable. He strained frantically at the seatbelt. Hugh nodded to Ken, and he touched a switch on the air-conditioner. White fumes flooded out of the vents, and the air reeked of acetone.

Ken's nose wrinkled up at the smell, but Perry acted like he was kicked by a mule. Hugh unclicked his seatbelt and climbed over the top of the seats, one hand holding a hypodermic.

There was no struggle. Once the drug took effect, Ken opened the windows to get rid of the acetone vapors.

He pressed another switch on the console.

"Molly?"

"Yes Daddy."

"Are the international circuits still up?"

"Yes, there was a glitch right when the bomb went off, but the hardened lines work fine."

"Good. We have our captive. Do you have the numbers?"

"Under lock and key in my diary."

"Fine. Send our report to Interpol HQ."

"Will do." She clicked off.

Ken pulled back onto the road. Perry was groggy, but he managed to ask, "What's going on?"

Ken glanced back at the work Hugh was doing, re-positioning the other seatbelts into a rather tidy web of restraints holding Perry in place. The contents of his pockets were dumped onto the center console, but nothing looked more lethal than a roll of antacids.

"Calm down Perry. There is nothing more that you can do. The invasion force from Beta Centauri 4 has attacked. You, as an enemy alien, have been arrested by the Earth Defense Force. When this is all over, you will probably be traded back to your people, so relax and enjoy the scenery. You won't be seeing much more Earth countryside after today."

"You knew?"

Hugh laughed. "Perry, your people watch too much TV. Earth has known about the coming invasion since the Eisenhower administration. Did you think we wouldn't be ready?"

Perry was having trouble holding himself upright. Muscle relaxants were keeping him more immobile than the straps. The Beta Centauri customized truth serum was having its effect as well. He started blubbering.

"I don't believe it. We have agents, all over the place. We would have known."

Hugh said, "We know about your agents, all 200,000 of them. All with good buddies ready to take care of them, just like we are taking care of you."

The car radio clicked on. It was Ruth. "Ken, are you okay?"

"We are just fine. Just like clockwork."

"Molly called in with confirmation on your report. Local agent captures are already in the high ninety percents."

"Good to hear it. Anything you want to say to Perry?"

"No."

Ken got a shiver from the tone of her voice. Mothers were the most deadly creatures on the planet when their blood was up.

Then, there were other voices in the background.

Ruth asked, "Ken, what is your location? The primary GPS transponders haven't recovered from the EMP." Her voice was all business. Hutto Band Boosters were the primary dispatchers for the area north of Austin proper.

"Half way to Manor from the dam."

"We just got a no-report from one of the Pflugerville teams. They haven't activated the main comm link."

"Gueeseet. He got away." Perry offered, with a giggle.

Ken pulled up a map to replace the instrument gauges. "We are going to assist. Notify air command."

"Wilco. Ken, be careful. Watch the restricted zones."

"I will."

He tapped commands on the displayed keyboard, and the whole sound of the vehicle changed. It was if a dragon had been sleeping under the floorboard and suddenly awoke.

"Hugh, get up here."

He climbed back into the front seat and strapped himself in. Ken pressed on the accelerator, and the Suburbanator took off.

"Whoo," came the response from the back seat as they climbed a thousand feet in thirty seconds.

"Are you okay back there?"

"You can't do this."

"Sure we can. Did you ever wonder why there were so many SUV's? It is all camouflage so we can keep these enhanced air/land hybrids on the road. A flight engine is too large to hide in a Geo Metro."

Ken banked to the left to avoid the air space over Manor.

Hugh pointed, "Look, they are taking off."

Perry cried, "What is that?"

In the little town of Manor were two water towers. The new one, like a giant golfball on a tee, was climbing rapidly on a long column of superheated water vapor. The old metal tower, made famous when it was climbed by Leonardo Di Caprio in the movie "What's Eating Gilbert Grape", was lumbering skyward at a slower pace, balanced on its cluster of smaller engines.

"Those are air to space interceptors. That is the cause of the water pressure drop this morning. Do you really think we needed all of these water towers? A cheaper, smaller, ground tank and a regulated water pump could to the job just as well. That is what we switched over to this morning. Phase 2 cold fusion is wonderful. No standby radiation. A little engine package and a tower full of water for exhaust mass makes a wonderful rocket engine.

"Look over there," he pointed over towards Austin, where there were too many white columns of vapor to count. "And over there." Pflugerville and Round Rock were sending their contributions to space. Everywhere you could look, from every city and town, interceptors were rising.

"Perry, I hope you don't have any family on the invasion transports. They won't be landing."

Their captive was whimpering. "Cold fusion?"

Ken nodded. "Yes, it was quite a scare when Pons and Fleischmann discovered it independently. We were afraid there would be someone who would confirm their report that couldn't be hushed up."

Hugh asked, "Perry, what will Gueeseet be doing now?"

There was no response for a moment, then he said, "I hope he makes it to the garage."

"What garage Perry? Where is it?"

"He will get to the boat. He will get away."

"Is the boat in the garage? Perry, listen to me. Where is the garage?"

"Private Warehouse. Looks like a boat."

Ken banked to the right. "I know the place." He touched the console.

"Ruth, are you there?"

"Yes. What do you need?"

"I think that the missing agent may try to reach an escape vehicle disguised as a boat, currently stored at a self-storage place on Highway 685, 'Private Warehouse'. We are en route. Get a ground team there."

"Wilco."

He had made the request according to procedure, but a minute later they were already decelerating, dropping down for a landing on the four-lane road. The tires squealed as they touched down, and Ken was very glad for the computer assisted steering.

They had barely slowed to a hundred, when Hugh pointed at a glow coming from the cluster of low storage buildings behind a chain-link fence. A canvas-covered Larson ski boat was rising from the parking lot of old cars, trailers, motor-homes and boats. It hovered for just a moment and then pointed bow up and accelerated. The canvas fell free.

"Go go, Gueeseet! Get away, get away."

Ken jammed on the accelerator. There wasn't much of the road ahead before it veered to the side at the bridge, but there was no choice. The dragon under the floor growled and his stomach sank to the floor as they arced skyward.

"You'll never catch him. Escape boats are fast."

"I don't know about that." The G-forces as they arced skyward were pushing the maximum that he could handle, but it was important to get every last BC spy. No telling what damage a rogue could do with the technology at hand.

Perry's confidence wavered, "What's that? Are they chasing Gueeseet, too?"

Ken glanced towards Round Rock, where hundreds of specks of light were rising in formation.

Hugh said, "No, those are air-to-air fighters. Robotic. They are coming from the car dealer lots. Did you ever wonder why car dealers had hundreds of shiny new cars on their lot when they never seemed to sell more than a handful at a time. They replaced inventory regularly, all the others were just waiting for the right remote commands. Some of your ships must have survived the interceptors. Those cars will engage them in the air."

Ken added, "My son is driving some of them."

"Billy?" asked Perry incredulously.

"Yes. You've heard of Commander? It's a multiplayer, first person shooter game, where the players are connected via the Internet. Well, this morning, Commander and all the other Internet games shifted to a new level. The best-trained remote-control operators on the planet are now joined en mass, piloting those fighter drones. They should see some seriously new high scores."

Ken could not hide the pride in his voice—pride for his family, pride for the human race. But it couldn't be denied that the ski-boat was accelerating faster than the Suburbanator.

"Hugh, can you target him?"

Hugh nodded, and popped open the glove compartment. The targeting scope and controls unfolded into has hands. He tapped a button and the headlights dropped away, to land in some cotton field far below. There was still another hum—like the big brother of a charging photo-flash unit. Ken tried to hold a steady course.

Hugh locked on the speeding boat, and the twin lasers flashed multi-gigajoule pulses. No ship could outrace light itself.

There was a flash above, and a cloud of vapor.

"No," said Hugh after the plasma dissipated enough to let a radar pulse through. "It didn't take him out."

Perry giggled again. "Ha. Ha. Ab. Ablative shielding!"

Hugh charged up the lasers again, but the distance was greater, and less of the escape boat's burn-away shielding was consumed. "No good."

"Ha. Ha. Ha. Ha." Perry was like a kid, tormenting his captors.

Hugh turned to the back seat and snarled. "Did you ever wonder why so many of you BC's showed up on the Jerry Springer show? We wanted to test your personalities under all kinds of stress situations. One thing we learned very well. You are not nice people. We don't like you. You would have made horrible conquerors."

Perry looked shocked. His eyes started to shine with tears.

Ken gasped. Hugh turned back to the radar. He probed through the new cloud of vapor. "He's gone. The ship exploded."

Perry moaned. "Oh! Poor Gueeseet. He must have lost his Tums."

Ken glanced at the collection of junk from Perry's pocket. There were two rolls of Tums, one peeled open and partially consumed.

He asked, pleasantly, "Perry, why do you eat Tums?"

"Have to." He grinned.

"Do you want some of these?"

"Yes. No."

"What happens when you don't take them?"

Perry giggled. "Gas. Lots and lots and lots of gas."

"All at once?"

"Yes. Oops. Wasn't supposed to tell."

"If you don't take the Tums, you explode?"

"Aw. You guessed it. Wouldn't want an autopsy, you know."

Hugh peeled off a tablet and pushed it towards Perry's mouth. "Here, eat this."

Perry twisted and squirmed, clamping his jaws tightly shut. Hugh climbed, once again, into the back seat. Ken concentrated on piloting the Suburbanator. They had climbed so high and so fast that the sky was black. Unfortunately, their engine was strictly a cold-fusion powered jet engine, not a rocket, and there was no atmosphere to run it.

With the lack of thrust, they were in free fall, and Hugh's struggle was complicated by the zero-g.

"Any luck?" He called over his shoulder.

"No! He has the jaw muscles of a bulldog."

"Knock him out. Force them down."

"How? I can't make him swallow."

"Perry! How much time to we have?"

He stubbornly shook his head. Ken looked back and saw the look on his face. Perry wasn't looking at him. He was looking past him. Ken turned back. The clock. Perry was watching the clock?

Ken tapped the console. "Ruth! Can you read me?"

"Yes Ken. What's the problem? Ground tracking saw you take out the escape boat."

"We didn't! The BC's have a suicide bomb in their stomach. They have to keep taking antacid tablets to keep it stable. The escapee's bomb took out his whole ship. Notify Headquarters."

"Oh Ken! There have been a number of reports of explosions. We have lost thousands. The word has gone out to strip the captives of everything, in case they had hidden bombs."

"Tell them!"

"Okay. Perry?"

"We're working on it!"

Ken looked out at the black sky, and the blazingly bright blue white expanse of home below. Up at the edge of the atmosphere, like them, a ship-to-ship battle raged. The dancing white spots of engines, and the even brighter flashes of ships being destroyed made a breathtaking fireworks display unlike anything he had ever seen. *Play hard Billy.*

"Hugh!"

"No luck."

"Get back up here. We don't have any time."

After a pained sigh, Hugh said, "Last chance Perry!"

Perry stuck out his lower lip and shook his head.

Hugh sailed lightly, in the zero-g, back into his front seat position, and strapped himself in.

Ken put a finger on a button. He looked at Hugh. The eyes staring back showed raw fear and raw courage. His own were probably the same.

"Ready. One. Two. Yell!"

He pushed the button and they both began a long drawn out scream. The left rear door of the Suburbanator snapped open, and the whole seat assembly launched sideways out the door, seats, straps, and Perry. All the air inside rushed out with him.

Their yell went on and on, as they emptied their lungs to the vacuum.

Ken felt his stomach bloat and pressure behind his ears. The roar and screams went to silence. Ken tried to concentrate on the second counter on the dashboard clock. For some reason each tick took hours.

The return of sound, and the return of air forced his glance back to the empty gap behind him, and the closed door. He gasped air eagerly, welcome for the blast coming from the air-conditioner vent.

"Ken?" There was a faint voice, lost in the roar.

"Ken, do you hear me." He could hear her voice, but all he could do was gasp.

"Ken! Can you hear me?" The returning air made the panic in Ruth's words clear.

"Ruth!" Ken gasped. "We are okay."

"What about Perry?"

"Jettisoned. See if ground tracking can find him."

Ruth relayed the request.

"Ken, are you okay?"

He didn't really know. He was grateful for the after-effects of the vacuum. It distracted him from what he did to Perry.

"I'm fine. Hugh is fine. I'm starting to pick up air in the engine. The controls are starting to respond."

"Come on home."

"I'll do that."

Ken looked at Hugh. He looked sick too.

Off to the left, there was the noiseless flash of an explosion. Perry's time had run out.

Hugh mumbled. "Self defense."

Ken nodded. "War time."

...

Ken pulled into the driveway. Molly was sitting on the back porch, talking into her portable phone. She got to her feet.

He turned off the key, and the sudden silence was oppressive. As he pulled himself out of the car, he realized that he ached all over.

"Momma will be home in a few minutes. She just called to warn us that they will be cutting the power." She handed him the phone, "Say hello to Jean Louis."

He took the phone and exchanged *bonjour*'s with the young man on the other end. He hugged his daughter and handed the phone back.

"Why the power outage?"

"One of the BC's big ships broke through the line and they're going to use the Resonator."

He nodded. "And Billy?"

"Still shooting and having a wonderful time. I don't think he has realized that it's a real war."

"Good. He shouldn't have too. Not yet."

Molly spoke a few words in French to her European contact and then asked, "Should I be worried about the uninterruptible power supply on the computer?"

He shrugged. "Either the UPS will work, or it won't. There is nothing we can do either way. Hugh is staying for lunch."

Molly nodded to the man. "It won't be much, we have been kind of busy."

"Anything is fine."

"I've got to run to a wall phone," she apologized, waving the portable. It would work when the power went down.

Her father nodded, "Go."

...

Ruth arrived a couple of minutes later, still talking into her head-set as she parked her car. Ken gave her a hug.

"Blackout in ten seconds." She looked tense.

"Where is the BC ship?"

"Near Fredericksburg."

Oh no. His thoughts immediately turned to the granite mountain near that town.

"You think they know about the base inside Enchanted Rock?"

She shrugged.

From inside the house, there was the sound of the alarm on the UPS. The house air-conditioner went silent.

Ken looked off to the west, but there would be nothing to see. All of the electrical power distribution system in Central Texas was being switched over to its alternate task. The power generators of the area started pulsing the intricate grid of wires in a sweeping frequency range. Computers watched the power coupling effects, and locked into the perfect frequency to feed Megawatts of power into the attacking ship. Once locked on, the signal was modulated to cause the very metal walls of the ship to ring.

Ruth put her hand to the earpiece. "It's working. Spotters are reporting aurora effects around the ship. The sound, even at ground level is deafening... Someone is reporting a flash. Their weapons systems are malfunctioning. Big explosion." She looked at him. "It's coming down."

There was a flash of light off to the west. Ken tried to make it out, but it was too far to see any details.

Ruth kept talking, "Lots of reports of fires. Dispatchers are moving rescue workers into the area. Not my zone, thank God. Some reports of metal chunks falling out of the sky. It's gone."

Ken asked, "Any more BC ships?"

"Just small stuff. Billy and his friends are taking care of those. It's all over but the clean up."

Power came back on, and the annoying whine of the UPS went away.

Molly came back out with her portable phone, "Europe is now clear. Asia predicts completion in another hour or less. Everyone else is still looking to see if there is anyone left to fight."

Hugh eased into a chair. "I don't think I'll make it in to the plant today. Morning has been good enough."

Ken nodded, "It has been a good morning, a wonderful morning."

Molly poked her head out the door. "We've got hamburger. If someone would fire up the grill."

Hugh waved his hand and got to his feet. "I'll do it."

Ken watched as Hugh rolled out the gas grill from the porch. "Make sure you've got the safety on."

Hugh nodded. They didn't need it to be anything but a gas grill. Not anymore.

In a Black Mood

I drive a Jeep Wrangler, and the roads seem friendlier as Jeep people wave at each other. What if there was a way to bring that person-to-person feeling to all the traffic?

The Honda Mood was the first car, outside of the labs, that used mood trim. As a geek, I had to have one.

`Img: Mycar.jpg Alt: Me and my Honda Mood in front of my apartment`

So for about 7 months, my ride was the apex of cool. The technology was simple. I put my hands on the steering wheel and the wide bands of trim on the car changed color according to my mood.

There was a big PR push, and soon everybody knew that if my black car had red trim, that they'd better keep their distance in traffic, but if it was yellow, then total strangers would wave and smile as we passed each other.

I didn't necessarily agree with the company's color scheme. Green for envy, okay. Gold for lust? I don't know about that.

But it didn't take long for the aftermarket companies to offer add-on kits.

The first time I saw a BMW sedan pass me in traffic with his Joy colors showing from a gadget on his roof like a taxi or a pizza delivery sign, I was confused, and my Mood probably showed a little red.

There were patent lawsuits. But Honda knew which way the money was blowing. The Mood was a great novelty car, but people wanted trunk space and energy economy—as well as a mood flag. So they sold licenses far and wide.

Soon I was seeing everything from rusty VW Beetles to the latest Lectros, all showing their colors.

My poor Mood started feeling a little blue in the morning traffic. At least I was. I felt like a sucker. Without the color boost making my drive special, I started paying more attention to the amount of time I had to lean on the pedal to get up to speed on the on-ramp. My car's basic color scheme, all black, even the bumpers, soaked up the sun and the AC was howling like a storm, just to keep the insides tolerable on a hot day.

There was a strip of trim that outlined the hood that was my only look at my car's colors. Two hours ago, it flared green when that jerk's foreign car, all low profile and rumbling more wasted horsepower than my Mood could produce on a good day, pulled across two lanes to wedge in front of me. Its trim was glaring bright red, and I instinctively slowed to give him some room.

California was pushing that law to make mood stripes mandatory. Supposedly, some university egg-head produced figures showing that traffic accidents dropped in direct relationship to the number of mood-enhanced cars on the road. It's true I certainly give angry drivers more room. Generally, I suppose most people paid more attention to the vehicles and the people around them because of the mood colors.

Then, the angry car turned right, heading for the Mall—unfortunately, because that was where I was headed as well. He pulled into the parking spot that I wanted, but I found another one just a few slots later.

The driver of the angry car was taking his time getting out, and as the door opened, I saw why.

The car should *not* have had red trim, it should have been gold. Because his passenger ought to turn every guy's car gold. She was enough to stop me in my tracks.

And the driver's face certainly didn't look angry either.

He let go of his steering wheel, but the stripes didn't fade. He reached to the dash and flipped a switch, and then the color died.

I circled around, partly I admit for the pleasure of watching her walk, but also to get a better look at his car.

Mood stripes weren't supposed to have any controls. They came on with the engine and faded with it as well. If you took your hands off the wheel, it would show. That was the whole point—a visible connection to the mood of the driver.

The car gave an irritated blip when I got too close. I moved back an inch, out of its sensor range.

Up under the GPS screen there was an aftermarket device in chrome with color bars and a slider switch, still sitting on red. "Mood-Setter" was the label.

Img: MoodSetter.jpg Alt: Photo through the cheater's window

There are times when colors don't do my feelings justice. The Mood car was an innovation. The strap-on kits were an homage, the licensing inevitable.

This hack was an abomination. I was steamed. Various fantasies of destruction flicked through my head, but I couldn't afford the lawsuit or the jail time.

But I couldn't let this jerk get away with claiming an extra slice of the road by gaming the Mood system, could I?

Video: Interview.mpg Alt: Interview with the driver of the hacked car

JKL - James K. Lesser - Staff editor of the Social OverView

UNK - Unknown driver

Camera pan from car to the approaching couple. Girl clings to man's arm while he carries shopping bags labeled with premium label stores.

JKL: Excuse me, sir. Is this your fantastic looking car?

UNK: Yep. Cost me a bundle too.

Camera image waves around.

JKL: I was just taking a phone video of it to share with the viewers on my blog, the Social OverView. I'm sure they would be interested in some of it's features.

UNK: Another time maybe. I have a guest and I don't want to keep her waiting, if you know what I mean.

JKL: I certainly do. I just wanted to share this new innovation with the public. How did you discover this Mood Setter hack that allows you do cheat the other drivers on the highway?

UNK: What! Who are you?

JKL: James Lesser of the Social OverView. When did you decide to game the mood system to make other cars give you more room than you deserve?

UNK: You turn that thing off! Right now!

JKL: I'm sure the public will want to be on the lookout for cars that attempt to...

End of video. Phone was smashed on the sidewalk. Interviewer was punched in the face. But the file was recovered.

...

Update: Well the Social OverView may never have a week like this again, but it's certainly been worth it! The video went viral with over two million hits so far. The comments quickly identified the driver and his former girlfriend. Although I am gratified that the public was as offended by this cheating behavior as I was, I will be glad when civility returns to the comment thread. The whistle blowing has done its job, and the California law is being amended to outlaw "false and misleading" versions of the Mood system.

On a personal note, yes the bruise is fading. I have gotten a replacement phone, and I carry it always. And my Mood is yellow.

Partly Murphy

Can you tell I wrote this during layoff season, back when I was working at Motorola? Luck is so ill-defined that it's no wonder that no one considers it worth scientific investigation. But maybe we would be better for it if it were.

The *blaaaaa* of the alarm clock drove Jim Oliver awake. With his eyes tightly shut against the morning glow, he slapped at the top of the clock, hoping to hit the five minute button. His aim was bad. He knocked it skidding off the night stand. Eyes suddenly wide open to catch it, he lunged. He grabbed, missed, and slid off the bed himself, landing on painful comers with his head trapped between the legs of the night stand.

At least the alarm had stopped.

"...Clear skies through Friday, with a twenty percent chance of scattered showers over the weekend," the familiar voice was saying. Jim just rested in his contortionist position, content to wait until it got really uncomfortable, or until he woke up enough to move, whichever came first.

"And now for the fortune report: The National Bureau of Statistics reports new activity in the Central Texas area. Expect partly murphy conditions through the rest of this week with a twenty-five percent chance of isolated byxcs."

Jim winced. "No. Not today," he thought. "I can't afford any bad luck today." He twisted his arm to get some leverage to help himself up.

A loop of power cord pulled tight around the leg of the night stand. With a crash, it toppled over on top of him.

...

"What happened to you, Jim?" Jess Hammer's voice rang out across the open office area. He was an hour and a half late and a dozen pair of eyes turned onto him like air raid searchlights, pinning him there with his coat and briefcase in hand.

Jim eased over to his cubicle and divested himself of the incriminating evidence. "What do you mean?" he asked Jess in all innocence.

Jess was a *large* man. The finger that he pointed at Jim's sore eye looked like a blue steel .45 pistol. "That. Who hit you?"

Jim fingered the tender area. "Is it showing? I had a fall this morning."

Jess chuckled. "If it were any darker, you would look like Red Beard the Pirate. Did you have to go by the doctor's office? I notice you are a little late getting in this morning."

"No. Just traffic. One of those gravel trucks had a slight disagreement with a cement truck on the Montopolis bridge. I was stuck there with an instant barricade blocking my way forward and two million cars backed up behind me. The police showed up pretty quick, but they were more concerned about getting the cement spill off the bridge and into the river before it set than they were about getting the traffic unsnarled."

Betty Walker stopped outside his cubicle as he related the gory details of the accident. She waited until he ran down, then handed him a photocopy of a meeting notice.

"Mandatory attendance. Eleven sharp. The General Manager is in town and he wants to see everybody there. "

Jim frowned. "What's the meeting for?"

Betty let an evil smile creep over her normally dour face. "You know the rumors. It's layoff season again. Some people are going to get the ax today. Parker flew in just for this. As General Manager, he figures it is his job to be the bad guy." She looked at him carefully, as if checking him for lice. "I would hate to be in your shoes today, Jim Oliver."

"Why? What do you mean?" He could feel his heart start to beat faster. He had been dreading this day. He was a good worker. Surely they wouldn't cut him.

"Have you heard the fortune report today?"

"Sure. Partly murphy. Some byxcs around. "

She nodded. "You've got a byxc. I watched cable news this morning. Want to know the common factor this time?"

He didn't want to know! He nodded "Yes."

"Men with red beards. Jim Oliver, you're doomed." She shook her head, and walked off with an amused little smile.

Jess frowned. "A byxc. Oh, great!" He eased a step back. "I was sure our working group would be safe from this cut. But with a byxc around... Jim, I would advise you to get sick and go home. I've got to go."

Moving quickly, the big man got out of his cubicle and out of range.

Jim turned to his desk. It was littered with a half dozen little yellow sticker notes. He had missed two early morning meetings, a call from his girl friend, and he had papers to prepare, due an hour ago. He sighed.

It was a *long* day's work getting to eleven AM. Everyone who walked past his cubicle glanced in at him. Everyone was aware of the byxc. Even his phone contacts seemed eager to cut the conversation short. He had a disease, bad luck, and it might strike anyone around him.

Jess came by, not stopping inside the cubicle. His face was grim.

"Jim, I talked to the boss about the byxc. He agreed it would be the best thing to send you home, but he can't. Word came down that he had to have everybody in the big meeting if he had to use a whip to do it.

"However," he continued with a grin, "we are going to try to isolate you. You are not to use the copier or the word processors, or the coffee pot. Steer clear of anything mechanical or electronic. Don't even go near the computer."

Jim said, "Do you really think that's necessary?"

The big man replied, "Sure! The phones convinced us."

"Phones?"

"Yes. They are all out. Didn't you notice?"

Actually, Jim had noticed the phone going dead on him during that last conversation, but it had been so much like all the other minor catastrophes that had been plaguing him all morning that he hadn't thought it was anything more widespread. Perhaps the injunction to keep away from the equipment was a good idea. His stapler was seriously jammed, his file cabinet had a broken key stuck in the lock and his paperclip-and-scissors drawer was a quarter inch deep in coffee.

He felt a wave of sadness, a burning knot that turned in his stomach. His world was falling apart. And in ten minutes, he would probably be fired.

"Jess," he asked, "this has to stop. I can't take this pressure."

"Hang in there," Jess said cheerfully. "It's just a byxc. It will fade in less than a day. Use some elementary caution and you will come out of it with nothing worse than an after-dinner story to tell."

"What do you know!" Jim bit back, "You aren't the one with the black cloud over your head—the demon waiting to trip you up."

...

"Easy Jim." Jess eased his big frame into the cubicle. He pulled up the spare chair and tested it, as if he expected it to collapse under pressure. When it passed, he finally trusted his weight to it.

"Jim, what do you think a byxc is?" he asked.

A hundred news stories and sitcom situations passed through his mind. "It's a bad luck cloud. It follows somebody around and causes all kind of accidents to happen to him and the people around him. The government figures out when they are going to happen and reports them just like the weather."

Jess gestured with his big hands, "Almost. Murphy weather—byxcs, they have always been around. They are just human-scale variations in small-scale statistical mechanics. They are times and places where normal statistics falls apart. There is nothing evil about it. There isn't even anything intelligent about it."

"Then why is it always a bad luck jinx?" Jim demanded.

"It isn't really," he shrugged. "Just *wrong* luck. We humans aren't dumb. Let a stone age hunter find rabbits to eat by traveling the forest path and let him find big toothed nasties to hunt him on the swamp path, just in the normal run of luck, and he would certainly hunt the forest. If a byxc came along, he would find nasties in the forest. Bad luck for him. But if he had taken the *wrong* path that day, then it would have been his good luck.

"We humans bet our lives on the run of the dice. If the whole world was trapped in a giant byxc for a hundred years, we would still prosper—we would just have to learn the new way the dice bounced."

Jim thought a moment. "Do you mean that I could get in my car and race through downtown at a hundred miles per hour and not hit anybody?"

"Maybe. I wouldn't try it myself, but it is certainly possible. Your luck is different now, for as long as the byxc lasts. Today is the day to bet on longshots. Las Vegas pays very close attention to the fortune report. If you walked in with that beard, they would very politely usher you out.

"But for today, take no risks. Don't trust anything mechanical or electronic. If your byxc doesn't dissipate by the end of the day, let me bring you some food and a blanket and you stay here over the night. Automobiles are too hazardous—for you and for any innocent bystander."

"Okay. If I last the day.

Betty rushed up, "Phones are out. The eleven AM meeting is postponed until after lunch. One, at the auditorium. Got to run."

...

The day dragged. The phones came back up, but no one called him. The word was out. It would be useless to trust Jim Oliver with a job today.

The one o'clock meeting was postponed again, until three. But it was definitely stated that the meeting would be to announce the headcount cuts. The delays were caused by paperwork snarls in the manager's office, but the meeting would be held, paperwork or no.

Jim had skipped lunch; why risk it? Following Jess' advice, he tried to minimize his risk. He sat in his cubicle. He tried to avoid using anything more complicated than a pencil, until his pencil snapped.

Sleep was impossible. Not only was the injunction to never sleep on the job written deep into his psyche, but other worries were enough to keep his mind working.

If he were fired, how long would his savings hold out? The whole industry was depressed. Could he get another job in his area of specialization before the money ran out? He was raised to be disdainful of people on welfare. Could he stomach collecting unemployment insurance? How would it feel to be a "client" of the Employment Commission? Should he starve for pride's sake?

Halfway through the afternoon, nature called and he left the cubicle. He was very careful. That didn't prevent him from scalding himself with the super-hot water that came out when he attempted to wash his hands.

He stared at his red-bearded face in the mirror as he ran cold water over the burn.

The bycx was attached to red-bearded men. What if he cut off his beard? He shuddered at the thought. He had been bearded since he left high school. He liked the beard. It was him.

But he remember the decision he made years ago. If he ever believed that his beard was keeping him from a promotion or hindering him in his job, he would cut it off. He knew his father feared that it was a disadvantage, but in all the time he had been with the company, he never felt any suspicion that anybody minded. Even his boss had a beard, and that was as good an indicator as any that the factors his father had seen working had changed for this generation.

So now, was it time? If he cut the beard off, borrowed a razor and shaved it clean, would that magically remove his name from the layoff list?

He stared at himself. His hand throbbed from the scalded place. He took a deep breath and shut off the water.

No. I'll keep the beard. I won't give in to a quirk of statistics. Besides, scissors and a razor were lethal instruments right now.

Jess came by to escort him to the auditorium at three, but the word came just as they were leaving that the meeting was being postponed for another hour. No explanations.

"A four o'clock meeting," Jess shook his head. "Closing time at four-thirty. If they delay it any more, then that's it for today."

"I wouldn't mind." Jim settled back into his chair, conscious of how carefully Jess checked everything out when they were together.

"I don't suppose any of us would mind. But people are going to be cut, and every day delayed means another body out the door."

Jess had a sour look on his face and Jim had a feeling it wasn't because of the byxc. Jess was manager to a group of about a dozen people on the production floor. Jim suspected that Jess was worrying about them more than he would about himself.

"Hey, Jess." Jim asked, trying to distract his interest. "You know a lot about physics. What are byxcs?"

He shook his head, "I don't know, Jim. I've heard a dozen theories, blaming them on everything from ghosts to Einstein's hidden variables. The only thing I do know for sure is that you can predict murphy fluctuations if you have a big enough super-computer and have enough base data. It is a whole lot like predicting the weather; that's why the government got into the job in the first place—researchers kept wanting to borrow time on NOAA's big weather computer. Once NASA got the idea that would be a good idea to check for byxcs before any space launch, the funding for a permanent fortune report finally came through.

"It was a very human thing to do—if the universe wants to play with loaded dice, then we'll calibrate 'em and predict 'em."

Jim shook his head. "Still, it would be nice to know why my luck has changed. I would also like to know when it will get back to normal!"

Jess looked thoughtfully, then said, "Get a calculator and divide six by three."

Jim fumbled through his disk drawer, jabbing his finger on a thumbtack. The calculator was a simple one, useful for calculating percentages and adding up his checkbook. He keyed in the simple division problem and read the result back to Jess. "Six divided by three is 102.111139."

He nodded, "Keep that with you and try it again every so often. When you get the right answer every time, then your byxc will probably be gone."

...

When Jim eased into the back of the auditorium for the four PM meeting, he still clutched the calculator like a set of worry beads. He had done over a hundred tests, with results as high as OVERFLOW and as low as -8.74535E12. He had even gotten a 2.00 every once in a while, only to get something outlandish the next try. The poor little electrons in the semiconductor chip weren't following their statistical laws at all.

The auditorium was large, but still, to get all the employees in at one time was an exercise in sardine packing. Up on the stage were several of the higher managers, having whispered conversations among themselves. The crowd in the seats and standing along the walls managed a respectable roar as hot rumors circulated through the unnumbered conversations. Statistically, there was only a very minute chance that everyone would stop talking at the same instant, but that's what happened.

For a long five seconds, that great mass of people were quiet. Everyone looked around for the reason everyone else had shut up, then in a renewed burst of noise, they all started talking at once.

Jim Oliver tried to keep out of everybody's way, content to play with his calculator. Four o'clock came and went with no one stepping to the microphone. Five minutes passed, then ten. The people up on the stage were plainly at a loss. Someone was sent off to check on the holdup.

Jim got 2.00 twice in a row, before it went crazy again.

A man with a worried look on his face came up on the stage. The group on the stage held an animated conversation among themselves. The crowd in the seats quieted down as everyone strained to overhear. Finally, the man from Personnel stepped up the, microphone and tapped it.

"I have just been informed that Dick Parker, our General Manager, has broken his leg. This meeting will be postponed until tomorrow."

There was a mixed roar—some cheers, some expressions of concern. But there was a great feeling of reprieve. The rear doorway where Jim was standing was suddenly flooded by people trying to get out. No one tripped. Jess spotted Jim being pressed along in the crowd, calculator held high. Jim waved and shouted, "Five times in a row!"

. . .

It was generally agreed that it was time to go home. Jim Oliver retrieved his briefcase and joined the flood of people heading out to the parking lot.

Outside, there was quite a mob. Jim pressed through the group to see what was going on. An ambulance was backed up in the No Parking zone and a gurney was being edged up to the back of it. Laying down on the gurney with his leg wrapped in white was Dick Parker, General Manager, working frantically with a pair of scissors, hacking away at his red beard.

The Christmas Count

Clay Phennicie introduced me to the idea of the Christmas Count ages ago, but just as this and other customs change, no matter where we live, whether on this planet, or on another, or even some place in-between, people will shape their lives in familiar ways.

Fred Jerret squinted his eyes against the light. The sun was a white band of light stretching high across the sky. The checkerboard fields of the farms he knew to be on the other side of the sky were washed out in the glare. There was no change. Winter should have come by now—it was past four PM

"Fred," his wife, Dot, called across the field to him, as she stood at the back porch of their gray stone farm house. "Fred, I need the list."

"Okay! I'm coming." Reluctantly, he stepped from furrow to furrow in the caked black earth until he reached the wide patch of grass he kept as a backyard for the kids to play in.

Waiting out in the field wouldn't make winter happen any faster. He had been a farmer for too many years to try to second-guess the climate control computer. The Piedmont Herald would publish the day, but no one knew the exact moment. The weather in their farming world was at the mercy of a real-time computer system far too concerned with solar flares and the heat balance of their self-contained space colony to give out predictions.

Fred had a couple of bucks down in the 4:15-4:20 spot in the betting pool that the boys at the general store were keeping. He had wanted four PM, but that spot had been taken. Just as well, he thought. Maybe I'll win anyway.

Dot had vanished back into the house, and he slowed his pace a trifle. He was born a farmer, and today he needed to be outside, soaking up the peace he knew was always there in his fields.

Joey had been gone all day, vanished at first sunlight. He had not asked to leave. It was a deliberate escape from the chores he knew he was responsible for. Fred thought of the scolding he would give the boy. There was a sick anger in his stomach. He had said those words before, when Tim, his oldest, was sixteen.

A distant metallic rumble, like the legendary pre-space locomotives on rails, stopped Fred in his tracks. It was difficult to see through the hazy sky that clouded the center of this cylindrical world, but he knew it was the sun shutters. Three great metal gates had moved on their courses, restricting and channeling the sunlight that entered the world of Piedmont, shifting the energy balance. For the next few weeks, more heat would be radiated from the back side of this enclosed world than would be let in through the great mirrors. It would get colder. Winter had begun.

Fred looked at his watch and shook his head. Missed it by three minutes.

Inside, Dot looked up as he entered. "Winter's come," he informed her. "Here's the list." He handed the clipboard to her. "I thought we had finished with the kitchen."

Dot gave him a twisted little grin. "Well... I have to reduce the roach count." She pushed the selector button on the clipboard a few times until the roach count appeared on the display plate. She subtracted two from the count and then gave it back to Fred.

He shook his head. "Dot, this is not the day to kill roaches. This is Christmas Eve. Today we count the beasties, not try to wipe them out."

She curled her lower lip. "But they asked for it. I had my pumpkin pies cooling on the cabinet and those two came after them. I wasn't about to let them get on my pies!"

Fred tried to hide a smile. "Pumpkin, hmmm. Well, if it was pumpkin, I won't turn you in. But don't tell David about it. He will take it as approval to go hunting the rats in the woodpile again."

Dot nodded, then looked out the kitchen window to the fields and the woods beyond. "Where are Kim and David? Haven't they finished yet? With winter here, dark will come sooner."

"Maybe I had better go looking for them. I've got all the livestock counted and I keyed in the changes in the acreages for the insect estimates." He sniffed the kitchen air. "How soon is food?"

"Maybe another hour. By the way, are you sure we won't have any guests for Christmas dinner tomorrow?"

He shrugged. "I guess not. I made the invitations, but everyone was taken." He was not terribly surprised. After all there were three farming families for every one of the city folk. Dot had come from Galvin, a manufacturing world that circled the Point in the same lazy orbit as Piedmont. The world she had grown up in was nothing but one big city. Even after all these years as his wife, living on the soil, she still tended to think of that city as a big place, rather than the handful of support and maintenance people it actually was.

He continued. "I thought Charlie from river maintenance might come, but his wife had already made other arrangements." Maybe it would be better with just family this year. If there was company coming, Dot would work herself to exhaustion to get the house spotlessly clean.

Outside, the air was already getting cooler. Fred looked over his fields, freshly planted and waiting for the winter to make its appearance, and then leave for the long growing season.

Fred expected the winter to be colder than usual this year. The ant infestation down by Southport had hurt a dozen farmers. A good solid freeze or two would wipe out the nests.

Spot came bounding across the fields to meet him. Fred clapped his hands together and the dog jumped high to snap the imaginary treat out of the air. Spot knew there was nothing there, but he liked to play the game. Sometimes Fred would fool him with the real thing.

Off to the east, a neighbor's dog barked. Spot lost interest in Fred and raced off, voicing his challenge. Fred could just spot the tiny figures in the next farm over. The curve of the ground rose enough to show a man building his Christmas fire. Fred glanced at his watch and hurried on.

The strip of woods that bordered the Jerret farm was partly on his property, so he was responsible for it in the count. It was the kids' job to help him with that.

The high-pitched shout of five-year-old David helped him locate them quickly. Kim and David were having a leaf fight. Fred adjusted his path slightly so he kept out of sight behind a stand of oak as he approached. Just yesterday, ten-year-old Kim had gotten a scolding from her mother about getting leaves in her hair. Fred waited until the last moment, then stepped out from behind a tree just as David was dumping a double handful of leaves onto his older sister's head.

"David!" Fred used his stern-father voice. Both kids jumped. David spilled most of the leaves off to the side of his target. He guiltily brushed his hands against his trousers.

"Yes, Daddy?" he asked timidly.

Fred let a moment of silence grow. But he had no intention of doing anything about the leaves. The kids would get the necessary dusting from their mother. It was her restriction, she would enforce it. Personally, Fred had nice memories of playing in the leaves when he was younger.

"David, you are going to have to help me with the fire. Have you two finished your counts?"

David pouted. "Why do I have to help with the fire? That is Joey's job."

"Joey is not back yet." His voice showed a little impatience. "Now did you finish your counts?"

Kim gave a warning glance at her brother. Now was not the time to complain about chores, not with Joey being out late again. Daddy was likely going to be in a bad mood until he came home.

She spoke up, "Yes. We counted twenty-two squirrels, and nine rabbits. The mice don't seem to be as bad this year, there were only ten in the sample square. I didn't spot the badger, but there were fresh signs."

Fred tapped in the numbers on the clipboard. "Are you sure all of these were on our side of the boundary line? We are not supposed to count the animals on any other property."

She nodded, "I'm sure. I think the rabbits moved their hole down by the gully since the last count."

"How about the birds?"

"I didn't see any crows, but I saw five orioles. David claims to have seen a cowbird, but I didn't."

Fred nodded. "If David saw it, we count it. The climate computer needs to know everything we see, so it can plan the right amount of rain to make and plan how many days of winter we need."

"And summer?" asked David.

Fred smiled. "Yes, and summer. That's why we have four counts: the Christmas Count, the Easter Count, the Earthday Count, and the Harvest Count. We have a small, special world here in Piedmont and the counts are one of the ways we take care of our home."

David's attention had already wandered off to something in the sky by the time. Fred had finished saying that. But Kim was older, and this time the words seemed to make some kind of impression on her.

David pointed. "Daddy, look."

Up high, halfway to the patchwork of fields on the other side of the sky, was a tiny speck moving south. A man-shape and a set of wings. It was too high for them to hear the sputtering of the tiny engine.

"A flier," Fred said, "trying to make the run to Southport. He'd better hurry." He looked at his watch. "And we had better run. Dark will come in five minutes."

Darkness, when it came, closed down over Piedmont like the lid on a large cedar chest. The distant rumble of the shutters followed as the sound hurried to catch up with the shadow, like black thunder chasing the stroke of darkness. With only the light leak around the sun shutters to provide a pale imitation of moonlight, they had to step carefully as they made their way back to the house.

David shouted, "Hey look! Lights in the sky!"

And there were. First a dozen yellow lights scattered across the far side of the sky, then more, as farmers all through Piedmont lit the traditional Christmas Eve fire. Dot came out of the house, rubbing her hands on the towel at her waist. She, too, started up at the sight.

"Hurry and help me, David," Fred said to his youngest. "We have to get our fire going."

"Aww. Why do I have to..."

"None of that!" Fred spoke sharply. "Santa is coming in just a few hours. This is not the time to act up."

"Yes, Davie," taunted his sister. "If you're naughty, Santa won't give you anything."

"Kim," commanded Dot, "come on and help me set the fireside table." Kim's face twisted as she realized she had trapped herself into helping her mother.

As the door closed, David heard his mother's voice rise sharply. "Kim Jerret, what is that in your hair?"

David giggled.

David was not really strong enough to help much with the fire building, but his father believed in chores for the children, even if it meant more work for him. They had the stack of wood placed in the fire pit, ready for lighting by the time the dinner was served.

"Can I light it now, Daddy?" David asked. Fred shook his head.

Dot looked up at her husband with a question in her eyes. He turned away, looking briefly at the road that led past the front of their property. Joey had been late getting home several times before. But it was Christmas Eve! He shook off a rising flood of anger and frustration. He couldn't let Christmas be spoiled for the other kids.

He said, "Let's just sit here for a little bit and enjoy the lights."

Dot insisted they eat while the food was still hot. Helplessly, Fred felt the liquid trickle of an old hurt as they watched the lights flickering above. Empty places at the family table again.

Joey was at a difficult age. His older brother had been the same—staying out later and later with his friends. The role and restrictions of being a child were too much for him to bear. The harder his father fought to keep control, the more Joey managed to slip away.

His brother Tim had vanished one day, leaving a note saying that he had left to apprentice as a shuttle pilot. That had been two years ago. Christmas that first year had been hard, with that vacant chair as a constant reminder of a part of them that was gone.

The second year Tim sent Christmas presents for the kids, and a letter for his parents. They wrote back, but it was clear that their son had left for good. He was a regular pilot, with a regular run among the different orbital worlds. He had a life of his own, and it did not include Piedmont. Fred's boy would never be a farmer like his father.

"Why do we light a fire on Christmas Eve, Daddy?" Kim asked.

His little girl was growing up, too. He smiled at her as she stared up at the display above.

"There are a couple of reasons. When I was a boy, my father told me that Piedmont had started the Christmas fires to remind us of the stars in the night sky of Earth."

"What is the other reason?"

Fred went over to the storage shed and picked up a bag of powder from the shelf. He set it down on the bench before the kids. "This is seeding powder. We put it on the fire and it helps the formation of raindrops. Piedmont is a special world and we have to take care of it in a lot of little ways."

David asked, as he stuck his finger in the grayish powder, "Does it make snow, too?"

Fred laughed. "Yes, it helps make snow, too."

"Good, let's light it!" David grabbed the bag and headed over to the fire.

Fred was quick on his feet and grabbed the bag before the boy had dumped it. "Okay. But we have to sprinkle the powder over the fire carefully."

Kim wanted to help, but Fred ruled that since David had helped build the fire, he ought to be the one to start it. They soon had a blazing fire and he showed David the proper way to toss the little scoops of powder over the fire.

In the yellow light, Fred noticed tears in Dot's eyes. He moved to her side. Christmas was a time for extremes. If you didn't feel wonderful, you felt horrible. He held her hand as they watched the flames.

He tried to smile, to feel as happy as his two little ones. But it was so hard. He squeezed Dot's hand. She squeezed back.

"Hey!" Kim pointed. "Here comes Joey!"

And sure enough, the bouncy white light of a bicycle on a dirt road was visible in the night. They all watched it as it pulled up and Joey walked up to the fireside.

He came right up to the flames and rubbed his hands. "This feels good. It's getting cold."

"Where have you been?" Fred tried to keep his voice level. There would be nothing good in having another shouting match like last time he returned home late.

Joey looked at his father's face and then looked back to the fire. "Mr. Grey, the scout troop leader, he asked me to help. Troop Two was supposed to handle the count on the Common." He shrugged, carefully watching the flames. "It took longer than we thought."

Fred nodded. He had heard it before. He sighed. "Dot, could you heat up something for Joey?" To Joey, he said, "David had to do your chores today. He gets your allowance, too."

David squealed in delight. Joey started to protest, then thought better of it.

It took an hour or more for the fire to die down to a red piping bed of coals. With Dot leading, they sang Christmas carols.

David asked, "How can Santa get to every house in one night?"

Kim eagerly explained, "He has a magic flier so he can land and take off real quick. He comes in a red shuttle and visits all the worlds in the circuit all in one night."

Fred always held his breath when the little ones asked about Santa. He dreaded the moment when they would ask if Santa was real. For David, at least, the moment had not yet come. He was just a little too young to guess at such a great conspiracy. At least his older ones were firmly coached not to give away the secret to the younger ones, at least not on purpose.

Across the landscape, like a metallic rolling thunder, the clank of the great doors of the Northport docking hangar clanked shut.

Kim and David started shouting, "Santa's here! Santa's ship is here!

Distant voices, far too distant to resolve into anything more than the sound of humanity, told of all the world's children cheering the coming of Santa.

Dot said, "Okay. Bedtime, kids. " She hustled them off to bed, giving David his medicine and getting Kim to wash her hair. Bedtime was never quick and easy with kids, not even on Christmas Eve.

It was much later that Dot came back to join Fred as he tended the bed of coals. "Woooo! It's cold." She rubbed her hands together before the warmth of the coals, then sat down on the bench next to him. He put his arm around her.

Quiet moments, and a spot of warmth on a cold night—that and love can drain the stress of the day. They sat and breathed the frosty air, and enjoyed the moment.

"Oh," Fred asked, "did you upload the clipboard file?"

"Mmm. I plugged it into house storage. The midnight poll will upload it to central." She leaned her head against his shoulder and laughed. "Did you see Kim's hair? She must have rolled in the leaves! "

"No, " he contradicted. "David dumped those on her. I caught them at it in the woods."

"Why didn't you tell me? I gave her quite a scold."

"If she didn't snitch on him, why should I? Besides, I would have liked to play in the leaves, too, if they would have let me."

She poked him in the ribs. "Impossible. Farm kids! And you're the worst of the lot."

Fred nodded. "Good kids," he said quietly.

"All of them," she agreed.

Then, a touch of wetness on her cheek turned Dot's eyes to the sky above them. "Snow! It's starting to snow."

Drifting down in lazy swirls, large snowflakes were suddenly filling the air. Minute by minute, the white stuff increased, until it became clear that they had to get up and go inside or get wet from all the snow melting on them.

"It will be a good snow this year," Fred said, getting to his feet and helping his wife up. "Good for snowmen."

"And don't forget Santa."

Almost on cue, they heard a strange sound faintly through the snow-muffled air. The sound of a flier. But no one would be flying on a night like this! And the sound was becoming louder, as if the flyer was coming down.

Neither of them spoke. Her hand gripped his tighter when the flier flickered into view at the edge of the field. The wings tilted up, the sputtering died. A man in a heavy suit, carrying a large bag over his shoulder, set the flier back on its struts. He walked toward them.

"Tim?" Dot spoke.

"Son?" Fred asked.

The young man's face, dimly lit by the rosy glow of the coals, was one big smile. "Mom, Dad. Sorry I'm late." Then words were lost in a joyous round of bear hugs and happy tears.

"I couldn't get here any sooner," he explained. "Northport control had me delay docking so that I could be Santa's ship this year. I'm sorry I didn't warn you I was coming. It took some fancy last-minute schedule swapping with the regular pilot to get me here. And then I almost got lost in the snow." He shook his head in embarrassment. "I had forgotten about the snow."

"Just so you are here. " His mother gave him another hug. "All my children are here."

"Dot!" said Fred, as the thought struck him. "Go correct the count, quickly before the midnight upload. Our family is six—in our Christmas Count tonight."

For more stories by Henry, look for more volumes of **Henry's Stories**, or visit

Henry's Stories online magazine

http://www.henrysstories.blogspot.com

Enjoy a collection of Young Adult Science Fiction Novels.

These stand-alone tales take high school aged adventurers from today's small towns as they take that step off into the strange.

Available from the usual online book sellers and the most perceptive of bookstores.

Beginning with **Star Time** in 2011, follow a mult-thousand year saga as humanity struggles to find its place in the universe.

Look for The Project Saga at your favorite book stores.

www.ingramcontent.com/pod-product-compliance
Lightning Source LLC
LaVergne TN
LVHW010056110826
845155LV00028B/368

* 9 7 8 1 9 3 5 2 3 6 4 5 0 *